The train bearing the girl and the Golem sped through the tunnel. Flickering shapes began to appear in the car, taking on a substance.

Stalin lay dying. Khrushchev grinned with pleasure.

The girl and the Golem were again enclosed by train walls. Suddenly the train faded.

Malcolm J. Neigh, President of the United States of North, South, and Canadian America walked out of the oval office. Three-thirty in the morning—the President was dressed in robe and pajamas. He walked down a hall. He pressed the button. Neigh had gone completely and irrevocably mad. . . .

Again the scene flickered and changed. Distorted images broke into frail wisps, blinked out.

The Golem eyed the backs of the other passengers. "These sights take some getting used to, don't they?"

The girl nodded silently.

"What do you call this?" the Golem asked.

"The nightmare express."

NIGHTMARE EXPRESS

by Isidore Haiblum

FAWCETT GOLD MEDAL • NEW YORK

NIGHTMARE EXPRESS

© 1979 Isidore Haiblum

Published by Fawcett Gold Medal Books, a unit of
CBS Publications, the Consumer Publishing Division
of CBS Inc.

ISBN: 0-449-14204-3

Printed in the United States of America

10 9 8 7 6 5 4 3 2 1

NIGHTMARE
EXPRESS

PART 1

Imagine a world shrunk to the size of a mere golf ball. Its gravity would be so compressed that nothing could withstand it. This is the black hole we must now contend with.

from *The Notebooks of Dr. James Ingram*

CHAPTER 1

Mark Craig

I came stumbling out of the alley.

Brother, what hit me? I couldn't remember. My mind was a blank, shiny slate, as useless as last year's lottery ticket. I seemed to have picked up a couple of other infirmities, too. Small specks like a platoon of deranged fireflies were shooting it out before my eyes. A very young and inept drummer was practicing his instrument somewhere in the back of my skull. The pavement lurched under my feet as though it had been carelessly built on a mound of quicksand. Aside from that I couldn't complain. There was no one around to hear me, anyway. The street was dark, empty. I was as alone as a mouse at a vivisectionists' outing.

Nighttime.

A chill wind sent loose debris scooting along the pavement. I shivered. I wasn't dressed for the occasion—whatever the occasion was. A flannel shirt and work pants were my main items of apparel. Hardly a suitable getup for a man of means. I hoped I was one. I didn't know.

All this stocktaking seemed to make my head ache even more. I was as alert as a punch-drunk pug down for the long count—but probably not as spry. I leaned up against a handy brick wall and waited for things to improve. They didn't. I realized I might have a very long wait. More than a body could stand. Certainly more than my body—in its present condition—could stand.

Where the hell was I?

A slum section of some kind. Dilapidated five-story tenements huddled together, shared the block with a barren, weedy field. Across the street a gutted factory hulked in the moonlight. The street lamps were mostly casualty cases; only two were lit, cast a tired glow into the darkness. A honey of a spot, all right. Most of the windows, I saw, were boarded tight. No light shone from the rest. I listened for signs of life. There were none.

And then, ever so faintly, I heard something.

I strained to catch what it was; it seemed important. Footsteps. From behind me in the alley. Slow, shuffling steps headed my way.

I didn't like it.

An instant ago I was ready to welcome all and any comers; I was Mr. Cordiality himself. Now, abruptly I changed my mind. Suddenly I wanted only one thing: to hide, to crawl off to some deep, dark corner where no one could ever find me. *What was going on?* I didn't wait around for a reasonable answer. There wasn't apt to be one. I moved.

My knees buckled when I tried to run and I almost tumbled to the ground. Not a very promising start. What I needed was a couple of orderlies with a stretcher. What I had was a pair of almost useless legs. I glanced back. The mouth of the alley seemed to be a black, swirling pit. I couldn't see a thing. But the footsteps had grown louder. That was enough for me. Something about those footsteps made me want to scream. I needed a hiding place fast.

The front door of the first two houses I reached were boarded up, but the third swung open to my touch. I staggered in, moved down a damp, peeling ocher hallway. One small bulb hung from the ceiling. All the doors including the rear one were nailed shut with long sheets of tin. This place was a grade A candidate for the wrecking crew. No exit on the ground floor except through the front. I'd be bottled up like a prize specimen if I stayed

9

put. But the last thing I wanted was to go back on that street. That street was a menace. The roof? What did I have to lose, except the rest of my strength? Slowly, clinging to the railing like a spent oldster, I started up the stairs. The only sounds I heard were my own footsteps and feeble efforts to draw breath.

The light was out on the second floor and I groped my way forward. I couldn't be sure but I thought I heard the front door opening down below. That was inspiration. I got to the next landing in double time—relatively speaking. A faint sliver of light crept out from under the last door in the hallway.

Someone home in this dump?

Not likely.

A bulb accidentally left on, probably weeks ago. But one that showed a door not yet nailed shut! If I could get in there, flick off the light, I'd become part of the darkness. A worthwhile scheme if ever there was one. I almost chuckled with relief.

Tiptoeing over I tried the knob. Quietly the door slid open. Success! I stepped through, closed it behind me.

One large room. Night came through lightly curtained windows that looked out on a fire escape. A single lit lamp on an end table. In its weak light I saw a kitchen table, two chairs, a sink, gas range and bed. A figure sat in a rocking chair near the window—an old white-haired woman. Deep-set eyes gleamed brightly under long white eyebrows. A black embroidered shawl was wrapped over stooped narrow shoulders. She rocked slowly back and forth, a thin veined hand clutching the shawl tightly around her. The musty odor of rotting wood came from the walls.

The woman turned burning eyes toward me; she spoke, her voice a creaking sly whisper. "What kept you, Mr. Craig?" Toothless gums grinned out at me from a seamy face.

I stared at her. Amazement wasn't the right word to describe my feelings. The right word hadn't been invented yet. I finally managed to crank my mouth open, to say something, anything that might make sense. Instead a thin giggle escaped my lips.

"You think it funny, do you, Mr. Craig?" the old crone asked. Laughter bubbled from her throat, wild hysterical laughter. She rocked back and forth in a frenzy, her black piercing eyes never leaving mine.

I put a shaky finger to my lips, pointed to the door. "Sh-h-h . . . there's someone out there . . . someone . . ."

"Of course there is," the woman cackled. "You don't think you can get away, do you?"

Behind me the door burst open.

I whirled.

It stood swaying in the doorway. Its shoulders were huge, its hands ponderous. It had no face, merely a large featureless oval for a head.

A voice was screaming, filling the room with unpleasant sound. *My* voice. I ignored it. Other matters seemed more important, demanded my immediate attention. And got it. I didn't hesitate. Turning, I made tracks for the window. The old woman sprang at me. I put a fist in her face, sent her sprawling.

Shielding eyes and face with my arms, I dived headlong through the window.

I opened my eyes slowly. I was on a bed in a small, white-walled room. Bright sunlight shone through the red and green curtained windows. Behind the closed door I could hear movement, voices. I tried to sit up. An error. My head felt as if it might topple off my neck onto the blanket; my stomach started bobbing like a piece of driftwood in the ocean. I knew when to call it quits. I lay back on the pillow; my eyes closed all on their own. I must have dozed. When I looked up again I wasn't alone; a man was standing by the side of the bed.

"Feeling better?"

"Better than what?" I managed to ask weakly.

That got a smile. Too bad it had cost me almost all the zip I had. My visitor was short, chubby, in his sixties with a round face and white hair. "Well-ll, it can't be too bad if we are joking about it, can it?" He had a soft, melodious voice.

"Don't bet on it," I said. "Who are you? Where am I?"

"I am Dr. Spiegel."

"This a hospital?"

The doctor nodded.

"No guesswork, Doctor. The way I feel it'd have to be. What's wrong with me?"

"Perhaps simple exhaustion."

"Nothing simple about it; I've got all the drive of a cadaver. What've I been up to?"

The doctor looked at me quizzically. "You do not know?"

I considered that; it didn't take long to reach a definite, if not very heartening conclusion. "No."

"Well-ll," the doctor said, "that makes two of us."

"Great. How'd I get here?"

"The police."

I raised an eyebrow. "No kidding?"

"You were disturbing the peace."

"How?"

"Screaming."

"I was mad at someone?"

"You were all alone. It was three-thirty in the morning. You were standing on a street corner."

I looked at the doctor; he looked back at me. "That's pretty weird," I told him.

"You remember none of this?"

"Not a thing."

"So-o, tell me, Mr. . . ."

"Craig. Mark Craig."

"Fine. Any drinking problems, Mr. Craig, drugs perhaps?"

"I don't think so," I heard myself say.

Dr. Spiegel wrinkled his brow. "You are not sure?" He peered at me quizzically.

"No."

"What do you do, Mr. Craig?"

"Do?"

"Yes. Your occupation."

A long embarrassing moment passed. I shook my head once. "I don't seem to remember, Doctor."

"Where do you live?"

I managed a shrug; it wasn't easy.

"Wife, children, parents?"

"Sorry," I said in a weak, tired voice that summed up exactly how I felt.

"Well-ll," the doctor said, "it appears you only remember your name, Mr. Craig."

"So it appears."

"It *is* your name?" Dr. Spiegel sounded dubious. I couldn't blame him.

"Uh-huh."

"How do you know?"

"I just seem to."

"You are positive?"

"No."

"So-o," Dr. Spiegel said.

In the silence that followed I asked, "What happens next, Doctor?"

"More tests."

"More?"

"You were examined twice since your admittance here."

"That's news to me."

"You were not too responsive. But we found nothing wrong with you."

"Nothing?"

"Nothing physical."

"What then?"

"Shock, perhaps. A trauma which has caused a temporary loss of memory."

"I'm glad you said temporary."

Dr. Spiegel smiled. "I trust, Mr. Craig, that you will respond adequately to treatment."

"Treatment? I can hardly wait; what kind?"

"Nothing that need trouble you. Rest, nourishment, talk. Along those lines, Mr. Craig."

"Sounds simple enough. What hospital is this?"

"State-City."

"Never heard of it, Doctor."

The face in the mirror looked beat, as used up as old rags. No surprise there. A squarish face pushing forty, the forehead faintly lined. Dark hair. Brown eyes with dark patches under them—earned, I hoped, in the line of duty and not while on some bender. High cheekbones. A straight enough nose. Full lips. A face I could live with; especially since I had no choice.

The body that went with it looked okay, too. A tall, narrow-waisted body with plenty of muscle. Just waiting —I hoped—to rest up and get going again.

While neither body nor face seemed overly familiar, they weren't all that strange, either. I was thankful for little things. Little things were all I seemed to have left.

I turned away from the bathroom mirror, closed the door behind me and made it over to the window, hardly working up a sweat. I stood there feeling woozy and blinking in the sunlight. I must've been up pretty high, maybe twenty or thirty floors. The view was something, all right. A lot of glass and metal glittering up a storm. All shapes and sizes too. As neat and spiffy as if it'd been uncorked just last week. I gave my eyeballs a good work-out trying to pick out something reassuring and familiar. Anything would do; I wasn't about to be choosy. No dice. I turned, made my way to the bed; my sight-seeing jaunt had taken a big bite out of whatever pep I still had. I lay down and closed my eyes.

That was a mistake, all right.

I could feel something happening. I didn't know what. A shifting of some kind. Maybe a dream. Maybe just dropping off to sleep. I didn't have time to find out.

I landed on the fire escape. On all fours. Like a cat who'd been booted outdoors.

Wind whipped at me. I hung on.

My pants were torn. Blood on my leg where a piece of jagged glass from the window had done its work.

I didn't worry about it.

I wouldn't last long enough to bleed to death. The thing was climbing out the window to get me.

Down below, a fenced-in courtyard. No exit that I could spot. No time to hunt around. I grabbed a metal rung—icy to the touch—hoisted myself up the ladder toward the roof. Only two stories to the top—if I could reach it.

The fire escape shook.

I glanced down. The thing was gaining on me.

I put on a burst of speed, heaved myself up the last rungs, rolled onto the roof. I got to my feet fighting the wind. In the moonlight I saw: some old canvas. An empty paint can. A dried brush. A long piece of board next to the chimney. The latter got my attention. I almost started to laugh. I lurched over, scooped up my prize. My hands were shaking. I wheeled to face the thing that was scrambling onto the roof.

I swung the board. I gave it all I had. It connected with the thing's oval.

A wet squishy sound as if a ripe melon had been crushed. Something dark oozed out of the wound. A soundless scream went off in my mind.

The thing swayed like a felled tree, fell back against the metal grid of the fire escape.

I dropped the board. I'd had it, my fighting days were done. What I had to do now was go away while I still could.

I stumbled across the connecting rooftops. A fire escape on the last house led down to the empty lot I'd glimpsed earlier. I paused for an instant, let my eyes sweep over the terrain below.

There was nothing cheerful about what I saw:

Deserted, narrow streets faded into darkness. Clusters of tenement houses were bent and shriveled in the moonlight. No traffic or people. No light from any of the buildings.

A wasteland.

Was it my imagination or did I really see a faint, reddish glow far off near the horizon?

A fire?

Behind me I heard a scraping noise. The blasted thing was back on its feet.

I started down the fire escape. Vaguely I heard something that might've been a train rushing through a tunnel. It came from a long way off.

From the field below blackness rose to meet me.

I came to as if I'd been rising out of a deep lake. I felt tired, discouraged and half dead. I just lay there, my eyes closed, hoping somehow that I'd gotten back to State-City —it beat the only other place I remembered by miles. I was sure, though, that I hadn't.

But I was wrong.

Dr. Spiegel said, "You hit him?"

I put a yes to that.

"And?"

"I ran across the roofs and beat it down the fire escape."

"And then?"

"Then nothing. That's it."

"So-o. A dream?"

"Search me, Doctor."

"You think it *more,* Mr. Craig?"

"This stuff in the alley, it's all I remember, all I've got. I hope there's something to it; that and what went on in the house."

"It all has significance, Mr. Craig; what of this old woman?"

"Nothing. She knew my name."

"You know her, Mr. Craig?"

"Afraid not, Doctor."

"But you know *your* name. How is that?"

"Beats me."

"So-o. And that is all you remember?"

"That's the size of it."

"It seems real and not real, both at the same time. Is that right?"

"Right."

"You actually *believe* any of this?"

"I feel it."

"What do you think?"

"Think? It had to be a dream."

"All or part?"

"All."

"Well-ll. That is progress, wouldn't you say?"

"Not especially."

Dr. Spiegel smiled. He folded his hands on his desk, peered at me good-naturedly.

I looked back, Old Stoneface himself. I was dressed in pajamas and robe. I could see the spit-and-polish city through the doctor's office window. It looked as normal as a three-headed butterfly. It made me feel creepy.

Dr. Spiegel said, "Actually, this is a good deal of progress. Your unconscious is speaking to you, Mr. Craig."

"Yeah?"

"Most certainly. But the unconscious speaks in symbols, doesn't it, Mr. Craig? The symbols might be termed masks. That is why the man had no face."

"That's why, huh?"

"Yes, indeed. And that is the start, of course."

"Of what?"

"A cure."

I grinned. "No kidding?"

"It may be slow."

"How slow is slow?"

"Who can tell? The mind works at its own speed, Mr. Craig. First there was little to go on. You were running from something. In fear. That is quite typical."

"Yeah. Just one of the boys, Doctor."

"Then came the symbols."

"That's important, huh?"

"Your mind, Mr. Craig, is telling us a bit more. Soon there may be no need of masks at all. Then we may know everything."

"Why masks in the first place?"

"Shock. Something happened which you wish to forget. Something terrible, perhaps."

"Uh-huh. Let me ask *you* something, Doctor."

"Of course."

"Was there anything in my pockets, a wallet, some kind of identification?"

Dr. Spiegel shook his head. "I'm afraid not."

"Great. What about those slums I landed in?"

"What about them?"

"I got a pretty good look at 'em. From the roof."

"They weren't real, Mr. Craig."

"I know. Let's just suppose."

"But what's the point?"

"For kicks."

Dr. Spiegel sighed. "Go on."

"That section was weird, Doctor; crooked houses; twisted streets; everything boarded up. Anything like that in town?"

"Nothing at all."

"How's that possible?"

"Must there be slums?"

"Most big cities have them."

"In fiction, perhaps."

"Okay. How about nearby. In traveling distance, maybe?"

"You're on the wrong track, Mr. Craig. You're looking in the wrong place, believe me."

"Where should I look?"

"In your mind."

I remembered going to sleep.

I was on a train. I could hear the motor's beat, the whir of wheels on metal rails as the car pitched from side to side. I looked out the window. Nothing. Only a thick syrupy blackness. The train, then, was speeding through a tunnel. The air inside the car was stale, heavy, the odor of cigarette butts clinging to floor and wicker seats.

I tried to see the other passengers. Their heads were all turned away from me. I wanted to know who they were. But I was somehow too sluggish to make the effort. I sat as if riveted to my seat. I couldn't even turn my head. But out of the corner of my eye I caught some reflections in the windows. It helped only a little.

The small redhead was the clearest of all. He sat two

seats away. A pointy chin. Glasses. He looked to be somewhere in his forties.

I saw a black-haired woman with glasses and a blonde farther away. I saw a broad-backed bald-headed man. I couldn't make out the others. I wondered if I knew them. I didn't know.

CHAPTER 2

Alexis Rike

Alexis Rike opened his eyes.

He was flat on his back. His muscles ached. Dull gray light filtered through a small barred window high up near the ceiling. He could hear the steady drip of water.

Rike lay very still gazing at the uneven stone wall, the barred window, the damp ceiling. He was in a cell. He didn't know why.

Rike sat up slowly, painfully, then climbed to his feet. He felt weak. Otherwise there seemed to be nothing wrong with him.

The cell, he saw, was small, damp, and empty. A rusted metal door with a peephole. Water trickling through a crack in one corner. A hole in the floor for a toilet. The toilet had not recently been used.

Rike went to the door, banged on it, waited. An echo vibrated from somewhere on the other side, faded away. No one came in response.

Rike moved to the makeshift fountain, washed his face,

cupped his hands, and drank. The water tasted metallic. He seated himself by the far wall to wait.

Who am I? he thought.

Alexis Rike didn't know.

They came for him some time later, three large burly men in coarse, not too clean, brown monk's robes. They didn't speak as Rike walked between them down winding, ill-lit stone corridors.

Alexis Rike was a slender, wiry man of medium height who looked to be in his late thirties. He had sharp, delicate features, thick black hair parted on the right. Green eyes were half hidden by heavy eyelids.

They came to a large wooden door. Rike was led into an open courtyard.

Men and women shuffled along, vacant-eyed, their clothes soiled and ragged. Some sat on the ground staring off into space. Others babbled to themselves. A few jerked and twitched as though stricken by palsy. A young girl with long matted brown hair pirouetted in a solitary dance at the courtyard's far end.

Rike paused, stared at them.

A madhouse, he thought in some wonder.

A heavy hand shook his shoulder, pushed him forward. Rike moved along.

Another door led into the building. The four-man procession slowly climbed stone steps, moved down a last corridor and into a huge, well-lit room.

A short fat man with a bald head, thick lips and small squinty eyes waddled toward Alexis Rike. He too was dressed in a brown robe. The man's thick lips parted, he spoke:

"So, the devil's helpmate has ceased his slumber." His voice was thick, slurred. He glared at Rike. "Your name!"

"Alexis Rike."

"What manner of name is this?"

Rike said nothing.

"Confess!" the monk roared, "Confess you plot with the devil!"

Rike eyed the monk silently.

"Confess! Lest you burn in eternal hell-fire!"

"What am I supposed to have done?" Rike asked.

The monk told him. It seemed that he—Alexis Rike—had popped out of nowhere at two-thirty yesterday afternoon in the village square. There had been lightning and thunder. The townfolk fled in horror. Except for a few who, taking their lives in their hands, crept back. Rike was still lying where he had fallen. After a suitable time elapsed and he had failed to move, they took heart and dragged him off to the monastery. Where he now was. The monk paused for breath.

Rike said, "*That* was my crime?"

The monk wiped his brow with a shaky hand. "Confess now," he whispered.

"To what?"

"Conspiring with the foul fiend!" the monk shrieked.

Rike thought it over. "Have you no magicians here?" he asked.

"Consider your immortal soul."

"It was a trick."

"Trick? You are a trickster?"

Rike admitted it.

"Do a trick," the monk commanded. "Now."

Rike began to explain very earnestly why he couldn't.

"You hesitate?"

"The stars are not in their proper alignment."

"Lies!"

Alexis Rike said, "You are making a grave error."

"Where do you come from, trickster?"

"From far away."

The monk smiled slyly. "You will not tell me, then?"

"There is nothing to tell."

"But there is. Ah, yes, there is so much for you to tell. And tell you will, my dear trickster. There are ways, you understand."

"No doubt."

"Ways that are by no means subtle. Or pleasant. *Who are you?*"

Rike shrugged.

21

"Well, you will not tell me. So be it. But you will surely tell *them*."

"Them?"

"Of course, they have already been summoned. They come."

"Who are they?"

"The inquisitors, my dear trickster, who else?" The monk laughed. But a thin coating of sweat glistened across his bald dome, sent rills streaming over fat cheeks, chin, and neck.

He's afraid, Alexis Rike thought. And so am I.

Back in his cell, Rike spent the next hour hunting for some means of escape; he found none. The door was barred from the outside. The stone walls were solid except for the one crack which leaked water. Using his fingers, Rike could not widen it. The barred window was too high to reach.

Alexis Rike sat down, his back to the wall, and tried to think.

He had no idea how he had gotten here. The episode the monk had recited made no sense.

He knew his name. He knew he did not belong here. He did not know much else. Memories, vague and insubstantial, drifted in and out of focus. Someone was screaming and calling. A milling crowd began to run. He saw flames. There were faces, too, flickering on and off; they were familiar, yet strange . . .

Some time later they brought him food: a thick soup with pieces of meat floating in it and a large wad of black bread. He ate hungrily. They weren't going to let him starve. At least not until he saw the inquisitors. He did not think he would like seeing them. He wondered if somehow he could avoid it.

The five monks who came for him that night were tall, hefty men. Alexis Rike decided to go quietly.

They went in a different direction this time, down a dark, winding corridor. The lead monk held a torch. They marched past other cells. Sounds of laughter, weeping, screaming came from behind the bolted wooden doors. Alexis Rike shuddered.

They reached a wide metal door. Two monks lifted the heavy bolt, swung the door open on rusty hinges. They went down a wide stone staircase. Cobwebs glittered in the torchlight. A large rat scurried by below. Long shadows flitted over walls, stairs, and the six men who moved steadily downward.

The basement consisted of huge pillars rising up into the darkness. The floor was earth, had a damp, sour smell. Whatever sins had brought him here must have been considerable, Rike thought.

A final door was unbolted, Rike pushed through. He was in a narrow passageway. The monks did not follow. The door swung shut behind him. Rike heard the bolt fall into place. He was alone. Dim light came from the far end of the passage. Alexis Rike went toward it, through an arch.

He was in a high domed room. Bright light shone from walls and ceiling.

Three men stood in the center of this room. One trained a long-barreled weapon at Rike's chest. The second simply stared at him. The third moved toward a machine at the far end of the room. None wore monk's robes.

"You are the inquisitors?" Rike asked.

"Quite right, Mr. Rike," the man at the far side of the room answered.

"You aren't from here," Rike said.

"Right again," the man said.

All three were dressed in black, form-fitting garments. The one with the weapon was short, stubby; the one next to him of medium height. The man by the wall who had spoken was tall, narrow-chested. Their faces were white, pasty-looking as if they had never been exposed to the sun.

"This is the inquisition chamber?" Rike asked.

The tall man smiled. There was nothing pleasant about his smile. "This is the chamber of truth, Mr. Rike."

The medium-sized man spoke in a flat, dead voice. "Let us get on with it."

The tall man touched a switch on the machine. "Stand still, Mr. Rike, this will be painless."

A thin sliver of light leaped from the machine, focused on Rike, widened.

"Try to relax, Mr. Rike," the tall man was saying. "Relax."

The man's voice seemed to come from a vast distance. The room grew smaller. Alexis Rike looked around for a nice, comfortable spot to fall down on. Then it didn't matter. He was plunging headfirst into a whirling pool of blackness.

Alexis Rike walked slowly through the square in plague-ridden Athens. It was 430 B.C. Bodies littered the ground. Some were still breathing, a few tried to crawl along the roadway. So far no one had shown up to help the sick, to sift the living from the dead.

Rike leaned up against a wall, his knees buckling. There was something he had to do here.

What?

He tried to remember.

He had come from the shrines. And they were filled with bodies . . .

Slowly, a curtain seemed to be lifting in his mind . . .

The war.

How stupid of him to forget.

The war between Athens and Sparta.

Refugees from the Athenian countryside had swarmed into the city, thousands of them; their makeshift shanties were everywhere.

A hot summer. The sun roasted the city. There was plague. Corpses lay in the gutters. The dying dragged themselves over the streets, piled up around the fountains as thirst ravaged them.

They rotted in the shrines, rotted in their shanties, rotted on the streets. There was no end in sight.

Rike stared at the square before him, seeing nothing. His tunic was wrinkled and sweat-stained.

Something still escaped him, something about the plague . . .

The blonde was suddenly by his side. She looked to be in her mid-twenties—a slender, curly-haired blonde with green eyes and ivory skin. She too wore a tunic.

"Don't leave me," she said.

"I won't," Rike heard himself promise.

"Ever," she said.

Alexis Rike nodded in assent. He knew this woman, was close to her in some way.

The blonde said: "We can stay here, darling—together. Always."

"Here?"

"A paradise," the girl whispered.

"It doesn't *look* like a paradise."

"Trust me, dearest; come."

Rike did trust this woman, wanted to go with her. Something seemed to hold him back. It was as if gravity had suddenly increased, pinning him here to this spot. He tried to fight the force, to struggle against it. Alexis Rike raised his eyes.

Beyond the city's rooftops, far away where the shallow hills merged with the horizon, a red ball of flame was rising. It spread slowly, sedately, like a massive balloon filling the sky. Its red-hot center grew brighter.

Rike looked away, shielding his eyes. He could move again, the magnetic force was gone. So was the girl.

Nothing had changed in the square. The bodies were still on the ground, the sick and dying still crowding the fountains. What had happened to the girl? Had he imagined it all? The red glow—if it had ever existed— was gone, too. Rike put a shaky hand to his forehead; it felt hot, feverish. Alexis Rike wanted to move, to leave this place. His legs shook when he tried to walk; his breathing was harsh, shallow; his head heavy. He had taken numerous precautions but, obviously, not enough. The plague, it seemed, was about to claim another victim.

Alexis Rike dived into a very black pool.

The voices in the whirlpool came from all directions, simultaneously near and far. There were many of them.

"Well?"

"It is as I feared, he is not from here."

"You are certain?"

"What else can it be? His memories are letter-perfect."

"And our agents?"

"Their report is substantially the same."

"Yet he is not the one we seek."

"He knows nothing!"

"Perhaps he is deceiving us."

"How?"

"He has buried his true self."

"You think this possible?"

"I do not know."

"What if his memories are a mere overlay, a ruse?"

"Then he has been placed here as a diversion, to traduce us."

"We must probe again."

"He would perish. His mind could not sustain it."

"Let us wait then. It is a mere matter of hours."

"He cannot resist the probe. We shall know all soon enough."

"In any case, this one is now harmless."

"What of the woman he spoke to?"

"There was no report of her."

"His mind may be disordered."

"Or our agents at fault."

"It is his mind."

"We shall see."

"Take him back.

Alexis Rike opened his eyes.

He was again in his cell. He sat up cautiously. Nothing wrong. He felt neither weak nor groggy. If anything, his mind felt clearer, sharper than before.

What had happened?

Rike wasn't sure. The inquisitors weren't monks—belonged in this place no more than he did. A light of some sort had flashed out at him; he knew that much.

And he had found himself in ancient Greece. During the year of the great plague. Or imagined he had.

Nothing in that, he thought.

Or was there?

He shut his eyes.

A strip seemed to be unreeling in his mind. He could picture Athens plainly, its streets and dwellings. He could see now what had come after the darkness. Only a moment had gone by:

He was in the square, probably hunting for the girl. Some people were making their way down the street, a small man with red hair in front. Rike stiffened. Apparently he didn't want to be seen. Rike managed to turn his back. He moved quietly down a side street and out of sight.

In his cell Rike opened his eyes. His shock at these memories was real enough. But something else was bothering him, too. *The memories were different, somehow.*

He had been part of the man in Athens, had walked through the square with him, spoken to the girl, shared his very thoughts.

But that was before. With the inquisitors.

Now he could still recall the Alexis Rike of Athens. But as an outsider. Someone watching another perform from a distance.

And he didn't know what the performance meant.

Rike closed his eyes, tried very hard to raise Athens again. From far off, he seemed to hear the rushing of wind through a tunnel, the beat of engines.

What the hell?

Something had gone wrong; he would have to put more effort into it.

The second time he tried the image came:

He was in one of the shanties, a dark, empty place. He moved stealthily, rummaged under a mat, came up with a bottle. Hiding it under his tunic, Rike started back toward the city.

The strip continued to unwind:

Rike saw himself creeping through a darkening Athens. The scene had changed little. Groups of men hurried by. If they spoke at all, it was in whispers. Some carried objects wrapped in blankets. Looters? Rike avoided them.

By the time he reached the first fountain the moon was out. Cautiously he removed the bottle from under his tunic, emptied part of its contents into the fountain.

Poison? Alexis Rike in his cell smiled thinly, his green eyes half closed. It was all right with him. As a mere bystander he could hardly complain.

Nine other fountains were visited by Rike.

At the eleventh, three men stepped out of the darkness.

One was tall, heavyset. Grunting, he swung a club at Rike's head.

Rike moved, caught the man's arm with one hand, lashed out with the other.

The man fell down.

Rike kicked the club away, turned to the other two. The one closest to him—a fat, gray-bearded party— hesitated. His green-tunicked companion lunged past him, a knife in his hand.

Rike stepped to one side, his foot caught green tunic under the knee, sent him toppling. Gray beard sprinted away into the night. Green tunic scrambled to his feet, made off in another direction. The club swinger still hadn't moved.

Rike stood motionless.

And the picture froze.

In his cell, Alexis Rike let out a long sigh. He could remember no more. The memories, or whatever they were, had hit an impenetrable wall.

Rike got to his feet, began to pace. What had he learned? Not much. A couple of scenes that could have been lifted from any storybook. In a way, what he had seen was almost wish fulfillment. He had handled those three without batting an eye. Not bad. If he could toss around the monks in a similar fashion, he'd be out of here in no time. Rike flexed a muscle; at least there was one. It didn't quite seem sturdy enough to do the job. But who could tell?

Rike seated himself, prepared to wait for his next meal or anything else that might present itself. Perhaps if he let his thoughts drift he might remember something else.

Rike half closed his eyes.

And the tapping noise began. It was coming from the cell on the other side of the wall.

Rike listened. Without knowing exactly how, he was able to understand the message perfectly. It was a simple message tapped out in basic Morse code; it read:

You are not alone.

CHAPTER 3

The Girl and the Golem

Long blond hair hung loosely around her shoulders. Her feet seemed to glide over the cobblestones. Her gown was white. Skin ivory. Eyes green jade. She moved as in a dream.

Past midnight.

The small crooked houses on either side of her were shuttered tight. No light escaped from their windows. The church steeple towered over the city like a silent, peering watchman.

The time was 1577.

The city was Prague.

The girl halted before the house of Rabbi Judah Loew ben Bezaleel.

In the attic of this house the Golem had stood speechless and immobile for over a decade.

The Golem. Created, it was said, by the rabbi himself. Fashioned out of lime. To defend Jews from those who sought to destroy them.

The girl's hand moved to the brass knocker. Sound reverberated through the house.

The man who presently opened the door wore a black robe and yarmulke. His beard was long, white. His cheeks sunken. His brow lined. He held a candle in one hand. Rabbi Judah Loew known also as the Maharal said, "What is it you want?"

She did not answer.

Slowly the girl began moving past the rabbi into the house as if following an invisible beacon.

The rabbi did not stop her.

She moved up the darkened staircase. The rabbi followed behind, his candle sending long shadows across the wall.

The attic door was not locked; it opened to her touch.

The figure standing in the far corner was hardly imposing. No taller than five nine, it had a double chin and a slight paunch protruding under its dark robe.

Approaching it the girl placed two fingers on its forehead.

The Golem opened its eyes.

"Come," the girl said.

"I have waited a long time," the Golem said.

The pair vanished.

"So be it," the rabbi murmured. "He has come and he has gone. Blessed be He who has created all things."

The city of gold and silver shook with explosions.

"This way," the girl said.

She and the Golem ducked into an alleyway. Armed troops ran by on the street outside.

"Why are we here?" the Golem asked.

"We seek the Prime."

"He is here?"

"Unknown."

"Still?"

"Still. Come. Stay close to me."

"I will remain at your side," the Golem promised.

The pair trotted down the alley, came to a gate.

"It is locked," the girl said.

The Golem took hold of the bars. And twisted. They bent like licorice sticks. He and the girl crawled through. They were in a garden. The sounds of combat came from adjoining streets. Before them a large dome-shaped structure rose above the trees and foliage.

"There," the girl said.

The couple followed a gravel path.

The Golem asked, "Why did you not come for me sooner?"

"I could not. The system is in chaos. You were beyond my reach."

The Goldem seemed shocked. "How did this happen?"

The girl shook her head. Blond hair swirled about her. "That, too, is unknown."

The structure now loomed before them. A locked door blocked their progress. The Golem put his shoulder against it. Wood splintered. They were in a white, gleaming corridor which spiraled upward. Light shone through transparent walls. They moved along the corridor. The explosions outside seemed far away. But the building rocked periodically as if a large hand were shaking it.

The Golem asked, "Which of the stations are still open to us?"

"It varies. At times no more than a quarter. And our control, even over these, is slipping."

"Then how did you find me?"

"Luck."

They had reached the top. A mechanized wall responding to their presence slid up into the ceiling.

The girl and the Golem stepped through into a glass-domed penthouse.

Part of the city was visible from here. Small and large fires gutted the urban landscape. Troops could be seen moving below.

The girl went into the next room. "In here," she called.

The Golem joined her.

The man who lay huddled on the bed had been dead a long time. Hollow-cheeked. Skin wrinkled and blemished. Hair white, unruly. The body was all but wasted away.

"It is Ingram," the girl said.

"Hardly recognizable. He is not the Prime."

"No," the girl said with a shake of her head, "he is not the Prime. At least not *this* Ingram."

The train raced through the tunnel.

The girl and the Golem sat in the last car. They had company. The unmoving figures who occupied the front section of the car and had their backs to them sat as though frozen in blocks of ice. The girl and the Golem ignored them.

"Your power has grown," the Golem said.

"Only to a point. I can shift at will, now. But I cannot control the circuit."

"For that we no doubt need the Prime."

"We may never reach him. The circuit itself seems to shift. New territory is uncovered, but old is lost."

"Indeed?" the Golem said. "Then how do you know they have not already destroyed him?"

"If that were true, they would be everywhere now."

The Golem shrugged. "Perhaps they are."

CHAPTER 4

From the Diary of Dr. James Ingram

March 4, 1935. I have moved again. The third time in five months. Now that I am so close to my goal I must take no chances. Perhaps it is my imagination but I see *them* on all sides. Dear me, yes, they appear to be everywhere. But are they? I find myself searching the papers for clues. I read: *Three Killings Linked to Rackets* and wonder is it *them?* There is no way to know. Perhaps I am setting my sights too low? Another headline proclaims: *Japan and China Draw Together*. That would certainly fit into their scheme. But are *they* actually involved? For all I know they may not have reached this time juncture at all. However, I must work under the assumption that they have. To do otherwise would place my entire project in jeopardy. And with it the fate of the human race. The responsibility is great.

March 6, 1935. I took the day off yesterday. A lark. Well, there wasn't much else I could do. I have begun to move my equipment from the warehouse where I have stored it to my present lodgings at 465 West 25th Street. I shall move a little each night—stealthily—so as not to alarm my neighbors, or attract undue attention. In a matter of weeks my laboratory will be reassembled. I have already hired what assistants I will need. All that remains to be done is wait for the fateful day of May 15.

Meanwhile I indulged my taste for the local arts by visiting the Radio City Music Hall. I saw *The Whole Town's Talking,* with Edward G. Robinson and Jean Arthur. Quite delightful. Tomorrow I hope to see *Devil Dogs of the Air,* with James Cagney and Pat O'Brien. A caption in today's *New York Times* caught my eye: *Lasker Triumphs over Capablanca. Veteran Chess Master Gains Notable Victory at Moscow.* A remarkable deed. Lasker is in his mid-sixties and his abilities should be declining. His achievement gives me heart. We are, after all, the same age.

March 11, 1935. It rained all day. Mostly I puttered in my laboratory. It is now beginning to take shape, although much of the equipment is still in the warehouse. My nightly trips there grow tedious. At times I do not return home till the small hours of the morning. Last night I missed both Eddie Cantor and "One Man's Family" on the radio. But tonight, because of the rain I decided not to go out and was able to hear "Kate Smith's Review." Earlier I had sent the Wilden boy from the floor below downstairs with two cents to buy a *Times*. Max Schmeling, I saw, had stopped an American, Hamas, in the ninth round of a boxing bout in Germany. The Nazis who filled the stadium cheered for many moments. They represent the worst elements of the human race, and yet they are as nothing compared to the aliens who at the very instant plot to enslave us all. So far, they have been stymied, their hopes frustrated. Now they try again. On May 15 they will surely make another attempt, but I will meet them head on. Oh yes. I have waited thirty long years for this day. The most significant day, surely, in the history of mankind. God help us all if somehow I have miscalculated again.

April 9, 1935. It is done! The final pieces of equipment were installed late yesterday. The laboratory is complete!

Again and again I have gone over the calculations. Always the results are the same. May 15 of this year, the black hole will re-emerge through time-space. It will slice through earth. And in its wake, the alien troops will pour like salt through a shaker—no doubt to subvert, rather than fight, for they are best at that. My notebooks are full of facts and figures. I describe the properties of a black hole, delineate its visual distortions. Important perhaps for a full understanding of the forces at work here, but far from complete. For the aliens' own energy system has merged with the black hole. Only thus were they able to launch their first treacherous attack. (How distant that now seems.) My calculations, of course, have taken this into account, but it is impossible to predict fully what alterations have occurred. Still, none of this should interfere with my counterthrust. I hope and pray for the best.

April 10, 1935. I stayed home last night and listened to the radio. I heard Ben Bernie's orchestra, then the comedian Ed Wynn and finally, Fibber McGee and Molly. It is strange how much at home I am in this culture, how close I feel to it. But perhaps not so strange, after all. I have spent half a lifetime here, haven't I? I would rather have gone out as is my custom. There is so much to see, to smell, to hear, and indeed I was tempted to forget caution. But there is no way to know whether the aliens or their agents are here. They would surely be on the lookout for me. And yet, I am not certain they would dare move against me. For since that moment when I first struck at them, have I not too become an equation in their energy system? Tamper with me and all *their* calculations might go astray. Still, I thought it best not to wander about the streets.

April 11, 1935. I have had a most disturbing thought. Again—in my mind's eye—I saw the City of Silver and Gold. I recalled what had happened there: My initial stand against the aliens was not taken alone. Others were there. I remember turning to them in that final moment.

35

"Listen," I said, "when the switch is thrown, this laboratory will go out of phase with the city. We will become part of the force field. We will be linked together but will be unable to communicate. Carry on if anything happens to me . . ." *Carry on.* But are we still linked even here? How can I know of their efforts or they of mine? Would this not change the equations once again, alter both my calculations and even those of the aliens? *And with what results?*

PART 2

Mark Craig

No light whatever could penetrate a black hole, so concentrated is its body. The hole would truly be black. It could plummet through the very earth itself.

from *The Notebooks of Dr. James Ingram*

CHAPTER 5

I awoke in total darkness. It took me a moment to get my bearings. Something was wrong.

What?

There were no sounds at all. As if while I slept the city outside had been whisked away, the hallway on the other side of my door rolled up and carted off along with doctors, patients, nurses, everything . . .

I turned my head. The window should have been visible in the east wall. Even on the darkest night the city sent a stream of light into my hospital room. Now there was nothing.

How was that possible?

I started to get off the bed. There was no bed. That did it, a clean sweep.

I was lying on a cold stone floor. It was damp to the touch. I shivered. And noticed something else. My pajamas were gone. In their place I felt a heavy shirt, wrinkled pants—the work clothes I'd worn in the alley!

I opened my mouth and shouted:

"Hello-o-o." Help, would have been more to the point.

My voice came echoing back. That was the only answer. I seemed to be in some deep cavern.

Jesus.

I climbed to my feet slowly, wary of the weakness that might send me toppling. Another surprise, this one not quite as unpleasant. The weakness was gone too, along with everything else. I seemed to be all right again. At least physically. That was about the only thing that was all right.

Had it all been a dream? Or was this the dream?

The spotless city I'd glimpsed through the window. The doctors who'd fallen all over themselves trying to help a man with no past *and no money*. Did that make any more sense than the faceless thing from the alley? Or the wasted, deserted slums I'd seen from the rooftops?

An image seemed to drift up from the chaos that was my mind:

I saw a ward with too many beds, a lot of shabby men, some of them screaming because they had the d.t.'s. A bone-weary intern looked in on them from time to time. Nurses were scarce. The food was lousy. And after a while the social worker would drop around and ask who was going to pay the bill.

I'd forgotten a lot, maybe, but I still had a couple of facts stored up. And my being in State-City Hospital didn't fit any of them. The trouble was my being here in total darkness was even less reasonable.

Was I lying drugged somewhere in a hospital ward this very minute? Or some jail getting over the effects of a king-sized bender?

I moved.

Slowly at first, one foot in front of another. I had enough trouble without breaking my neck. I came to a wall, ran my hand over it. Large stone blocks, damp and partly covered with something that could have been moss.

I began to wonder if I'd lost all my marbles. For keeps.

I started walking, following the wall. It seemed to go on and on.

After a while I sat down to rest. I was dizzy. I must have fallen asleep.

The sun was shining.

I got to my feet slowly, shielding my eyes against the sun's glare, looked around. I was in a field. Grass, trees, shrubs. Blue sky overhead. A sprinkle of white puffy clouds. Small hills were visible in one direction, level plains in the other. I turned. Structures which might have been a city perched somewhere near the horizon. I could see no road. But I was alive and well. Who could complain? I started hiking—cross-country—toward the city. Soon I reached a gravel road. A sign pointing down it said Old York. Old York it was.

My name was Mark Craig. I was a registered Double M, a middle-man, one of the many who discreetly handled the numerous payoffs in the shakedown trade. I ran a solo office on Center near Main. I'd have done better with one of the bigger outfits but I valued my independence too much. The thought of punching a time clock, going on salary and a five percent commission depressed me. I was pushing thirty-six. My parents had died when I was six in the infamous Sherwood Square tenement blaze. The rest of my growing up was done at the city orphanage. A place I couldn't recommend even for a short visit. I'd put myself through college the hard way working the swing shift as a typesetter at the City Gazette. I'd done a couple of stints with the larger Double M agencies before hanging out my own shingle. I'd never married. I had a couple of drinking pals—including Clive Western, who held down an editor's desk at the Daily Sun—but no really close friends. Sometimes I wondered why. Usually I didn't think about it. I rented a three-room flat off Grove Street. I was hale and hearty, which was more than could be said for Old York itself.

I got over to a tree—no small accomplishment—and plunked down against it. My legs were shaking. I was dumbfounded. It was as if a strong wind were scattering the last wisps of fog that had spitefully hidden my past from me. Now I knew it all. All, it occurred to me, wasn't so damn much. I put my hand in a pocket, dug out a wallet, a set of keys. How about that? The ID in the wallet said I was Mark Craig, registered middle-man, and a photo—one bearing my face—seemed to prove it. I had around thirty bucks on me, too. And I remembered the keys, and the three-room flat they belonged to. My memory had made the fastest comeback on record. State-City Hospital and the fancy buildings I'd spotted through the window were just so much eyewash. Nothing like that had ever existed around here—that was for sure. And probably nothing ever would.

So here I was.

I sat there mulling it over. And wondered why I still felt rotten. I didn't think I'd enjoy finding out.

CHAPTER 6

The alarm clock jangled me awake the next morning.

It took me a second to figure out where I was. I made sure by turning my head toward the window. It was all there. Under a gray, overcast sky I could see the ramshackle five- and six-story walk-ups, all in need of paint jobs. Peeling fire escapes added that special touch. Down below crowds of denim-clad factory hands scurried along the cracked pavement. They didn't look any too chipper. Horse-drawn food and ice wagons rolled noisily over the tar roadway making their daily rounds. A typical morning in Old York. All perfectly familiar, of course. And yet I felt funny as hell looking at it. I tried to shrug the feeling away.

Climbing out of bed, I padded into the bathroom, fed the greenish pump its nickel ransom and was rewarded with a spurt of lukewarm water. Hateful, just as always. I grabbed a quick shower and shave before the damn thing died on me.

Dressing quickly, I draped myself in a wrinkled blue denim pin-striped suit, blue cotton shirt and wide denim

41

tie. I ran a comb through my hair, double-locked the door behind me, and carefully made my way down three flights of dingy, crooked staircase. I could hear my neighbors going through their usual rousing maneuvers: couples arguing, kids yelping, dogs barking. It never varied. The odor of perking coffee filled the hallway, along with the smells of disinfectant and insect poison. A thoroughly disagreeable blend.

Outside, I hoofed it two blocks to the corner carriage stop, flagged an express coach, managed to squeeze into the last of the three wagons and was carried downtown. The horse team moved plenty fast.

Presently the business section drifted into view, a cluster of dreary red and yellow brick office buildings anywhere from six to fifteen stories tall. A sight which had very few inspirational qualities. I had a fourth-floor, twelve-by-eight cubicle. My windows overlooked Center Street. Whatever sights there were I could see. I didn't consider myself all that lucky.

I ate breakfast across the street at the Swank Diner, and downed an extra cup of coffee to celebrate what I hoped was my return to sanity. Just to be on the safe side I swapped a couple of words with the waiter.

"About yesterday, Charley."

"Yes, Mr. Craig?"

"I think I forgot your tip."

"Nope," the waiter said.

"You sure?"

"Uh-huh."

"How about the day before?"

"No sir, Mr. Craig. You never forget."

"Not even last Monday?"

"Monday was the same as always," he beamed at me.

"Glad to hear it," I said, doubling his tip to a big twenty cents.

Charley thanked me and I went back into the street. I bought a tabloid from the corner newsie, who was also sure I'd paid him yesterday.

So much for that.

The three days I recalled spending in State-City Hospital were a pipe dream. I'd been *here,* not *there,* going about my regular business. Suddenly it was sharp and clear. A heavy work load had kept me hustling till all hours. I'd come in contact with scores of people and I remembered them all, just as they would probably remember me. I had a ledger up in the office and could check on each one if I had to. I didn't think I'd have to.

Standing in front of my building watching the wagons and pedestrians stream by I wondered why I still felt so queasy.

The alternative to State-City, of course, was that I had gone stark raving mad for a while! Maybe that was it.

I bent down quickly, touched my leg, felt the half-healed cut through my clothing, the one I'd gotten jumping through the window with the faceless thing at my heels.

And how *had* I gotten six miles out of town last night?

The door to my office was open.

Two men were waiting for me. One was tall and thin. He had a long horse face, hooked nose, high cheekbones and close-cropped sandy hair. He was seated in my chair, his feet up on my desk. The other was soft, short and round with a cupid's mouth and shiny black hair. He got out of the client's chair as I came in, went to stand by the desk. Both wore gray denims, narrow blue ties, the unofficial uniform of the plainclothes squad. I could see the bulge of their shoulder holsters.

"Mutt and Jeff," I heard a voice murmur sourly; my voice.

The tall one spoke without moving his lips, "Mean anything to you, Watts?"

The little man's round lips quivered; he replied in a high, flute-like voice, "Not a thing, Nickerson; it's pure gibberish."

"That's good," the man called Nickerson nodded. "That way there's no need to take offense, is there?"

"Not if he doesn't mean anything by it," the little one agreed. "That would be unjust."

I stood there wondering what I *had* meant. Mutt and

Jeff? I didn't know any Mutt and Jeff. Reluctantly I brought my attention back to my visitors. They looked like a pair of refugees from some chintzy cabaret troupe, but of course they weren't. I didn't have to hunt through my memory to know what was coming next.

"Take a load off your dogs," Nickerson said amiably.

I was too disgusted to do anything but stand there. "How'd you get in?" I finally asked.

"It matters?" Nickerson asked, exercising indisputable logic.

Watts said, "Show him the badge."

Nickerson got his feet off my desk, flipped a hand into his jacket pocket, removed a small worn leather card case, opened it and showed me the badge.

I said, "You've got a search warrant, of course?"

Nickerson looked at me as if I'd just asked for the next waltz.

Watts wagged a manicured finger my way. "Tut-tut," he said. "Search warrants are anachronisms."

"This may sound petty, fellas," I told them, "but I looked up my rights once, and guess what, I got some. Why don't you two scram?"

"A wise guy," Nickerson said sadly. "He understands just one thing, I bet: trouble. We can give him plenty of that, can't we?"

"Certainly. But perhaps we've got him wrong, Nickerson?"

"He thinks he got rights," Nickerson pointed out. "What gives you such dumb ideas, Craig?"

"A bum education?" I asked.

"Could be," Nickerson agreed.

I sat down in the client's chair. "You boys bringing charges of some kind? You better, because I'm not paying."

"Charges?" Nickerson said. "What's that, something like rights?"

Watts said, "Look, Mr. Craig, adults should be able to settle their differences amicably. There should be no need for charges, for arrests."

I looked around to see where the adults might be hiding. "Arrests, yet," I said. "Listen, chums, I hate to tell you but half the force out there is busy spending my dough. All the way from the boys on the beat right up to the captain. The take can only go so far."

"It's gonna go further," Nickerson said. "Wait and see."

"This is a special case," Watts assured me.

"Special? Listen, you're talking to a Double M; special cases are my bread and butter. And I can tell you boys *I'm* paid up fair and square."

"Almost," Nickerson said.

"Except possibly for one very small item," Watts said.

"I can hardly wait," I told him. "I bet it's a beaut."

"It has a certain charm," Watts admitted.

"We did a routine check," Nickerson said, "when your license came up for renewal."

"A mere formality," Watts said. "Imagine our chagrin when you turned out to be an unperson, Mr. Craig."

"A blank," Nickerson said.

"Meaning what?" I asked.

"Meaning," Nickerson said, "that up to a couple of years ago, no one had ever heard of you."

I sat there and looked at them. They looked back at me. Outside I could hear wagons and coaches rolling by, the sounds of pedestrians on the go. Sunlight made irregular patterns against the walls. A thin layer of dust I saw covered the floor. "How's that possible?" I finally asked.

"How indeed?" Watts said.

"We were gonna ask you that very same question," Nickerson said.

"No records?" I asked.

"None."

"Maybe someone stole them," I suggested.

"Maybe," Nickerson said. "But we don't want to pry, do we, Watts?"

"Perish the thought," Watts said.

"Thing is," Nickerson said, "the way it stands now, it's illegal. We could dig some, but why push it; no need for all that leg work, all that trouble."

"Not among friends," Watts said.

"Friends," Nickerson said, "that's an okay word, ain't it, Craig? Where would we be without it?"

"Broke, probably," Watts said sadly. "Old friends, new friends, what does it matter, as long as they're dependable friends."

"I guess that's me," I said. "You fellas seem to have come up with a brand-new wrinkle."

"Told you so," Watts smiled.

"Well," I said, "no one's more dependable than me when it comes to helping a friend. How much help you fellas figure you'll need?"

"How much you got?" Nickerson asked.

"Business is lousy," I said.

"What isn't?" Watts asked.

"I might manage twenty apiece," I said.

"Fifty would be neater," Nickerson said.

"Fifty would mean true friendship," Watts said.

"Fifty would bust me," I lied. "What does twenty-five buy?"

"We nod when we pass you on the street," Nickerson said.

"I could live with that," I told him.

Watts wagged his head. "You drive a hard bargain, Mr. Craig."

I reached into my wallet. Money changed hands.

The two cops rose to go.

"See, Craig," Nickerson said, "the bite wasn't so bad, was it?"

"And this way," Watts said, "you remain a man of mystery."

"I'm not really a man of mystery," I said.

Watts shrugged. "Suit yourself, Mr. Craig." He and his partner went away. I stood there looking at the closed door. I'd lied again. I *was* a man of mystery. Especially to myself.

CHAPTER 7

I went to my filing cabinet, pulled it open. A lot of empty space greeted me. I ruffled through what was left. Sure enough, everything before two years ago was gone. Fifteen years on my own and all I had to show for it was a lot of memories and a crummy twenty-four months' worth of case records.

I went back to my desk, got out the folder that should have contained my personal papers. Empty. The drawer holding my old ledgers was empty, too.

Some vandal had really had a field day, done a bang-up job. An absolutely senseless one, as far as I could figure. What use could all that stuff be to anyone? Unless, of course, Nickerson and Watts were trying to set me up for a big score. Some laugh. I was only a couple of steps ahead of being a pauper myself just like most everyone in Old York. And if the coppers had swiped my files, they sure as hell knew that. Any way you cut it, I'd have to take time off for a visit to the Hall of Records. A glance at my desk calendar told me even that wasn't going to be a cinch. I was full up. And if I let my cases go begging I really *would* end up a pauper. Well, I'd have to squeeze out a couple of hours whenever I could. The thing to do now was put Nickerson and Watts from my mind. Forget my missing files. Ignore State-City, the cut on my leg and all the rest of it. What I had to do was concentrate on the business at hand. It was going to be some trick.

Bridget Mercer was only ten minutes late.

She was a trim, thirty-ish woman with long black hair. Her eyes, behind round, wire-rimmed glasses, were brown, warm and large. She had on a tan suit, high heels and silk stockings. When she smiled I saw her teeth were small, even and very white.

She didn't waste any time getting on with it.

"You were recommended to me by Bob Hoffman at the Woodward Company," she told me in a soft, low voice which vaguely reminded me of whipped cream.

I nodded. I had done a job for Woodward a couple of months ago.

"Bob tells me," she continued, "that you are enormously discreet, Mr. Craig."

I admitted it.

Bridget Mercer smiled at me.

I smiled back, said, "It boils down to this, Miss Mercer: the larger agencies put your job through lots of hands. It's conceivable that someone might drop a word—in the wrong place. Here you've got only me to worry about. And since everyone knows that and I like to go on turning a buck, I keep my mouth shut."

"Bob told me you talked like that," Bridget Mercer said.

"Bob was right."

"Well, my partner, Victor Spalding, left the matter of retaining a Double M entirely to me. You're it, Mr. Craig."

"Thanks," I said. "What's the job?"

Mercer and Spalding, she told me, were real estate brokers who were planning to renovate one of their downtown properties. "We'd like to add about four stories to the building, but zoning laws prohibit it. So we must either change the laws or bribe the inspectors. Whichever is less expensive."

"Easy enough," I said. "Any time limit on this?"

"We'd hoped to begin work in the next three months."

"No problem. You'll probably have to settle for bribing the inspectors; it'll take close to six months the other way. And it won't come cheap. There're a lot of mouths to feed when you start fiddling with the legislature. The thing is, once you fix it in the Chamber, it stays fixed. Going the inspector route is a bit more chancy."

"You mean they might continue to ask us for money?"

"They might. But not so it'll hurt. That's where I come into it. I get a line on which inspectors are up for handling your zone. There's more than one team usually, and the guys who claim our building get it. I check out their track records and try to pick the ones who behave themselves. Then I give 'em the word on the QT. The boys know that, of course, and it helps keep them honest. Everyone's looking for an extra buck."

"Forgive me, Mr. Craig, Victor and I are new to this. How many payments will there be?"

"You can count on a big one at the outset, Miss Mercer, and after that, maybe every three, four months. That's just pocket money and nothing to worry about. If it gets out of hand, you call me, and I'll scoot over and read 'em the riot act. All part of the service."

"Sounds as if you have it down to a science, Mr. Craig."

"It's what I get paid for."

We spent the next twenty minutes or so going over the details, adding up the expenses and agreeing on my fee.

"That should do it," I said when she put her signature on the third copy of my contract.

"When shall we hear from you, Mr. Craig?"

"Anywhere from three days to a week."

"Good."

Bridget Mercer rose to leave.

"Miss Mercer," I said.

"Yes?"

"You've never seen me before, have you?"

She wrinkled her brow. "I don't believe so. Why? Do you think we've met somewhere?"

"It's a possibility."

"Really? Where?"

"I don't know."

We tossed around the names of a few dozen people who might be mutual acquaintances. No soap. None of the places—restaurants, clubs, bars—which I ticked off drew a nod of recognition.

"The theater, perhaps?" she said.

I shook my head. "I don't go in much for that."

We exchanged addresses. It turned out that Bridget Mercer lived halfway across town in a ritzy section I hardly ever visited.

"It's hopeless," she laughed.

I admitted she might have a point.

I walked her to the door.

"Anyway, it's been a real pleasure, Miss Mercer. And I don't mean just for business."

"Why, thank you."

The door closed behind her and Bridget Mercer was gone.

I managed to get back to my desk without passing out, a grade A stunt if ever there was one. I sank into my seat like a stone hitting rock bottom on a dusty canyon floor. My hands were doing a shimmy all on their own and my stomach was trying to crawl out through my belly button. Aside from that I was all set to take a bow. Why not? I'd put on the show of the century. I hadn't let myself think of my troubles, or scream, once. Not even when it occurred to me that my new client was the spitting image of the black-haired woman I'd spotted on the train. Of course, I'd only seen her from the back, then, and I couldn't be sure. And anyway, it had all been a dream in a dream. But there was something about seeing my dream-mate walk through my office door that made me want to cut my throat.

I got out the old office bottle and gave it a whirl. After a while I was feeling better, almost as flighty as a ladybug on a summer's day, if not quite as bright. I didn't mind. I could use the break. A glance at my desk calendar told me that the Yancy payoff was next on the agenda. That gave me a couple of hours to sober up. I wondered if I could face *anything* sober.

CHAPTER 8

The coach carried me out of town.

I'd cashed Yancy's check, put the money in my pocket next to my Colt Special and now I could concentrate on feeling tanked up for another hour and enjoying the trip.

Green fields, trees and fences took the place of tenement houses. The horses kicked up a gallop and we made good time. The coach passed a sign pointing the other way; it said Old York. I sighed; it was tough keeping my mind on business. Somewhere around here I'd come crawling out of a hole not twenty-four hours ago. I hadn't even known who I was. Now I knew. But I still had no idea how I'd gotten stuck in that hole in the first place—not to mention the weird goings-on I seemed to remember. Some of which had to be real, I knew, because the cops were in it and my records had been hit. And it had all happened here in little old Old York. Yeah. But how *could* it be real?

I let it go. I could almost hear the gears forcibly shifting in my bean. Business was business. And that's what this jaunt was all about. I rearranged my thoughts and after a while they almost seemed to fit the occasion.

Oliver Littlefield ran the Old York bail bureau—a lucrative niche if ever there was one. The crooks who got out on bail and vanished wanted their records to vanish along with them. An expensive proposition sometimes, but much less so than bribing the trial judge, a jury or the warden of the state pen. Payoffs went to the station

51

house, the arraignment judge, the DA's office, the bail bureau and anyone else who had a make on the suspect. Some guys had been through the revolving door so often they were cross-eyed. All it took was dough.

Except sometimes.

Tim Yancy's gang had blown one safe too many, got themselves pinched. The Downtown Jewelers' Association —a favorite Yancy victim—held a meeting, decided they'd had enough, raided their kitty and bought off the DA's office. Assistant DA Gardner wouldn't play ball when Yancy's Double M showed up with the usual bundle. Gardner was going to prosecute the case. The rest of the boys in on the take didn't like that one bit. The Jewelers' Association had thoughtlessly neglected to come up with their end. Very unethical. But an obvious saving. Gardner was too much a big shot to knock off so some of Yancy's boys came around one night after office hours, broke down his door and helped themselves to the works— namely, all the records that had anything to do with Yancy. Now it was Gardner's turn to see red. He put a slew of gumshoes on the case, had them stake out the other departments. But Yancy had moved fast, paid off the judge and precinct captain. Oliver Littlefield was out of town that day. Of all the city agencies, his was the only one that still had anything on Yancy. Gardner had started court action to get those records, but it would take months. Gardner didn't have months. Meanwhile Littlefield's price had gone up. But with the DA's coppers on the watch things were sticky. If Gardner could catch Littlefield—or his agents—in the act of making a trade he could put the bail chief on the spot. Such agents—myself included—were safe enough, exempt under state law. But Littlefield could end up paying off half the city, or even land in the hoosegow himself if he— or his agents—got caught.

I didn't intend to get caught.

I switched coaches at a way station. Only two passengers came with me, an old lady in worn, shiny black denim and a small round man in a blue denim suit and red vest. They seemed harmless enough. We rode past corn and wheat fields, small hills and valleys, an occasional ranch house. At four-thirty in the afternoon the coach pulled into Hornsville. I was the only passenger to get off.

Hornsville was a small jerkwater hamlet with a main street that consisted of three blocks of run-down houses. One of them said Carlton Hotel. I headed that way.

A stooped oldster with a seamy face and hairless dome checked me in. I asked for room 205 and was handed the key.

I rode up the rickety elevator, unlocked my door, went in.

I glanced over the room: a scruffy dresser, a skimpy single bed, a chair and closet. I strolled over to the wall on the right, tapped it three times. The wall tapped back once. An instant later a grinning Charley Frost ambled into my room through the connecting bathroom.

Frost was a medium-sized man with a ruddy complexion, wide moustache and thinning blond hair. He was a Double M. We shook hands.

"Not bad," Frost said grinning. "Damn coach was right on the button. Anyone tag along?"

"How?" I asked. "On horseback? What about you?"

Frost shrugged. "Safe as a babe in the cradle. Only ones to get off here were a small little guy and an old lady."

"Funny," I said, "that sounds like the pair who transferred with me to the Hornsville coach. Only they didn't get off at my stop."

Frost said, "There's no shortage of old folks, chum. Or stops in this burg."

"Sure," I said. "So what? Got the stuff?"

Frost said he did, handed me an envelope. Tim Yancy's records were inside. Digging into my pocket I came up with Littlefield's payoff. We both signed receipts, completing the exchange. Another chapter in the annals of Old York skulduggery. Anyway, it was a living.

"Not bad," Frost said, "for a fast buck."

I agreed. "Coming to this burg was a brainstorm, all right. Keeps us out of Gardner's way. And makes it real tough on anyone trying to shadow us."

"Who would want to do *that?*" Frost grinned.

"Only the bad guys," I leered back.

"None around here."

"Yeah. I noticed. The natives look docile."

"Why shouldn't they?"

We were set to go.

A sound came from the window.

Frost and I turned. Out on the fire escape an old lady and a middle-aged man in a red denim vest peered into the hotel room. Both held guns.

The bathroom door opened.

An old woman and man stood there—a pair identical in every detail to the ones by the window. They held guns, too.

Frost twisted sideways, a large automatic springing into his hand; he used it. The room shook with sound. The man on the fire escape fell from view.

Three guns emptied themselves at Frost.

I didn't hang around to note the results. I dived out the door into the corridor.

No one was there.

I turned a corner moving faster than I knew how. I could hear sounds behind me—running feet.

I pulled at my pocket trying to get the Colt out; it was stuck.

A door on the right said exit.

Exit was what I needed.

Plunging through I found myself on a staircase. I took the stairs four at a time, hoping I wouldn't break a leg or my neck in the bargain.

By the time I reached the ground floor, I'd gotten the gun out of my pocket and into my hand where it belonged.

I kicked open the door that led to the lobby.

The elderly desk clerk was there, facing me, a large automatic clutched in his hand. This just wasn't my day.

I did a belly dive to the floor. His gun did things to the wall behind me. I put a bullet somewhere through his side. The clerk screamed and sat down on the floor.

Scrambling up on hands and knees, I headed for the front door.

Behind me, the door through which I'd just come burst open.

The two old ladies charged into the lobby.

I ducked behind the reception desk as they cut loose with a barrage.

I ran down a side corridor, forgetting about the front door—I'd never reach it. These old ladies were some old ladies.

A man jumped out at me from a side door—a stranger.

I slashed at him with my gun.

He fell back into his room.

I ran over him.

Daylight gleamed through a dusty window. I crashed through it, glass flying in all directions.

I was in an alley.

I ran around the side of the building out onto the main drag.

The hotel door popped open as my murderous trio dashed out onto the street. I tossed a shot in their direction, missed, sprinted back into the alley, ran around the back of the hotel, up a narrow passage between two brick walls.

I was back on Main Street.

My would-be killers were nowhere in sight—probably dogging my tracks around the building. That gave me a second or two.

I took off down the street.

People, in clusters of two and three, had come out of stores and homes to see who and what was causing the racket. They watched as if they were all idle spectators at some sporting event. If there was any law in these parts, it wasn't showing itself.

By now the trio had rounded the hotel, was back in the chase. For a pair of old ladies and a middle-aged guy, they weren't doing so bad.

I was doing better. But for how long? I had no idea what was going on, whether these goons belonged to DA Gardner's crew or if they'd slipped out of a loony bin on their own. The identical twin bit was a nice touch, but what did it mean?

Down the block a sign said livery stable.

A notion spun through my head.

I popped a bullet over my shoulder, made a beeline for the stable. Inside, a burly man, the proprietor no doubt, started to get off a cot.

I showed him my gun.

He got back on the cot.

I ran out back where they kept the horses. None were saddled. I managed to climb onto a large black and tan stallion. Wrapping my arms around his neck I said giddy-up. When that got me nowhere I planted a shoe in his ribs. The stallion snorted, reared up and jumped over the corral fence.

I went with him.

The three assassins out front ducked for cover.

We rode by them, heading out of town.

No one followed me.

After a while, I got the horse to slow down. We stopped. I crawled off. Most of me still seemed intact. We were somewhere in the country. The horse looked at me, wandered off. I let him.

I put the gun I had been clutching like a life preserver in my pocket, made sure I still had Yancy's envelope and started hiking.

Presently, I reached a dirt road. A sign said coach stop.

Finding a shady spot under a tree, I seated myself and waited. An hour later a coach came rolling by. I flagged it down, climbed aboard and was carried off. I transferred twice and arrived in Old York after dark. None of my fellow passengers on any of the three coaches had tried to shoot me. It was a welcome change.

I dialed a number:

"Yancy?" I said.

"Yeah," a flat voice told me.

"It's me, Craig."

"How'd it go, Craig?"

"I got the stuff."

"Yeah? Burn it!"

"You want the receipt?"

"Uh-huh."

"I'll mail it to you. We had trouble."

"What kind?"

"Frost got downed."

"Frost? That's Littlefield's pup."

"Right."

"How come?"

I told him.

Yancy cursed. "You figure Gardner for it?"

"Who else?"

"That gums the works."

He had a point. The payoff racket kept everyone in pocket money. Murder was bad for business.

"What do you aim to do?" I asked him.

"Sit tight."

"That sounds okay."

"Hell, they ain't got nothing on me now. If that Gardner comes looking for trouble, he'll get plenty. You shoot back, Craig?"

"Yeah."

"Pot anyone?"

"The hotel clerk; he was in with them."

"That's it?"

"Uh-uh. Frost got one, too; his swan song."

"Sounds like a swell party."

"It was."

"The law show up?"

"Nope. I'd guess someone paid them to be elsewhere."

"How'd they know to do that, Craig?"

"Littlefield's office, probably. Someone heard we were heading for Hornsville—and passed it on."

"What's the world coming to, Craig?"

"It's going to hell in a barrel, Yancy."

"Ain't that a fact. You clear in all this gunplay?"

"I think so. Can you get hold of Littlefield, fill him in?"

"Yeah."

"Okay. I'll ask around, try to get the dope on this. Anyway, you're covered, no matter what. It's the law."

"I know."

"I know you know."

"You get back to me?"

"Yeah. As soon as I can."

"Okay, Craig."

I hung up.

The street lamps glowed a dull yellow. I trudged along past old tenement houses whose peeling fronts gave them an acned look. Men in shirt sleeves, women in light summer dresses sat on stoops, some chatting, others staring into the darkness as if hunting for some private signal. Kids played at games, scooted around buildings, out onto the tar-paved streets. Ice wagons rolled by even at this time of night. Pushcart vendors sold watermelon, ices, lemonade. Newsboys hawked the early edition of the *Globe,* their voices drifting in over the rooftops from far-off streets. They sounded plaintive as hell. The odor of horse manure hung in the air like a soiled blanket. The clean-up crew—with shovel and wagon—would hit the streets after midnight.

The day's doings kept kicking around in my noodle. The shoot-out was bad enough. Hard to recall anything like it, in fact. Roughhouse meant rocking the boat with a vengeance, was apt to get everyone in dutch. I couldn't see Gardner pulling it, either. Only who else was there?

Worse yet were the twins.

Two pairs of identical killers was really too much. The mere thought of it gave me the heebie-jeebies. It made me remember my dreams: had they somehow spilled over into the workaday world? That'd put the skids under me once and for all. I didn't even want to think about it. Tomorrow I'd start checking into this Nickerson and Watts opus. One step at a time. If that turned out to be a dud I'd go get some help in the dream department, maybe drop in at the local clinic.

Something had to give. I just hoped it wasn't me.

CHAPTER 9

Gray daylight seeped through the window shades. I cut off the alarm clock, rolled out of bed. Another morning. So why didn't I feel great? There was probably a reason. I would think of it by and by.

No cops were waiting for me when I reached my office. That was something, at least. The Hornsville fracas must have been hushed up. To make sure—always a smart move—I dialed some pals at police headquarters. No reports had come in from Hornsville during the night. We chatted awhile and said our good-byes.

I placed a call to Yancy, who wasn't in. I called the Buildings Department, remembering I still had to turn a buck, got a list of inspectors who were qualified to handle the Mercer-Spalding property. Then I called a guy who could give me a line on the inspectors. He did; we agreed on a small gratuity, swapped so-longs.

By now it was ten o'clock. I put off bracing the inspectors for later in the week, locked up the office, went across the street for a cup of coffee and hopped a coach. For a while I was going to be my own client. A sure way to end up in the poorhouse if ever there was one.

The Hall of Records was on South Street. An express carriage brought me to Municipal Square in jig time. I got off along with some high school kids taking the tour and a stout party dolled up in monocle and spats. A dull, gray day. People moved briskly along the crowded street.

I went past the large globe in the lobby. The elevator man took me up to the ninth floor, where I cooled my heels in line for ten minutes before reaching my destination, a small window stuck in the wall. Sliding my ID across to the short, bald-headed clerk in the green eyeshade, I asked for a copy of my birth certificate—a reasonable request. The clerk gave me a form to sign, asked for fifty cents, returned my ID and told me to come back in the afternoon. Reasonableness was winning the day. I wondered how long it would last.

I went down two flights and filed for copies of my back income tax statements. Then I went downstairs and took another ride.

The City Orphanage was pretty much as I remembered it: an old six-story brick building—surrounded by a high stone wall—with an overgrown lawn, scraggly garden and a couple of bent trees. The halls were scuffed and smelled of cheap green soap. The kids looked about as jolly as polar bears vacationing in the tropics. The staff I saw was dressed in somber shades of gray denim, which was probably all they could afford on their salaries. They were all strangers to me. That was okay. City institutions always had a huge turnover and a lot of time had drifted by. Less okay was the clerk's failure to turn up my records. Vice-Principal Hatch explained it to me: a fire had destroyed some of the orphanage files; mine was no doubt among them. Unfortunately, there were no copies. I thanked him and went away.

Neither Fairview College nor the *City Gazette,* my old employers, had had any fires, but the results were pretty much the same. They had files galore, but I wasn't in them; a sorry oversight. I knew no one and no one knew me. My college profs were all gone—either dead or unknown. A clean sweep. Dr. Stephen Grange had been president of Fairview in my day, and still was, but the prexy wouldn't know me from a hole in the wall. Bill Bradshaw, the *Gazette* union boss who used to wave a cheery hello, had died more than a decade ago. None of the typesetters rang a bell. There were no holdovers from the good old days—whatever those were.

Running down the pair of agencies I'd broken in at—Morgan Inc. and Henry Orway—took almost no time at all. The city directory showed no such listings. Agencies come and go. Lord knows I hadn't kept track. But no-show for both would have given me the willies for sure—if I hadn't had them already.

A couple of years ago I'd had an office at 60 Warren Street, a faded eight-story yellow brick building that had seen better days. Scanning the lobby register, I couldn't come up with a single name that seemed even vaguely familiar. Both the janitor and elevator operator had been on the job only a short while. I caught a downtown coach to Urban Realty. They had no record of my ever renting any office in their building. But their records were incomplete. Silven Inc. had once owned the building, but had since given up the ghost. I didn't bother tracing the remains of Silven Inc. I had lost confidence in office buildings. I decided to try a more personal tack:

A couple of years ago I'd rented a flat on Dexter Avenue. A local coach took me there. This time I really got an eyeful. Not merely the building, but the entire block was gone—razed to the ground. Weeds shared the terrain along with a lot of empty tin cans and soda pop bottles. I hiked around the neighborhood hunting for a friendly face, someone I might know. The corner bakery, grocery or butcher shop should have been good bets. They weren't. Neither was anyone else. Three blocks over I caught the North Side buggy and let the horse team carry me back to the Hall of Records. I was glad to go.

The tax people were still trying to dig up my old returns, demonstrating an admirable persistence. The vital statistics folks had tossed in the towel; if they'd ever had my birth certificate, they didn't have it now.

It was way past lunchtime, but somehow I'd lost my appetite. I wandered around the crowded downtown streets, like a lost puppy. I hoped what I had wasn't catching. I looked around at the midtown crowd, glad for the company. That's when I saw him.

He was short, slender, somewhere in his mid-forties. His hair was red, his chin pointy and he wore glasses.

As far as I knew, I had never laid eyes on him before—not in the flesh, anyway. But then I didn't know a whole lot these days, did I? He was the redhead from my dream—or his blood brother—one of the passengers on my dream train. I could see his reflection clearly in a plate glass window. He was strolling behind me, almost, but not quite, lost in a sea of pedestrians. He wore a black raincoat that contrasted nicely with his hair. I stopped to admire a show window full of drab denim clothing. Behind me, the small man had stopped, too.

It meant nothing. I had seen him only once in a dream I'd had at State-City Hospital. But State-City Hospital was a dream itself. And the three days I'd spent there a delusion. My office wasn't far off and I could have passed this redhead lots of times without fully noticing him; he'd probably gotten stuck in my unconscious and popped up in a dream.

It could be as simple as that; maybe it was.

I continued walking, crossed the street, turned some corners. Twenty minutes later the small man was still behind me. It wasn't so simple, after all. But then, what was, these days?

Pat De Marco looked up from behind a pint-sized desk when I entered his office, his mouth twisted in an unpleasant grin. "The Double M; how's tricks, big shot?"

"So-so," I said, helping myself to a chair.

Pat De Marco was short, dark and dowdy, with a permanent sneer etched into his narrow face. Behind him one lone window stared out glumly at a brick wall black with years of soot. Out front, four flights down, was Mason Street. Pushcarts, food stands, trash cans and a tired collection of bums, hobos and panhandlers. The decal on De Marco's door said: Investigator.

"One of your suckers getting shafted, Craig? Need some help?"

"Uh-uh," I said.

"No? Maybe you got a problem yourself, big man?" De Marco leered; he seemed to enjoy the prospect.

"Could be," I admitted.

"Well, well, ain't that a shame." De Marco grinned from ear to ear. "Okay, spill it, what kinda jam you in?"

"I've picked up a tail."

"So? How come?"

"Beats me."

"Had a row, maybe; someone lookin' to even a score?"

"Uh-uh."

"Trim a client, then?"

"No more than usual."

"So who's sore at you, Craig?"

"Damned if I know."

"Like that, ah?"

"Uh-huh." I described the redhead. "You can't miss him, he's been dogging my heels for the last hour."

"Whaddo I do?" De Marco asked with interest. "Give him the heave-ho? A lead pipe over the noggin, a smack in the kisser? Maybe a boot in the crotch?"

I shook my head. "Nothing like that. I handle kid stuff on my own during off-hours."

"Wise guy," De Marco said. "So whaddya want, I should give him a medal?"

"Just string along behind him quiet like; pretend you're a pro."

"Screw you," De Marco said. "That's all?"

"That's all."

"Suit yourself. Just cough up the jack. Ten a day plus expenses."

I counted out the money. "What I want is a line on this guy, who he's in with, where he holes up. The works."

"I get the drift."

"Only see no one tumbles; I don't want to wise up the marks."

"It's your dough."

"Right," I said. "How long we been doing business together, pal?"

"Two years."

"That's what I figured."

I didn't bother glancing behind me as I crossed the street. I hoped the redhead was on the job. I knew De

Marco was. What I didn't know was anything else. Maybe I could find out.

Back in my office, I used the phone. I'd missed too many business appointments and now I gave my excuses and tried to come up with new arrangements. I managed to get it done without losing more than a couple of clients, a real accomplishment under the circumstances. Maybe the only one of the day.

I took a swig from my trusty office bottle and tried to settle down for the work at hand. I was a bit jumpy but I figured I could remember enough names, numbers and clients from my elusive past to make a stab at finding *someone* who had known me way back when. I dialed the numbers of two old girl friends, a former client, an ex-boss and a guy I'd known on the handball court. I was only sweating a little. I connected with a grocery store, a movie theater, two strangers and an ice delivery service. I was sweating a lot more now but I still had a trick or two left. I reached for the city directory. Three hours later I'd run clean out of tricks. I closed the directory, cradled the phone and sat there like a stiff.

Putting out the desk lamp, I swiveled my chair to face the window, got my feet up on the sill, took a deep breath, leaned back and stared out at a darkened Center Street. Nickerson and Watts had been right after all. I *was* an unperson. And damned if I knew what to do about it.

CHAPTER 10

The night grew darker. Yellow light peered out from a maze of distant windows—too far away to offer much warmth or comfort. I was all alone. I didn't like being alone. A man who's just lost most of his past needs company. I reached for the phone, dialed a number. Clive Western was still at his editor's desk at the *Daily Sun*. We chatted awhile. I asked him to meet me at Lucky's, a local pub, in half an hour. Western said sure. I sat around for a while staring into the darkness. Rising, I shrugged into a lightweight raincoat, doused the lights, locked up shop and went off to Lucky's.

The pub was thick with smoke. Glasses clanged, voices murmured. Western was at a corner table.

"Well, go on, spill it. I know something's eating you," Western said after I'd pulled up a chair. "You've got that look." Western took out a cigar, lit it. He was a slim, bony man in his early fifties. His eyes were black, hair gray, face red. He looked tired.

I said, "Someone or something seems to have skipped off with my past."

Western appeared mildly interested. "Do tell. Someone snatch your diary, son?"

"Worse than that." I gave the editor a brief rundown of my day's doings. Western sat still, his eyes fixed vaguely on the customers who filled the pub. When I was done, Western looked at me.

"That's the nuttiest thing I've ever heard," he said.

"You wouldn't be trying to pull my old leg, by any chance?"

"Scout's honor."

"I take it you haven't seen the little shavers lately." Western blew gray smoke into the air, sat back in his chair. "You've gone cuckoo, of course; you know that?"

"It's occurred to me."

"What you need," Western said cheerfully, "is a good rest, or a good doctor; both perhaps. Obviously, you've imagined the whole thing."

"Obviously. But my peculiar lack of history has already brought an official visit. *That* was real enough."

Western tapped his skull with a bony finger, smiled sweetly. "So you say."

"I didn't exactly get a receipt, but there *are* ways of checking."

"No doubt. Perhaps your two callers can do with some help, too."

"Actually," I said, "I was hoping for a bit more than sympathy from you."

"Such as?" Western raised an eyebrow.

"Well, you might assign a couple of your boys to run down a list of names."

"What names?"

"Past clients of mine, firms that don't seem to exist anymore. And a couple of agencies I've worked for that've also beat it. You've got the resources, can check the paper's morgue. I'd do it myself, but it'd be smoother this way. Besides, I don't think I can stand any more."

"Why would I want to do anything as silly as all that?"

"To get at the truth?"

"Frankly, I don't think I could bear the truth—not your version, anyway. Nothing personal, you understand."

"Sure. How about for old times' sake?"

"Well, that would be about two years, wouldn't it? That's not very old."

"Everything seems to go back two years," I said. "It's very discouraging."

"I'll tell you," Western said, lowering his voice conspiratorially, "the thing is, if any of this starts looking even remotely reasonable, I'll know I'm ready for a padded cell, too."

"Too, eh?"

"There, there," Western said, "I'll have the boys look into it if it really means so much to you."

"You will?"

"Why not?"

"True," I said. I got busy compiling a list. When I was done, Western gave it a casual once-over. "Ring any bells?" I asked hopefully.

Western raised his eyes from the piece of paper, shrugged. "Nary a one, son. Sorry."

"Me too."

We downed some more booze, chewed the rag. After a while we went into the night. Western went away. I headed home.

Hanging my coat in the closet, I hightailed it to the icebox, got out a bottle of milk, some ham, a loaf of rye and grabbed a quick bite.

It was nine-thirty.

Settling down in the living room in a large stuffed easy chair next to the phone, I started thumbing through the city directory. I didn't expect much, but it gave me something to do. I found Mrs. Emma Landry's name at eleven-fifteen.

I grinned sourly. It was only a name. There was no chance that this was *my* Emma Landry.

Emma Landry would be in her nineties by now.

Still, what did I have to lose?

The phone rang eight times.

"Hello?" An old woman's quivering voice sounded half asleep.

"Emma Landry?"

"Yes?"

"Emma Landry who used to live on Decker Street?"

A moment's hesitation, then, "Yes," and peevishly, "Who is this? Do you know what time it is?"

"I'm sorry," I heard myself say. A pulse was pounding in my ears. "It's me," I said, "little Markie Craig."

"Markie Craig?"

"You know me, don't you, Mrs. Landry? The little boy from the second floor. The house on Decker Street . . ."

The voice on the other end of the line was suddenly alive. "Dear me, dear me, is that really *you*, Markie?"

I noticed I'd been holding the phone in a death grip; I loosened my fingers. "Yes, it is, Mrs. Landry, it really is."

"Goodness gracious, Markie, it's been such a *long* time, hasn't it?"

"Thirty-two years," I said. I was having trouble keeping my voice under control. "Do you remember the others, Mrs. Landry, our neighbors on Decker Street, the other people who lived in that house?"

"Heavens, yes, I should hope so; why I was there for close to forty years, you know."

"Who were they?"

"Why, let me see. Mrs. Swingle, on the first floor. Dear Mr. Murry—he moved from the top to the second floor. Although that may have been before your time, Markie; he died, you know. About fifteen years ago, poor man. Then there was Lester and Elaine Benning, Mrs. Welch and her son Irving. Mr. and Mrs. Dobbs, such a sweet couple. Dr. Tompkins. And that awful Mr. Rile who drank so much . . ."

"What happened to them, Mrs. Landry, where are they now?"

"Now? Why I'm not at all sure, Markie; is it important?"

"I think so, Mrs. Landry."

"Goodness, we do lose touch, don't we? All those years gone by. Why it seems like only yesterday. You know, Markie, I can't promise but I do believe I have some of their addresses. Mrs. Welch and I always send cards on Christmas. And I used to visit Mr. and Mrs. Dobbs. But I don't get around much now. Dear me, no. The addresses must be in one of my trunks. I could look if you'd like."

"Would you?"

"Why, Markie, of course. It's all packed away. Would tomorrow be all right?"

"That would be fine, Mrs. Landry."

"But, dear me, here I've been chattering away and I haven't asked about you; how are you, Markie, what are you doing with yourself? Gracious, you must have a wife and children by now. And you always wanted to be a lawyer, didn't you? Is that what you finally became?"

"I'll tell you all about it, Mrs. Landry—when I see you tomorrow."

"Tomorrow? Here? Why, Markie, that is *so* nice. I hadn't dreamed you might want to come for a visit."

"I'd like to very much."

"How exciting," Mrs. Landry said.

I verified her address and said I'd be there by mid-morning; we exchanged good-nights.

CHAPTER 11

Five-thirty A.M.

The alarm prodded me awake. I climbed out of bed, showered, shaved, perked up some brew, got dressed and went out into the street. Still dark. And raining. I put up my umbrella, walked over two blocks to the coach stop and waited. Street sounds, shifting and wind-swept, washed over me. A blurred necklace of globed street lamps stretched down the block, dwindled to doll size before being snuffed out by the Christy Street rise. After a while, the coach came. I climbed in and was carried away. Only a few passengers, mostly factory hands, inside. Some dozed, others sat vacant-eyed and staring. The clip-cop of horses' hoofs splashed through puddles. Rain beat on the carriage roof. The night and its sounds slid by outside like refuse rolling down a river. Storefronts were dark, vacant places, padlocked against the night and its intruders. Occasional lone neon lights blared their silent message across the empty streets. I watched through the window as one neighborhood gave way to another, changed shape and size like a kaleidoscope.

I got up at the last stop, took a transfer and stepped back into the rain. Dawn put stray whisks of gray into the darkness. I shivered, watched the water puddle at my feet and wished I'd brought along a hip flask.

Another carriage came along and I hopped on. This one was more crowded. The day was starting to unwind. I settled down between an elderly lady in white and a denim-clad factory hand holding a lunch box on his lap. The horses began to gallop, rocking the carriage from side to side. I closed my eyes and dozed.

By the time I left the carriage an hour later, the sky was a dense gray sheet. The rain had turned to a steady drizzle. I watched the carriage roll away, let the circulation trickle back into my legs and started hiking. I was on East Second Street. I turned a corner and started down toward the river. The houses grew shabbier, more crowded together. Rusted fire escapes ran up the faces of five- and six-story tenements. Trash cans leaned against blackened brick walls, blocked cellars and doorways. I passed Stiles and Greenwood streets. There was nothing to see, only the rain, ragged street and dilapidated houses. Then I was on the last block, in sight of the waterfront, and there was the house: a five-story job composed of weathered boards and shingles; Mrs. Emma Landry's home.

I went up three lopsided steps and into the alcove. There were no names on the doorbells or mailboxes. I pushed open the door, found myself in a damp hallway. One dim bulb glowed in the ceiling. I started up the stairs. No light on the second floor. I groped my way along the landing, found the stairs and continued my climb. I reached the third floor. The rain was inaudible here but I could still feel it in the air. The dampness clung to me like a wet sheet. It was pitch-back. I felt in my pockets, dug out a match pack, broke off a match, lit it. Long shadows flickered over the walls. I went to the last door in the hallway, knocked.

"Who's there?" an old woman's voice quivered.

"It's me," I said, "Markie Craig."

"Come in, Markie."

I blew out the match, pushed open the door.

I was in one large room. A heavy curtain was drawn over the window. A single lit lamp sent faint yellowish light over a table, two chairs, a sink, a gas range and a bed. A shadowed figure in a long dress sat in a rocking chair near the curtained window. I couldn't see her face. A black embroidered shawl was wrapped over stooped narrow shoulders. She rocked slowly back and forth, a thin veined hand clutching the shawl tightly around her.

"Mrs. Landry?" I said.

Slowly she turned toward me. Light slid across her head. I saw white hair, two deep-set black eyes. She grinned, slyly, exposing toothless gums. "What kept you, Mr. Craig?"

A whirlpool seemed to spin around my feet. I was being sucked under.

I heard mindless laughter.

The room tilted sideways and I fell against a wall.

I was back in the nightmare.

The black eyes danced in the seamy white face. "You didn't think you could get away, did you, Mr. Craig?"

The old crone was right. I could never escape. No matter where I went, what I did, I would always return here to this spot, to this moment. And sooner or later the thing would get me.

As if on cue the door burst open.

It stood swaying in the doorway. Its shoulders were huge, its hands ponderous. It had no face, merely a large featureless oval for a head.

It moved toward me.

Old York had been nothing more than a digression. Clive Western, Nickerson and Watts, Pat De Marco and my bundle of vanished memories a gigantic ruse. State-City was only an interlude. I was a man without past or future. Riveted to this instant in time. It was my sole reality. And now I would die.

The whirlpool was all around me. I had sunk to its very heart. I had eluded Faceless before by reaching the window. But now the window was a distant shimmering dot, bobbing and weaving far out of reach.

My strength was gone. I could hardly lift a leg, let alone sprint to that window. I'd had it. An almost irresistible urge to close my eyes swept over me. I would sleep. And then there would be nothing.

Faceless hulked over me. An umpleasant sound was filling the air. Apparently I was screaming. At least I had good reason.

The door swung open a second time.

Little Pat De Marco stood in the doorway. He glanced around sharply with narrowed eyes. The light seemed to flicker and fade. De Marco, I saw, had a gun. He used it, opened up at Faceless. Faceless turned on De Marco. I wagged my head good-naturedly. Faceless had neglected to kill me. Maybe it would kill De Marco instead. I started crawling toward the window. Behind me there were more gunshots. I was too busy to pay much attention. I had enough trouble inching my way through the darkness. Sooner or later, I'd come to the window, then I'd leave all this behind. The room seemed to tilt again. That gave me an excuse to rest. I looked back over my shoulder. It was very dark now and I could barely see the struggling figures behind me. Faceless had Pat De Marco by the neck. De Marco didn't look pleased. The old crone was nowhere in sight. Just as well. I hadn't liked her anyway. Time to continue my jaunt. I got my muscles working again and moved on. I reached the window just as the lights went out. Uh-oh. The moment called for drastic measures. I made a fist and swung at the window.

There was no window.

My fist hit empty air. Momentum sent me spilling. I toppled over onto the ground like a broken statue off its pedestal.

I lay there for a while wondering how I'd managed to

miss the window; quite a trick, if not exactly on a par with some other recent events.

Lying there, I noticed something else. All sounds of activity had stopped. I cocked an ear waiting for the fireworks to resume—certain they would any second now.

Nothing. Not a solitary peep.

How about that?

I ran my hand over the floor. An instant ago it had had the feel and texture of worn floorboards. Now cold, damp stone was all I felt.

I thought that over very carefully, like a man who's just discovered a spike stuck in his back. The thing with an oval for a face had already run my nerves ragged, pushed hysteria to its very breaking point. Not much more could be done in that direction. But what little could be done, this new twist would probably accomplish.

No need to hurry now.

I got to my feet with all the enthusiasm and vigor of a very old man going to inspect a cemetery plot. I put one foot in front of the other like a polio victim learning to walk again. My hands were stretched out in front of me like an overaged child playing blindman's buff.

I came to a wall. I wasn't surprised to find damp, moss-covered stone. I opened my mouth and yelled. Sure enough, my voice came echoing back.

I'd been in this place once before. It had no doors. No exit of any kind. I'd gone to sleep and awakened in a field six miles from Old York City. I had neither the energy nor gumption to go hunting through this blackout now. The thought of trying to figure out what was happening was even less inviting.

I did the sensible thing. I'd have done it even if it was dumb.

I lay down and went to sleep.

PART 3

Inside a black hole the familiar laws of nature would totally cease to exist.

from *The Notebooks of Dr. James Ingram*

CHAPTER 12

Mark Craig

I opened my eyes to semidarkness.

It didn't take any guesswork to know where I was. I could see the gray rectangles that were the windows and the lights of the city beyond.

No mistaking that city. Buildings that reached to the sky. A humdinger, any way you sliced it. And I was right back in its center. I'd never even asked what city this was. Probably, I'd had other things on my mind.

My bed was a darn sight more comfortable than the stone floor I'd taken to napping on—a habit I'd have to break if I didn't want a sore back. Along with a lot of other complications. My pajamas felt swell, too. I was glad I hadn't gone to bed in my work clothes.

But then there never had been any work clothes, had there?

And it would be Monday. Again. Because the four days I'd spent in Old York had never happened.

Old York didn't even exist.

Only a phantom of an overheated mind groping for its identity.

A yarn spun by my unconscious in a frantic effort to tell me something.

Too bad I didn't know what.

I knew more about the Mark Craig of Old York than I

did about myself. But that was hardly astounding since I knew nothing about myself at all.

The whole crew back at Old York were the only people I could remember. And I wasn't exactly crazy about any of them, now that I thought about it. Even Craig. He'd been in a doozy of a racket, all right. The kickback was a going concern in Old York, as aboveboard as selling candy somewhere else.

Not that I was so sure what went on somewhere else. Still, you had to hand it to old Craig; he'd come out a winner. He had his own shop. He knew who he was even if no one else did. Yet Old York was a mess by anyone's reckoning; what kind of future could Craig expect there, even without his other troubles? Here, at least, they knew how to keep their buildings clean. *And here I was.* Even if I wanted to get back *there,* how would I go about it?

The whole thing was academic. Old York—along with Western, Nickerson, Watts, De Marco, Mrs. Emma Landry, the whole insane caboodle—never was! And that went double for Old Faceless, the derelict buildings and the lightless cave or whatever it was.

None of it was real.

I wondered how long it would take to cure me.

"Not long," Dr. Spiegel said.

He sat behind a wide, impressive desk. We were in the outpatient wing of State-City. I relaxed in a plush leather easy chair. Indirect lighting glowed down on us. Five neat rows of leather-bound volumes climbed one wall. The other—facing west—was glass, looked out over the city. More glass glittered back at us from skyscrapers, high rises, along with a variety of gleaming metals. The day was clear and cloudless. I'd been up and around for eight hours now. It was Monday afternoon. Again.

"You can't prove it by me," I said. "I've felt worse physically, so I've made some progress there, but my memory's still not worth a damn."

Dr. Spiegel wagged a finger at me. "You forget your latest dream," he told me in his soft, melodious voice.

"I wish I could."

The doctor made a steeple of his fingers, fixed me with his sharp blue eyes. "You are wrong, Mr. Craig. There are untold clues in this dream of yours. Its seeming length, its richness of character and detail are remarkable. Doubtless you feel somewhat uneasy. Which may be an indication that you are closer to recalling your past than you realize. There is, let us say, still some resistance on your part. All quite natural, I might add. A portion of your mind, however, insists on drawing back the curtain, desires that you know who you are."

"That's just swell," I said.

"Well-ll," Dr. Spiegel said, "let us see what we have."

"A mess," I said.

"A repetitive dream, Mr. Craig."

"Just a small part," I told him, "is repetitive."

"True. But the important part."

"And it's still a mess."

"Perhaps. But that part which repeats itself may be the key to your problem."

"How?"

"Your memory loss, Mr. Craig, was the result, we believe, of a traumatic incident."

"So you've said, Doctor."

"Yes. This incident is symbolized by the faceless man who pursues you. His lack of features, Mr. Craig, is a thin disguise."

"That's some disguise."

Dr. Spiegel held up his hand. "Wait, you have also pointed out that even this part of the dream is not totally repetitive. There are significant permutations."

"They'd be hard to miss, Doctor."

"Precisely. In time, Mr. Craig, it is our belief that this man will acquire features—will be shorn of his disguise, and the event in which you both participated will reveal itself for what it was. At that moment, Mr. Craig, you will fully regain your memory."

I sat back in my leather chair, folded my arms and looked at the doctor. I was feeling just edgy enough to spring it on him. "This memory business isn't the only thing bothering me. It's Old York. I know it all has to be a dream. But it doesn't seem like one. What it seems like is about as real as my sitting here talking to you."

Dr. Spiegel smiled. "Well-ll," he said, "considering your current state of mind, Mr. Craig, that is hardly surprising. Of course, your dream appeared remarkably vivid. Why should it not? It might be called the mere tip of an iceberg. Buried beneath its surface, Mr. Craig, is a lifetime of experiences; *yours;* only now presented in a manner that is incomprehensible to you. Have patience, Mr. Craig, the pieces will fall into place. The persons whom you think dwellers of this dream city will shortly assume their true relationship to you. Moreover, their actions will no longer be a riddle; the symbolic content will become obvious."

"And everything will be hunky-dory," I said. I was beginning to sound bitter.

The doctor shrugged. "Surely, Mr. Craig, you do not *really* believe in this city of yours?"

"I suppose not. At least my head doesn't."

"Well-ll," Dr. Spiegel said, "perhaps the heart will listen to reason, too."

"I wouldn't mind," I told him.

"Your sense of history, Mr. Craig, it is more or less intact, is it not?"

"Who knows? Probably. With the exception, of course, of recent events. Although right now I wouldn't bet on my knowing my left hand from my right."

"Fair enough. You are familiar with the horse-and-buggy era, are you not, Mr. Craig?"

"Uh-huh, I know what it is."

"Fine. In terms of transportation, your Old York is quite unique."

"Go on," I said.

"The horse-and-buggies have all the characteristics of an old bus or trolley route. Most peculiar. History records no such transit system."

"Sure," I said. "What else?"

"The phones, Mr. Craig. Surely there were no office phones in the horse-and-buggy era."

"I guess not. While you're at it, don't forget the denims."

"Thank you. I was not about to. It is, of course, impossible to chronologically pinpoint Old York. But I believe it is quite safe to assert that denims were not a universal mode of attire in, say, 1880."

"I'll go along with that."

"Excellent. Now, perhaps a word concerning your, ah, Double M profession."

"Don't bother. There never was and never will be a racket like that."

"Very good, Mr. Craig."

"And a private eye like Pat De Marco is a bit ahead of his time, too, wouldn't you say, Dr. Spiegel?"

"Quite. The entire free enterprise system as you have described it to me, Mr. Craig, is extraordinary for that decade."

"What decade, Doctor?"

Dr. Spiegel shrugged. "Why, the 1880s, I should think."

"But it isn't," I said. "No problem with the date, Doctor, just everything else. I bought a paper, had a desk calendar, filled out a couple of forms that needed dating. Ask me when Old York was, Doctor."

"Very well, Mr. Craig, when?"

"Not the 1880s; not even the Gay Nineties. I've got a very weird unconscious, Doctor. The year was 2074."

Dr. Spiegel laughed. "You see, Mr. Craig, you are your own best witness. What you have been describing is a terrible hodgepodge. You have a number of elements which could only coexist in a fantasy. This must be obvious to you."

"It's obvious."

"Well-ll?"

"It doesn't *feel* obvious."

"Your feelings are in a state of confusion, Mr. Craig."

"So am I."

"Give yourself time, Mr. Craig. Believe me when I say these dreams represent progress."

"I don't have much choice, do I, Dr. Spiegel?"

The doctor grinned good-naturedly. "None whatsoever, Mr. Craig."

"What year is it?" I asked.

"Why, 2074. You were quite right. But where are the horses, the carriages, the denim-clad workers off to their daily grind? I can assure you we have no ice wagons here, no pumps which require a nickel to operate. And there are certainly no slums."

"Congratulations."

"There have not been any for more than fifty years."

"And you take drifters off the streets and treat them like royalty?"

"There are no drifters and there is no royalty."

"What is there, then?"

"Citizens, Mr. Craig."

"Just that?"

"With various rights and obligations. One of which is the right to treatment in the event of illness."

"For free?"

"Of course."

"Not bad. You won't catch me knocking it, Doctor. What town is this?"

"We are the main metropolis on the eastern seaboard, Mr. Craig, not quite what you would call a town."

"The place has a name?"

"Certainly."

"You're going to make me guess?"

"But you already know, Mr. Craig."

"I do?"

"Think."

"Old York."

"Close, Mr. Craig."

"New York."

"Not quite. Try again."

"York," I said.

"Bravo, Mr. Craig."

York it was.

CHAPTER 13

Alexis Rike

Caligula smiled.

From the vantage point of a darkened corridor, Alexis Rike had an unobstructed view of the proceedings. The emperor was speaking to someone, a man who had his back to Rike.

Caligula smiled again, moved closer to his companion. Carefully, the emperor reached under his toga. His hand emerged clutching a long-handled dagger. Swiftly he plunged it into the man's chest.

The man screamed.

He came tripping, stumbling directly toward Rike, his mouth gasping, his eyes rolling. Gurgling sounds escaped from his lips. Blood bubbled from his mouth. The black handle of the dagger stuck in his chest. As the man fell, his eyes lifted toward Rike—their gaze locked.

Alexis Rike saw himself!

The man crumpled at his feet.

Rike backed off down the corridor, turned, began to run.

Two palace guards started after him, their swords drawn. Caligula had seen him, too, was shouting orders.

Rike turned a corner.

Two more guards were there. Rike's fist caught one in the face. The other swung a heavy spear. Rike went down.

Rike opened his eyes. He was lying flat on his back, a

pile of straw under him. He was in what appeared to be a small, dank cell. He wasn't alone.

"How are you?" the man across from him asked. He was seated on the ground.

"I've been better. Head feels as if it's split."

"A mere bump, my friend."

"Mere?"

A corner of the man's mouth twitched. "In here, even a split head is not considered a very serious complaint."

The man got to his feet, stretched, scratched himself. "Lice," he murmured. He was large, fleshy, with thick features, wavy black hair, round shoulders.

Rike asked, "Where am I?"

"Caligula's dungeon."

"That," Rike said, "doesn't sound so good."

"It isn't. Few leave here whole. Many not at all. Who are you, my friend?"

Rike gave his name, identified himself as a merchant. "And you?"

"Gaius Sabinus, a colonel in the emperor's guards. Your speech has the ring of a foreigner."

Rike admitted it.

"Where are you from?"

"The distant provinces." Rike named a city halfway across the world.

Sabinus shook his head. "It is unknown to me."

"It is very far away."

Sabinus nodded. "And what brings you here?" His lips twitched in what might have been a smile.

"I was a witness to a killing," Rike told him.

"Whose?"

"It hardly matters. The emperor's hand held the dagger."

Sabinus sighed, said nothing.

"And you, Sabinus?"

The colonel shrugged. "The emperor thinks I mean to kill him."

"Do you?"

"Yes."

"Good," Alexis Rike said. "Then perhaps I can help you."

Darkness began to close over the pair.

"How?" Sabinus said, his voice seeming to come from a vast distance.

"By helping you to leave this place." Rike's voice was very faint now.

Total blackness came.

Again the voices spoke from the whirlpool around him.
"Well?"

"These memories are troublesome."

"Is there no accounting for them?"

"Assuredly. They may be a perfidious falsehood in order to ensnare us."

"Would not the probe expose them as such?"

"Perhaps."

"You possess doubts?"

"Our way here is uncertain. The stratagems of those who oppose us are cunning. This specimen may yet retain other memory levels, none of which would necessarily be truthful."

"Then what is our course?"

"The probe again. The memory levels will, in due time, deplete themselves. Then we shall know."

"But what if they are real?"

"It is of small concern if these paltry recollections are all he possesses."

"Still . . ."

"He could have been swept along in one of the upheavals. This would be a simple explanation."

"Then the probe is our best recourse."

"Precisely."

"When?"

"Soon."

"Take him back."

Alexis Rike sat up.

Nothing had changed in the small cell. He was still

among the monks—if that's what they were. Perhaps they weren't.

He leaned back against the damp stone wall, took a deep breath and tried to relax. Water dripped languidly onto the floor.

Monks.

Greeks.

Romans.

These were the only memories he had. And none of them fit together.

None!

The memories *must* be false. But how and why?

He didn't know the answer to the first question. He could guess at the second.

What better way to drive a man insane?

Alexis Rike thought it over. He didn't *feel* insane. If that was their aim, they certainly weren't doing a very good job of it. And there *were* better ways of driving a man insane—only at the moment he couldn't think of any. There were numerous things he couldn't think of, including who he was. Perhaps it would come to him later. He didn't seem to have much control over it, one way or the other. Or did he?

Rike tried to recall more about Caligula, Gaius Sabinus, his other Roman self. In Rome he'd spoken of some way to escape the dungeon. And no matter how far-fetched, knowledge of that sort couldn't hurt right now . . .

Alexis Rike had managed to squeeze out an epilogue to his Greek memory, but nothing Roman would come. Perhaps it was his fate to remain eternally trapped in his cell with Sabinus, waiting for a miracle which could never occur. More likely, whatever had concocted these bogus recollections had simply run out of material and called it quits.

There was, however, another difference between his Roman and Greek selves: Alexis Rike in Athens had been, in some ways, as befuddled as Rike was now.

The Roman Rike was something else again. His thoughts had proven impenetrable.

He had, at least, seemed more self-possessed. But what did it mean? Rike shrugged. As far as he was concerned, it meant nothing.

Rike got up to tap on the wall. Whatever code had been used, he seemed to have understood it well enough at the time. So why could he remember nothing now? Another mystery. One that didn't matter:

There was no answer from the other side of the wall.

CHAPTER 14

The Girl and the Golem

The train bearing the girl and the Golem sped through the tunnel.

Outside, the darkness poured by them like molten tar. Inside there was only the engine's purr, the washed-out gleam of overhead lights, the statue-like immobility of the other riders.

Flickering shapes began to appear in the car, take on substance. For an instant the car was transformed into a shadowed bedroom.

Stalin lay dying. Khrushchev grinned with pleasure. "We're rid of the old fool!" Stalin raised an eyelid. He might yet survive and he had heard his assistant's words. Khrushchev reached for a pillow to smother the dictator. And was gunned down by a security guard. Stalin would live . . .

The bedroom was gone.

The girl and the Golem were again enclosed by train walls, could see the darkness flash by outside, could hear the hum of engines.

The train faded.

Malcolm J. Neigh, President of the United States of North, South and Canadian America, walked out of the Oval Office. The White House was still. Three-thirty in the morning—the President was dressed in robe and pajamas. He walked down a hall. Behind him, on his desk, he had left a note explaining everything. That no one would be alive to read this note shortly after he pressed the button did not especially concern him. Neigh had gone completely and irrevocably mad . . .

Again the scene flickered and changed.

Professor Ingram turned to face the group which had gathered in his laboratory. "This is the moment," he said. "We have tried before and failed. We will not fail again." Ingram extended his hand, pulled the switch. The room exploded.

Distorted images broke into frail wisps, blinked out. Again the train reasserted itself.

The Golem grinned. "The possibilities are restless tonight. Restless but futile."

The girl said, "We've got to find the Prime. These things *could* become real."

"Indeed. But the Prime is elusive, more so than we suspected. A blessing, perhaps, when you think of it."

The girl brushed a lock of golden hair from her forehead; green eyes stared quizzically at the Golem; she smiled. "In what way?"

"Were it a simple matter to locate him, *they* would have done so long ago. We, however, do possess certain advantages. *They* have scant knowledge of those who were close to the Prime. If these persons could be found—"

"If," the girl said.

"What choice do we have?" The Golem eyed the backs of the other passengers. "These sights take some getting used to, don't they?"

The girl nodded silently.

"What do you call this?" the Golem asked.
"The nightmare express."

CHAPTER 15

From the Diary of Dr. James Ingram

April 21, 1935. More and more I have become convinced that others too are involved in the crucial struggle against the aliens. But *who* are they and *where?* In what time juncture? Are my dreams a clue?

April 22, 1935. I have dreamed again. I see faces of both men and women. Only two are known to me, the rest are strangers. The dreams began over a week ago. Always the same dream figures. They grow more vivid with each succeeding night. They gain in strength as we approach May 15!

I do not think these are mere dreams. Are they some sort of message? The force field must still link me to my old laboratory, my former associates. Could it be that the impending re-emergence of the black hole has opened the channels again?

April 23, 1935. I no longer doubt that the channels are open. My "dreams" are full of these strangers and aliens. It is hard to make sense of it all.

April 24, 1935. The channel widens, the broadcasts

grow stronger! There is a voice too now, one that constantly speaks of a "prime." The word is unknown to me.

April 27, 1935. I have been too heartsick to take pen in hand these last three days. I have come to understand the meaning of Prime. God help us all. My entire project has been put in question. Yet I have no choice but to see it through. For it is impossible to calculate how the Prime figures in my equations, or those of the aliens. He is a wild factor. It is obvious that my old colleagues have moved ahead on their own—for what else can it be?—that somehow their efforts have resulted in a new player in our game: the Prime. Who is he? One of my dream figures? Someone else? I cannot tell. More important: *where* is he? For he is linked by the same force field which embraces both my energy system and that of the aliens. And unless his whereabouts are known, no definite calculations are possible.

Can I be sure of this? No. The voice itself is far from clear and I have had to guess at its meaning. Who or what *is* the voice? Again I am at a loss. Are the frantic dream figures agents of my former co-workers? Is their mission to locate the Prime, return him to my old laboratory and thereby balance the equations necessary for my counterthrust on May 15? But how would they even know about May 15? Unless the widened channel allows them to monitor my activities. If so, are these dreams the best they can do to alert me? Or have I misread everything? Is something wholly different occurring?

Or is all this perhaps the work of the aliens themselves?

CHAPTER 16

Mark Craig

I became an outpatient the next morning.

"No reason now you lie here all day," a Dr. Wolf, poking his head into my room, explained. "Physically you well."

"That's nice to hear," I admitted. "What do I do, just walk out the front door?"

"See Dr. Spiegel, he fix everything."

"Everything, huh? This I've got to see."

Dr. Wolf smiled, withdrew. It was eight thirty-five. I cleaned up, dressed, breakfasted in the State-City cafeteria and went off to see Dr. Spiegel in the outpatient wing.

"Well-ll, Mr. Craig." Dr. Spiegel smiled, running his hand through his white hair. "There is no good reason why you should remain here, and every reason for your swift discharge."

"Not that I'm complaining," I said, "but name one."

"Being out in York may help your memory. And it will enable us to take concrete steps to find out who you are."

"Fine. No chance, I suppose, that these dreams of mine might get out of hand?"

"Frankly, Mr. Craig, I do not see how. They are, after all, merely dreams. Exceptionally vivid, I'll grant you, but still dreams. You were not observed sleepwalking. You neither fell out of windows nor crashed into walls.

It is doubtful if you even went so far as to wave your arms or kick off your blanket."

"Very peaceful," I said.

"Precisely. So we need have no fear on that account."

"Okay," I told him, "but I'll be wandering around out there without a trace of memory or a penny to my name."

"Hardly without a penny," Dr. Spiegel smiled.

Eric Hughs was short, stoop-shouldered and wore thick glasses; he had steel-gray hair and tired lines under his eyes. His office was three floors below Dr. Spiegel's. Hughs nodded me to a chair, introduced himself. His voice, surprisingly, was clear, crisp. "So, you're our latest memory case, eh, Mr. Craig?"

"Yeah. You've got others?"

"We get a few. From time to time."

"How's that?"

Hughs shrugged. "It's an illness like any other, Mr. Craig. People want to forget something, maybe themselves."

"I thought this place was paradise."

"Perhaps it is. Maybe that's what people are trying to forget." Hughs smiled. "There *are* other reasons, of course, like getting banged on the head."

"Sure."

"Still," Hughs said, tapping a brown manila folder with a stubby finger. "Your case does have its peculiar side. You seem to have blanked out on most of what's going on out there, Mr. Craig."

"It shows, huh?"

"Oh, brother. What's this, Mr. Craig?" He was holding up a two-by-three red plastic card.

"Search me."

"Money, Mr. Craig. Ever see it before?"

"Nope."

"Sure you have. This card is the one thing you've *really* got to know all about."

"That's not very encouraging."

Hughs waved an arm. "Don't worry, it'll come back to you."

"Yeah. What happened to the folding stuff?"

"You mean paper money?"

"Uh-huh."

"Went out around the turn of the century," Hughs smiled. "It's just possible you're some kind of a historian, Mr. Craig? Sound promising?"

"Who knows? Anything's possible. How's the card work?"

"It's called a swiftie. You just slip it into a checkout slot—they're just about everywhere, Mr. Craig—and it taps right into bank-central." He tossed me the card. "Your swiftie, Mr. Craig." My name was already on it, I saw.

"Thanks. How could I possibly forget a thing like this? You give it away for free?"

Hughs chuckled. "There'd be no end of takers, both of us included, eh, Mr. Craig? What you've got there is a thousand dollars' worth of credit. From the York emergency loan fund. That should hold you till we get a line on your identity."

"What if I turn out to be a pauper? How do I pay this back?"

"Don't worry. You're probably rolling in the stuff, Mr. Craig. There are no paupers, you know."

"Actually, I hadn't known."

"Take it from me. You'll turn out to be some kind of historian. Anyway, even if you can't pay it back, there's a provision for that too."

"What is it, debtors' prison?"

Hughs rolled around in his chair laughing. "You should go on the Tela-vista, Mr. Craig, you'd break 'em up. You've got a real talent there. Why, if you're short of capital, what we do is find you a job."

"Sounds about right," I admitted.

"Of course. Feel up to managing the city on your own? We can find you a companion."

"I'm okay."

"Fine," Hughs said cheerfully, "that's the spirit. I'm going to give you a visitor's map of our fair city, it'll help you get around. I've reserved a room for you at the

Brooks; it's circled on the map. So is the SEC; drop in there first chance you get. They'll do a check on you, maybe clear up your problem right on the spot."

"Nice," I said. "What are they, the local witch doctors' club?"

"Better than that as far as you're concerned, Mr. Craig. The SEC is the Securities Exchange Commission. They control money; that is, they regulate the swifties and credit ratings. They've got more data on where you've been, what you've done and how much you earn than anyone else."

"I'll look 'em up," I promised.

York:

Green glass and metal skyscrapers lined the main drag. Mobile ramps hustled pedestrians on their way, slid out of underground tubes to spiral upward across the tips of buildings. Ramps and feet seemed to be the standard mode of locomotion. The few vehicles I saw looked official. Automat cleaners swept streets and structures, kept them spotless. Most folks wore tight-fitting, gaily colored outfits, except for a few who went in for more somber shades. Hughs had supplied me with a two-piece red and green striped suit which ended in flopping bell trousers. My shirt was white silk with an open-necked, fluffy laced collar. I felt like a walking peppermint stick. No one took any special notice of me. I blended in just right with the rest of this crowd. Old York had occasional patches of smoke-filled sky. York had no smoke at all. Silent aircraft drifted by overhead. Store windows glittered with fancy duds, furniture, appliances. Only some of the items were familiar. Old York was a dream, but one I could live with: its narrow streets and beat-up tenements had had a comfortable feel to 'em like an old smoking jacket. Probably because my unconscious had cooked up the whole shebang and was thoughtful enough to include a batch of phony memories. But York was real and I remembered nothing about it. No doubt I'd turn out to be a lifetime resident with a history a mile long—as soon as my brains got unscrambled.

I wondered what I was going to do with myself till then.

CHAPTER 17

Alexis Rike

The noise woke Alexis Rike from a deep sleep. He sat up. No light came through the high barred window. Sometime in the middle of the night. The large door of his cell, he saw, was being pushed open.

The short, fat, bald-headed monk who had first interviewed him stood in the doorway, a torch in one hand. His round face appeared yellow and vacant in the flickering light. Three tall, silent monks, almost lost in shadow, stood behind him. "Remain here," the fat monk said, stepped into the cell, swung the door shut behind him. Placing his torch in a wall receptacle, the monk turned to Rike.

Alexis Rike stood up.

The monk took a hasty step back, glanced sideways toward the door; his small eyes seemed to reflect terror.

Rike said earnestly, "I won't hurt you."

Standing stock-still, the monk whispered, "How can I trust you?"

Rike said, "You must trust me already or you wouldn't be here."

The monk nodded slowly. "You are not of the devil, are you?"

"No."

"What then?"

"Whatever I am," Rike said, "I am not with those you call the inquisitors."

The monk crossed himself. "God grant it be so."

"They are not of your order?" Rike said.

The monk shuddered. "No, though they claim to be from a far monastery."

"You know that to be false?"

"Merely to see them is to know."

"In what way?"

"The crates which they bring contain hellish devices."

"You saw for yourself?"

"But briefly. It was more than sufficient, however." The monk had begun to shiver. "Their voices, their faces speak of evil. Even their carriage denotes overweening pride. *Who in God's name are they?*"

Rike said, "They may very well be the devil's helpers."

Again the monk crossed himself. "I am in great fear."

"You plan to do something?"

"What *is* there to do?"

"For a start," Rike said, "you might consider releasing me."

"Would it were possible."

"Why isn't it?"

The monk took a deep breath. "If you truly require my aid, is this not proof that you cannot withstand their power? What then will happen to us when you have departed? Will these fiends not wreak a terrible vengeance?"

"I don't think so. Their chief interest seems to be me."

"For what reason?"

"I'm not sure."

The monk shrugged. "Their men roam our monastery at will. They are everywhere. How would it serve us to help you?"

Alexis Rike said, "I'm not sure. Why have you come here now?"

The monk spread his hands. Dark shadows leaped over the stone walls in the wavering torchlight. "I did not know what else to do. I was afraid."

Rike nodded.

"Who is in the next cell?" he asked.

"No one. It is empty."

"Can you come to me tomorrow night?"

"Yes. I will try."

"Perhaps we will find some way to help each other, then."

"God willing."

The monk took his torch and left. The heavy door swung shut behind him.

Alexis Rike sat down again, stared off into the darkness. Where the hell could I go, anyway? he thought.

CHAPTER 18

The Girl and the Golem

The Third Avenue el rumbled by overhead. Down below, the street was half hidden in shadows. Tenement houses, storefronts, pedestrians and traffic congested the block. A poster on a wooden fence read: Buy War Bonds. It was November 3, 1943.

The girl stood on the northwest corner of Third Avenue and 78th Street. When the light changed, she crossed to the east side of the street, walked to a house at mid-block.

The front door of this building was not locked. The girl entered, went up a flight of stairs. She rapped on a door.

"Who is it?" a voice called.

"Miss Darling, from the Compensation Board," the girl replied.

A stooped, elderly woman opened the door. Her eyes were dark, gleaming, her hair white and tied in a bun. She had on a long black dress with a white lace collar and cuffs. "Won't you come in," she said.

The girl stepped into a bright, orderly living room. Potted plants on the windows. Fresh flowers in two vases on small end tables. A magazine rack piled with back issues of *Life, Collier's, The Saturday Evening Post*. A large floor model radio stood next to a stuffed easy chair. A daytime serial, "Our Gal Sunday," was just beginning. The elderly woman turned it off.

"You are Mrs. Emma Landry?" the girl asked.

"Yes, indeed."

"You are the Emma Landry who lived at 465 West 25th Street?"

"I am."

The girl smiled. "As I explained over the phone, Mrs. Landry, my name is Ann Darling. I'm with the Metropolitan Compensation Board."

Mrs. Landry nodded brightly.

"There was a fire at that address—"

"A fire?"

"Many years ago. Quite a large one. The date was May 15, 1935."

Mrs. Landry chuckled. "Of course. Dear me, I should have remembered at once."

"The Board believes that some of the tenants may be eligible for compensation."

"But, my dear, that was so long ago."

"True. But the law says we must investigate, even now, if the circumstances warrant it."

"I see."

"The landlord himself, Mrs. Landry, called our attention to the case; he may also be in line for some compensation."

"My goodness," Mrs. Landry said, "am I to receive money, too?"

"Quite possibly."

"Dear me."

"The fire may have inadvertently been started by Mr. Logan, on the fourth floor. Do you recall him?"

"The nice white-haired gentleman, with the moustache?"

"Yes."

"I can't imagine what poor Mr. Logan did to start such a frightful blaze. Why, the entire two top floors were burned to cinders. Everyone thought a gas pipe had exploded."

"He was conducting experiments."

"In his apartment?"

"We believe so."

"Whatever for?"

"We don't know, Mrs. Landry; that is perhaps one of the things we will find out."

"Mr. Logan died in that blaze, you know."

The girl nodded gravely. "Along with two other tenants."

"Mr. Karp and Mr. Jordan. It was frightful."

"Can you tell me what happened on the night of the fire?"

"Of course. Would you care for a cup of tea, Miss Darling?"

The girl said she would, followed Mrs. Landry into a yellow-walled kitchen. The table at which she seated herself was next to a window. She could see patches of snow in the yard below.

Mrs. Landry spoke as she prepared the tea. "It must have been sometime past ten. I had been listening to the radio when someone knocked on my door. It was Miss Ryder, who lived on the floor above. She said she smelled smoke. We went up together to her rooms and I could smell it too. Gracious me, we had no idea how serious it was. We began to climb to the next landing. The smoke became very thick. We couldn't go on. I went down to call the fire department from the hall phone while Miss Ryder began knocking on neighbors' doors. The other tenants took to the street and I joined them. We were all down there when the firemen arrived. By then we could see the flames through the windows of the top floor. It took them more than two hours to put the fire out. Even when the top floors were rebuilt, Miss Darling, you could still smell the burnt wood. You could smell it for years afterward . . ."

The girl sipped her tea. "Do you think, Mrs. Landry, that you could provide me with a list of tenants?"

"I'd be glad to, my dear; as many as I can recall."

"And their descriptions, perhaps?"

"Of course."

CHAPTER 19

Mark Craig

"Wait here," the clerk said and hurried away. Presently he returned with an elderly, gray-haired man in tow. I got to my feet.

"I'm Jennings," the man said. "Mr. Hughs' office has already informed us of your problem, Mr. Craig. If you will be good enough to follow me . . ." I followed him down a wide corridor and into an elevator that took us to the ninth floor of the SEC building. I was led into a small room with no window, a desk and a chair. Jennings himself gave me the works. I was photographed, voiceprinted, fingerprinted and told to wait. I waited. Ten minutes later a pink-cheeked lady dropped by to get a sample of my handwriting. She left and I waited some more. Jennings stuck his head into the room and motioned I follow. We went back to the elevator and rode up to the fifteenth floor. Jennings saw me to a waiting room where a pert receptionist let me hang around for another ten minutes. I began to see how my dream world was based on solid fact: my trip through the Old York Hall of Records had taken no less time. Maybe Dr. Spiegel was right: getting around in the city *would* jog my memory—if not improve my mood.

A buzzer sounded; the receptionist said Mr. Lardner would see me now, and I went through a door on the left. I found myself in a large office. A glass wall looked out on the city. A very fat man sat behind a huge desk fingering a sheaf of papers. He looked annoyed. I made my way across a thick carpet to his desk.

"Mr. Craig, is it?" Lardner looked up.

I said it was.

"Sit down, Mr. Craig. I have some rather distressing news for you."

I sat down.

"There is no record of your ever having held a job, of your ever renting a house or apartment. You have no credit rating, no medical coverage, no retirement insurance. These, sir, are merely vastly improbable. You were never issued a swiftie, sir, never; now *that* is plainly impossible. What have you got to say for yourself?" The fat man glowered at me.

I opened my mouth and closed it. I was stumped, not exactly a startling development. Finally I said, "You've checked out everything in less than half an hour?"

"In less than *three minutes*, sir. We checked and double-checked. Confound it, if it were not completely impossible, I would suspect fraud, sir."

"Why isn't it possible?"

"Signatures may be forged, facial features altered." The fat man wriggled a finger at me. "But not fingerprints. Not voiceprints. Sir, you are . . . you are . . ."

"An unperson?"

"Yes, sir, indeed!"

"I've had some slight experience with the word," I told him.

The fat man shook his head. "We shall get to the bottom of this, sir. Have no fear. It is conceivable that you are a foreigner. Although you do not *sound* like a foreigner. Our computer is in alignment with Immigration.

Immigration has no record of you. It is equally conceivable that you are an illegal alien. Our borders are open to most persons except those who have committed certain crimes. Perhaps you are one of those, although if that were the case, you would most certainly be on file at Immigration as an undesirable. We have queried overseas. Overseas takes twenty-four hours. I expect to see you back at this office promptly at two-thirty tomorrow." Mr. Lardner nodded. "Good day, sir."

I spent the next couple of hours touring the city. It wasn't a pleasant trip. I traveled up and down the mobile ramps, looked at big and small buildings, down side streets, peered into strangers' faces, went walking in two of York's green, leafy parks and generally hunted for a sight that looked as if I had seen it before. If any such sights existed they were doing their best to avoid me.

I called it quits after a while and went hunting for more reasonable game.

I used my swiftie to land a toothbrush, comb and shaving kit. I bought gray trousers and a blue sports jacket at a local haberdasher and had them toss in a pair of shoes, some socks and a change of underwear for good measure. I carted my finds off to my new hotel, checked in, was given a room. I shaved, showered, climbed into my new getup, eyed myself in the mirror, lay around on a too soft bed watching the Tela-vista do its tricks, got up, snapped it off and went back down the elevator and out onto the street. I was beginning to miss my nutty Double M racket; at least it had given me something to do besides bite my nails. I was as restless as the very last dodo hunting a mate. And my prospects were about as hopeful.

I let my feet carry me where they would.

I passed glass skyscrapers, something that looked like a Greek temple, a handball court; the shouts of kids came from a nearby playground. A tall bronze building bore a large gold-silver shield over its front doors; I didn't bother reading the inscription. Music came from far off—an outdoor band by the sound of it. I followed the music.

Soon I was passing large, colored posters. The posters proclaimed something called Time Festival. That seemed as good a destination as any. I liked the name.

Lights winked and blinked. Music blared. Crowds streamed through multicolored gates. As far as the eye could see Time Festival stretched across the landscape.

I swapped some swiftie credits for a pocketful of loose change at a booth inside the fairgrounds and headed down the midway.

Trees lined some of the streets, those veering off into rural America of the 1800s. Squat, round and towering structures competed for attention on the other byways. All the ages were on display here. The crowd—some in celebrity face masks—filled pavements, high-rise walks and spirals. I moved through the crowd. Signs pointed toward the 1700s, Dark Ages, 2060s, Ancient Rome. Booths sold face masks, snacks, souvenirs. A sign pointed toward a mobile ramp, said: 1930s set. I boarded the ramp, was carried down into an underground tunnel. Passengers wore Julius Caesar, Barbra Streisand, Karl Marx face masks. A teen-ager had the face and long beard of Johannes Brahms. Side ramps led off to Ancient Greece, 1960s, an Indian reservation. I got off at the 1930s, rolled up into daylight.

I was on Broadway and 42nd Street. A billboard read: Rearranged to Form a Composite View.

The Fifth Avenue Public Library was on the left side of the street. Part of the Central Park Zoo had been put next to it. A large shaggy lion was roaring, adding to the din. Monkeys capered frantically in their cages. The giant Camel sign blew huge smoke rings over Times Square. The Coca-Cola sign glowed a bright red.

People, bare-faced and masked, went by; masks of James Cagney, Bette Davis, Mae West, Gary Cooper, Clark Gable . . . Newsstands held papers whose headlines proclaimed:

Garden Throng Boos Roosevelt for Bonus Veto
Mussolini Rebuffs Geneva on Ethiopia
Britain to Triple Air Force by 1937 in Reply to Hitler
Theater marquees lined the Broadway midway. *The*

Thin Man was at the Little Carnegie. *The Bride of Frankenstein* at the Roxy. Charlie Chaplin played the Plaza.

A white, shiny Studebaker and a black Ford were parked down the block. Fred Allen, the dry-voiced radio comic, broadcast out of a large floor model radio replica, next to the Ford display. Krazy Kat, Popeye, Mutt and Jeff life-size cutouts formed an honor guard outside the Comic Book Hall of Fame.

I stood there, let the sights, sounds and smells of the thirties strip wash over me. I knew this place, all right, knew the names of the cars, the voices on the radio, the cutout comic book characters. I remembered the movies on the marquees, recalled their story lines, the actors who strolled through them. My memory had scored a bull's-eye.

But so what?

It proved nothing. Only that I'd been here before, on this very strip, just like the hundreds of other paying customers streaming by.

The doctors at State-City were right.

Old York was a hodgepodge made up of bits and pieces. You didn't have to be an expert to know the ins and outs of yesteryear—all it took was the price of admission to *this* place. I'd lifted a lot of stuff from the thirties set, but I'd borrowed from the other sets, too. It was all here, everything I wanted to know about my dream world. And all it added up to was a lot of hooey. I still didn't have any idea who I was. Or how I'd wound up an unperson.

Dusk began to fall. Lights were snapping on all over the midway: red, blue, yellow. I moved with the crowd.

There was no special destination. No pressing business demanded my attention. One place was as good as another. As long as my swiftie credits held out I was a man of leisure.

The bar was on a side street. Pale neon lights spelled out: Frank's. A thirties dive—identical to the ones I remembered from Old York.

I hadn't noticed any bars in York proper. But then I

hadn't been looking, had I? Something that felt like a touch of nostalgia seemed to prod me. That was silly because Old York was only in my mind. Silly or not, I pushed open the swinging doors.

The lights were dim and sawdust covered the floor. A few men sat on stools at the bar, others farther back at small tables.

I took a seat up front at the bar, ordered a whisky. The barkeep, a large meaty guy, gave me a shot; I asked for a second and third. The minutes slipped away like raindrops down a pane of glass. Maybe I wasn't making much progress, but it didn't seem to matter anymore. I could sit here and nurse my drink and let things take care of themselves. Things would anyway. Because nothing I did or thought made the slightest difference. That was the long and short of it.

I raised my eyes to the mirror behind the bar. I looked tired and done. Not a very inspiring sight. I shifted my gaze to the men at the tables.

They didn't look like tourists. They didn't look any too happy either. They sat hunched over their drinks silent and gray-faced in the dim light. Maybe York had a couple of drawbacks, after all. Maybe some of these guys felt better off in a fake bar on a carnival midway.

I looked at them and they all seemed to be off in their own dream world; they sat motionless as though they had been carved out of gray soap, their eyes downcast or staring into space. All except for one man who sat at a corner table. It was too dark to distinguish his features fully, but a sliver of light fell across his forehead. I could see his eyes. And they were staring directly into mine.

We sat there ogling each other. I expected whoever it was to look away. Nothing doing. If anything, now that he'd caught my attention, my unknown pal was really working the routine. I took a last swallow of booze, turned on my stool to face the tables.

Still too dark for a clear view. But I could see my admirer hadn't given up. Maybe I'd hit pay dirt of a sort. There was just the chance I had accidently run into someone who knew me. Or at least had seen me before. Either one would do.

I got to my feet, slowly walked across the sawdust-covered floor to the corner.

A white-faced, haggard-looking Pat De Marco sat staring up at me.

CHAPTER 20

Alexis Rike

Alexis Rike glanced over his shoulder. The noontime crowd hustled along, poured out of small storefronts, office buildings. A street sign read: East Broadway, Essex. The *Jewish Daily Forward* building loomed over the neighborhood like a huge lighthouse. Rike glanced at a newsstand. IKE READY FOR WHITE HOUSE a *Herald Tribune* headline proclaimed. He crossed the street, went into the corner cafeteria. A babble of Yiddish, Polish, Russian, English. Orders of kasha, chicken and pea soup. Customers crowded the small tables, many of them journalists and printers from the *Forward* and its rival down the block, the *Jewish Day*. Getting on line, he ordered pea soup, flanken, mashed potatoes, a glass of tea, and carted them off on his tray to the side dining hall. Fuller was seated in back, pastry and coffee in front of him, his suit jacket flung over the chair opposite him. Alexis Rike handed Fuller his jacket and sat down. Over the clang of glasses, dishes, a symphony of voices, Fuller said:

"You were careful?"

"Reasonably so. I don't think I was followed."

"Think!" Fuller snapped. "You've got to be positive!"

"Perhaps," Rike said, "I'd do better if we stopped playing these little games and you got to the point."

Fuller smiled out of one corner of his mouth. He was a thin, nervous-looking man in his late forties. A brown moustache under a long crooked nose gave his tapered face a vaguely sinister cast. His brow was furrowed and there were black lines under his gray eyes.

"That's what we're here for," Fuller said.

Alexis Rike nodded, started in on his soup.

Fuller said, "I can help you, Rike."

Without raising his eyes, Rike said, "Yes?"

Fuller grinned. "I know about you, Rike, know how you live."

"Really?"

"Sure. It's tough earning an honest buck when you're on the blacklist, isn't it?"

Rike shrugged. "I get by."

"Sure. But a little dough wouldn't hurt, would it? A little something extra?" Fuller reached for his jacket, pulled a bulky envelope from the inside pocket. "I figured you might need some convincing. Take a look in here."

The envelope changed hands. Rike took a look. "How much is it?" he asked.

"A grand! Go on, take it."

Rike placed the envelope very carefully on the table. "Fuller," he said, "what's this all about? What the hell am I supposed to do with your money?"

"Not mine, Rike. Never was. It's yours, buddy. Yeah—just like that. A little something to show we mean it."

"Mean what?"

Fuller's face twisted into a grimace. "Listen to me, Rike, we're talking about the Reds, the Commies."

Rike said, "What about them?"

"Those scum are out to get us. You, me, this country, the works. They don't care about the rules, about any high-minded ethics. They just want to win—win big. They're a conspiracy, Rike, not some goddamned political party. And we're going to break their backs."

"Yes?" Rike said.

"Our boys are doing it in Korea; we're going to do it here."

"You and who else, Fuller?"

"The agency, Rike."

"*What* agency?"

"Don't push it," Fuller said.

Alexis Rike smiled, shook his head.

"Look at the money, Rike. That's real, isn't it?"

Rike shrugged. "What does it buy?"

"You."

Rike's smile broadened. "That's not much."

"Sure," Fuller said. "But it's your reputation we're interested in, Rike."

Rike laughed. "Now I know you're nuts."

"You've got a lousy reputation, Rike."

"Yes?"

"It's that college bit that did it. You got a big play in the papers when they bounced you. For a while, Rike, you were a name."

"That was a long time ago."

"Controversy," Fuller went on with satisfaction. "It's the stuff folks remember. Even when the details are vague. Funny, Rike, but in a lot of minds, old buddy, you're down as a Red. Remember Bruno? Rudolph Bruno?"

"I didn't know him."

"Right. But he knew you. Graduated a year before your little incident."

"I knew the face."

"Sure you did. You bet. He was in the service too. About the same time you were, only in a different company. Same base, though. You know that?"

"Perhaps. I may have seen him once or twice."

"Know anything about him?"

"How should I?"

"Why, he was a Red. Get it? He was there when you got tossed out. And you know what that makes you in his book, don't you, Rike?"

"I suppose you're going to tell me even if I don't ask, right, Fuller?"

"Right. A Commie."

"So what?"

Fuller grinned. "And I'm sure he wasn't sorry to find you an employee of that leftist sheet, either."

"He knows about that?"

"Of course. Of course he knows. And so do we, Rike. It's our business to know."

"What are you? A government agent, Fuller? Is that it?"

"Now you've done it. You've let the cat out of the bag. Hell, it's tough keeping a secret around here, isn't it, Rike?"

"And you want me to do what?"

"A job, Rike; we want you to do a very simple job for us. You're going to help us exterminate a rat, and then blame it on the Commies."

"Anyone special?"

"A senator. A rat who'd sell out his country for a dime."

"I'm going to help you kill him?"

"That's right."

"And Rudolph Bruno?"

"Rudolph the Red, they call him. You and Rudolph are going to be great buddies. That's very important. Because we're going to pin the job on him; him and his pals."

"And if I don't?"

"We get you too, Rike."

"You're insane, Fuller. If I go to the police, they'll have you locked up."

"You really think so, Rike? Who'd believe you?"

Rike stared at Fuller, picked up his by now lukewarm glass of tea, took a swallow. "A thousand dollars isn't enough for that sort of thing."

"Of course not," Fuller agreed, grinning. "It's just a first installment. A down payment. You game, Rike? You going to play ball with us?"

Alexis Rike shrugged. "Why not?"

He was falling through darkness, head over heels in a dizzying spiral. He knew it was only an illusion, that actually he was standing or lying down. *They* had caught him in their beam again. Another memory or story or whatever-it-was had run its course through his mind. He would remember and perhaps, if he was lucky, learn from it. *And so would they.* The churning whirlpool was all around him. The voices—those of his interrogators, no doubt—would be speaking. The sounds their voices made were flat, nasal. He did not know what language they spoke. He was not sure what language he himself spoke. It did not matter. Perhaps nothing mattered. He could no longer tell. The more he found out about himself, the less he seemed to know. Perhaps if he listened very closely he would hear something new. He listened:

"Well?"

"I am, frankly, at a loss."

"You think his memory false?"

"Too soon, too soon to judge with accuracy. But should it prove so, it would mean nothing less than a direct assault upon us—here."

"How could they have penetrated to this juncture? Our defenses are intact. And what could they hope to gain? How can this one individual strike out against us?"

"He cannot."

"Do you think him then to be the Prime?"

"The Prime? That is nonsensical. Is he not our prisoner?"

"He is feeble, too."

"There is a dark riddle here."

"We shall solve it!"

"We probe again?"

"Assuredly."

"When?"

"Within three hours."

"Let him remain here, then."

"Good."

CHAPTER 21

The Girl and the Golem

The Golem smiled at Brewster. "Yes," he said, "there may be money in it."

"That'll be the day," Brewster said. "What did you say your name was?"

"Reginald Meerlue," the Golem said.

"And you're with *what* board?"

"The Metropolitan Compensation Board."

"You got any proof, mister?"

The Golem flipped open a leather card case, showed his identification, one purchased in a novelty shop. It bore what appeared to be the city seal and in bold letters read "Metropolitan Compensation Board."

"Hurumph," Brewster said, stuffing tobacco into his pipe. "Go on, ask what you want."

The Golem seated himself in a hard-backed wooden chair. Brewster, a thin, sixtyish man in wrinkled trousers, undershirt and flannel robe, sat on a worn couch. The radiator hissed steam. Outside the sounds of traffic could be heard going by on Canal Street.

The Golem said, "I know, sir, that it was a long time ago. But think back. Were there any new tenants in the building? Or perhaps someone subletting an apartment? Someone who moved in after Logan and was there the night of the fire?"

110

Brewster puffed on his pipe. "Read off that tenants' list again, will ya?"

"Certainly." The Golem read the list.

"Yeah," Brewster said, "I thought so. You forgot Harry."

"Who?"

"Old Harry Henderson. Moved in a month before the fire. Wasn't around very often. But we swapped a couplea words sometimes."

"Ah!" the Golem said. "You wouldn't happen to have his address?"

"Yeah. Got it here somewhere. Lemme go look."

"You are Mr. Harry Henderson?" the Golem asked.

"Right."

"I am Reginald Meerlue."

"What can I do for you, Mr. Meerlue?"

"I am, sir, an investigator with the Metropolitan Compensation Board."

"You don't say?"

"I should like to speak with you."

"There ain't no such outfit, brother."

"Ah, you are aware of that?"

"Uh-huh."

"Very well then, Mr. Henderson, I will be frank with you."

"Sure. Why don't you?"

"I am investigating a certain fire—for private parties, let us say—one that occurred eight years ago. I believe you can be of some assistance to me."

"Assitance, eh? You got an expense account, Mr. Meerlue?"

"I most certainly do."

"How much assistance you figure on needing?"

"Fifty dollars' worth."

"This going to take long?"

"There are only a few questions."

"That sounds okay. Come on in."

The Golem left the dim hallway, entered a small flat. It was clean but sparsely furnished. A table. Some chairs. An easy chair, reading lamp and radio. The door to the bedroom was open, the edge of a quilt-covered bed was visible.

The Golem withdrew his wallet, extracted two twenties and a ten, handed them to Henderson. The money disappeared into Henderson's pocket.

"Pull up a chair, Mr. Meerlue; let's hear what's on your mind."

"Thank you, sir." The Golem seated himself on a hard-backed kitchen chair. Henderson remained standing, hands jammed into his pockets. He was a chubby man of medium height, with a wide nose, gray hair and a double chin. He had a small scar on his left cheek. He was in his sixties. "In April 1935," the Golem said, "you moved into a flat at 465 West 25th Street. A fire occurred there the following month."

Henderson grinned. "And you think I started it?"

"On the contrary, sir. I *know* you did not. What I do *not* know is what you were doing there."

"Well, that isn't too tough a question. I was shadowing a guy."

"Dr. Ingram."

"Right." Henderson smiled quizzically. "How'd you know?"

"I have been employed by Dr. Ingram's family. They wish to know his activities prior to his death."

"It took 'em a hell of a long time to get going, didn't it?"

"Ingram was not his real name. His family did not know what had happened to him; but when more than seven years elapsed they took action to have him declared legally dead. A safe-deposit box was opened under court order. It was then that the Ingram identity was uncovered. Ingram had engaged in experiments, it seems. The authorities believe that these led to the fire. At least two lives were known to be lost in that conflagration, a Mr. Karp and a Mr. Jordan. There may have been others. The family is well-to-do; they would like to make amends. They would also like to know as much as possible about Ingram's last days."

"Yeah," Henderson said, "I get it now. But I don't know how much help I can give you."

"Anything at all, at this stage of our investigation, would be useful."

"Well, it's like this. I was just a hired hand. In those days I got by by doing odd jobs, anything that came along; the Depression was going full tilt. I was supposed to keep tabs on this Ingram, report on his comings and goings, who he saw, stuff like that. And that's just what I did. Until the fire; that ended the case."

"Do you remember any of these persons, sir?"

Henderson laughed. "After all these years? Look, it was just a meal ticket for me. I made out my reports and forgot 'em."

"You remember no one?"

"Uh-uh. I wasn't even there full time. There were two other birds. We took turns."

"Who were they?"

"You got me. We all had keys to the flat. I only saw them maybe two, three times. We used to nod, that's all. They did most of the shadowing while I stayed put. Like I said, Mr. Meerlue, it was a job, and a lousy one at that. I must've had hundreds like it. I probably remember it just for one simple reason."

"And what was that, Mr. Henderson?"

"There weren't three people killed in that fire. Nine or ten was more like it. They all trooped up to Ingram's before it happened. And I didn't see any of them come down."

"And you told no one of this?"

"What was to tell? I wrote it all up in my report. Only none of the bodies were ever found. Don't ask me why. I never figured out that part of it."

"Who hired you, Mr. Henderson?"

"Ace Investigations. You can look 'em up. They're still in business, Mr. Meerlue."

CHAPTER 22

From the Diary of Dr. James Ingram

May 3, 1935. Three days into the month of May. For more than thirty years I have waited and planned for this month, but now I am filled with trepidation. The dream figures which fill my nights still go through their frantic paces. Only two—my former co-workers—are familiar. The rest, I feel, should be, but aren't. The aliens too are present. Each night this host plays out a game whose rules I do not understand. Each night the images grow stronger, the voice grows louder.

It is the voice which disturbs me most of all. For it speaks of a greater upheaval than I ever imagined. Could it be that the onslaught of the black hole and the alien energy system have somehow dislocated time and space itself? How is this possible? There is no hint of such an occurrence in any of my calculations.

May 4, 1935. I spend my days readying my equipment and my nights the prey of fearful images. I will be thankful when this is over one way or the other. The voice has become more explicit. The Prime, it tells me, is the key to my equation, the essential ingredient in repelling the aliens. For the Prime has become enmeshed in the force field which binds my energy system to that of the aliens. He must be found for my equations to become whole, my counterthrust successful. But how can I find someone I know nothing about?

May 5, 1935. The voice has told more. The Prime is himself unstable, flits from one time juncture to another. This complicates matters greatly.

May 6, 1935. Again there is more. The voice hints that the aliens have also penetrated through time. I thought them merely clustered about certain areas such as the emerging black hole. But if they have gone beyond that, why haven't they struck? Could it be that this Prime has somehow undermined their efforts?

The dream, too, has begun to change. There is a red glow over everything now.

CHAPTER 23

Mark Craig

De Marco and I trudged along the midway. We had left the thirties set. Asphalt paving was under our feet, but bushes and trees were on either side of us. The clatter of horses' hoofs, the grind of coach wheels on gravel roads sounded through the trees. We were somewhere on the nineteenth century set. The twitter of birds, the chirp of crickets couldn't quite drown out the more enthusiastic sound tracks of nearby eras.

"Damned if I know," De Marco said for maybe the tenth time.

"There must be *something*," I said again. I had said it so often during the last twenty minutes that I was starting to sound simpleminded even to myself. My chat with De Marco was proving less than totally enlightening.

"It was a feeling, get me?" De Marco said. "Like I had to be there."

"All you did at Frank's Bar was sit around?"

"Yeah."

"Didn't you wonder what was making you do this, De Marco?"

"Sure. Whaddya take me for, a sap? That's all I did was sit there an' wonder: *what the Hell is goin' on?*"

"But you kept coming?"

"Sure. I felt even worse stayin' away. What can I tell you, Craig? It was like a . . . a *compulsion.*"

"And this has been going on for two whole months?"

"Yeah, around that."

"Ever take the Time Festival tour before?"

"Sure."

"What happened?"

"Nothin'."

"You a thirties buff?"

"No more'n the next guy. Maybe a little."

We walked in glum silence for a while. Glum silence seemed the appropriate mood, all right. I said, "Any plans now?"

"What plans? I keep comin' back to Frank's. Maybe it'll wear off."

"No job, no family?"

"No family. I work outta my own office. I can take a break, if I got to. Looks like I gotta, huh?"

"What's your racket, De Marco?"

"Hunting down the swiftie-sharps."

"I thought there were none."

"Nothin's perfect."

"What're the angles?" As a phantom Double M, I took a vague professional interest.

"Well, there's tombstone swifties. Some guy kicks the bucket—see?—but by the time he's made the books, some sharpy's got hold of his swiftie an' run up a big score.

116

There're phony swifties, too, only that's tougher to swing. And lifted swifties—mostly one-shot cons."

"You're something of a private eye, then?"

De Marco grinned sourly. "That's for the old-time flicks. I'm licensed by the SEC."

"The cops don't run down cheaters?"

"Yeah, sometimes. Maybe if there's a whopper, right? With us it's quieter. The SEC likes to keep things quiet."

"That figures. But your hanging around the thirties doesn't."

"You're tellin' me. It's got me up a stump."

"See a doctor, De Marco?"

"I ain't *that* wacky. Not yet, Craig."

I knew what he meant. I could probably have written a paper on it. I asked, "Still sure you don't remember me?"

"Hell, I ain't sure of nothin'."

"You may have seen me somewhere in York; maybe just passing on the street."

"Look, Craig, when I first seen you I was *dead sure* I knew you. And you me, right? Only don't ask me when or where. I don't know. That whole thing's haywire."

We came to a small park. A stream ran through it. There were wooden benches, gaslit street lamps.

"Let's sit down awhile," I said. "I want to tell you about *Old* York."

De Marco sat staring into the darkness as I laid it out for him, ticked off some of Old York's main features. The tar streets. The ratty tenement houses. The denim attire. The horse-and-buggy transit system. The sweatshops. My own Double M racket. It took me about twenty minutes.

"Sounds screwy," De Marco said when I was done.

"It *is* screwy."

"An' that's *all* you remember, this creepy dream? Hell, you're worse off'n me, Craig."

"Uh-huh."

"All that stuff, this Old York, it comes from *here* and the Tela-vistas."

"Maybe. But I can give you chapter and verse on how that place works. Right down to the orphanage. Which is a darn sight more than I can do for here."

"So?" De Marco said.

"Well, you figured you knew me. Only you don't know from where."

"Yeah."

"I know. Old York."

"Shit," De Marco said.

"You were a private eye in Old York. You did odd jobs for me."

"For Chrissake—"

"On the level. We've done business for years, De Marco."

"It's a pipe dream. Maybe you seen *me* in the street somewhere; maybe you imagined the whole thing. Maybe you even got a screw loose, pal."

"Sure. Only you felt it too. *There's some kind of link between us.*"

"You're talkin' crazy!"

"Right, but so far this link is all I've got. You haven't exactly been behaving normally, De Marco."

"Aw, that's one thing, but this—"

"You want to hear about the last couple of times we met?"

De Marco shrugged. "Anything you say, pal."

"Okay." I spread the deck, told him about being braced by Nickerson and Watts—Mutt and Jeff; only the Mark Craig of Old York couldn't've known about Mutt and Jeff. I told him how I went hunting for my mislaid past and came up empty, then spotted the little guy: a short, slender redhead whose only previous appearance in my life—as far as I could remember—was in the dream. "This little guy was tailing me. That's where you came into it, De Marco."

"You hired me."

"Uh-huh."

"How much was my asking price?"

"Ten a day plus expenses. For shadowing."

De Marco waved a hand. "That settles it. You got the wrong guy, pal. I ain't never worked for chicken feed."

"Ten bucks bought plenty in Old York."

"Sucker's pay."

"Yeah. Well, after I sicced you on the little guy, De Marco, I went about my business, which seemed to get worse by the minute. I never even made it back to my buddy Clive Western, an editor at the *Daily Sun,* who was going to hunt through the morgue for me."

"There ain't no *Sun* in York, Craig."

"Old York isn't York."

"But you an' me *were* in this Old York."

"Right."

"Jesus!"

"You've got my sympathies, De Marco; I don't feel any better about it than you do, worse probably. Anyway, let's wrap it up: I began checking on everyone I might've known in Old York. All I found were blanks. Like here, I had no past. But there was a difference. In Old York I knew who I was. Or thought I did; here *everything's* down the drain. Anyway, I finally landed someone who knew me, an Emma Landry, my only witness to a vanished childhood. She must've been in her nineties. Great, huh? But Landry was really the old crone from one of my other recent nightmares—one where I'm being chased by a faceless man—and if you, De Marco, hadn't been on the job, tailing me and the redhead, Old Faceless would've nailed me for sure. Yeah, he showed up in Mrs. Landry's living room and you came in behind him pumping lead."

"Hooray for me," De Marco said. "You really expect me to buy all that bull, Craig?"

"No," I said. "It sounds worse when you tell it."

"It sounds like you oughta be put away."

"I know. I guess I don't believe much of it either."

"Much!"

"There's still you at the bar; we know each other."

"Two to one, there's an explanation."

"I'm the only guy that looked familiar to you in all those two months?"

"Yeah, just about."

"What do you mean, just about?"

"You're gonna jump all over me, Craig; try to hold it

down, it's probably nothin'."

"*What's* nothing?"

"Well, it wasn't like with you, Craig; I wasn't sure I ever seen this guy before. Only at first I think maybe I have. He's been in a couple of times. Only he never gives me a tumble. So, I figure, what the hell. And I ain't lookin' for no one. Right? But this cock-an'-bull story of yours, Craig—it kinda reminded me. This guy, he coulda come outta your dream."

"Who was he?"

"A redhead, Craig; a little redheaded guy."

The buzzing of the phone brought me out of a deep sleep. I groped for the nightstand lamp. *Where was I?* It took me a moment to figure it out even after the light came on: the Brooks Hotel. As safe and sound as a babe in its crib. And just about as knowledgeable. I flicked on the phone. Pat De Marco's face appeared on the two-by-three screen.

"He's here," De Marco whispered. His face was flushed and bright-eyed.

It took a second to register. "The redhead?" I heard myself say.

"The same, pal. Look, you want me to put the screws on him?"

"*Don't do anything!*"

"It's your show, pal."

"You're still at Frank's?"

"Where else?"

"The Festival runs all night?"

"Uh-uh. Closes down at midnight. Some of the spots work the swing shift. Lights out here around three."

I looked at the clock: one thirty-five.

"Do me a favor."

"Sure. You want me to string after our pal here if he takes off. Without wising him up. Right?"

"Right."

"Uh-huh. Same deal like in Old York if I got you straight." De Marco grinned. "Only this time it's on me. I can't use no lousy ten bucks."

120

He winked. The screen went opaque.

The Time Festival was dark.

I went past the empty change booth, down the darkened midway. The moving ramps slid silently by. An occasional neon light blinked in the distance. I stepped onto a ramp, was carried to the thirties set.

The lights were still on at Frank's. About fifteen men sat at the bar or at tables. They didn't talk or move much. For all I knew this was the same bunch I'd left over five hours ago. De Marco was sitting at a table by the door. I pulled up a chair.

"Over there," De Marco nodded.

I raised my eyes, looked over there.

I had first seen him in a dream. We were on a train together, traveling through a dark tunnel; we were going somewhere, but I didn't know where. He was seated in front of me. He hadn't moved or spoken. The next time I'd seen him was in Old York. On the street near the Hall of Records. He had been tailing me then; now he was seated at the far end of the bar nursing something in a tall glass. He hadn't seen me yet. And odds had it that when he did, he wouldn't know me from Adam.

But I knew him, all right.

Red hair, a pointy chin, thick glasses, a short, slender guy in his mid-forties—my man to a T.

"Wait here," I told De Marco.

"You're the boss, pal."

I got to my feet, walked across the sawdust-covered floor.

The redhead saw me in the mirror. His eyes seemed to grow large. His mouth dropped open as if his jawline had sprung a wide crack. He half turned to face me.

I had hoped for some reaction, a sign of recognition, but I'd bargained for nothing like this!

I put out a hand, parted my lips to say something.

The redhead shrank back against the bar. "The man from the nightmare," he croaked in an awful voice.

His eyes seemed to rise into his forehead.

121

Silently he slid off his stool, fell to the floor.

I almost joined him.

Two guys got up to fuss over the redhead. The barkeep leaned across the bar to follow the goings-on. The rest of the customers stayed put; it took more than a stricken boozer to interfere with their drinking.

I stood where I was, glad to still be on my feet. It was an accomplishment. My head was doing a hoedown; little pins and needles in my arms and legs were giving me a good going-over. I felt as agile as a rusty wind-up toy, creaky and out of whack. All that was missing was a swift, hard kick to the guts. That would probably come next.

Pat De Marco's voice sounded in my ear. "You okay, pal?"

"Yeah," I managed to mumble; my mouth felt as if it were full of dried mush. "See about him."

De Marco bent over the redhead, whose eyes were starting to open, asked, "How are you, pal?"

"I'll be fine," the redhead said. He didn't sound fine. An optimist. The redhead glanced over at me, his eyes wide and frightened. Some of the optimism seemed to drift off, like fog over the waterfront. Only much swifter.

De Marco and another guy got the redhead to his feet, helped him over to our table. I followed along like a dazed wino in search of a handout. The waiter brought drinks. The customers went back to theirs.

After a while I said, "My name's Mark Craig. This is Pat De Marco." My voice sounded strange, but the words came out in more or less their proper order. I liked that.

The little man was busy staring at me as if one of the bar stools had begun to engage him in earnest conversation; I figured I knew how he felt. I said, "Take it easy; you're not the only one climbing walls. All three of us here may be in the same boat. You've got lots of company."

"Speak for yourself," De Marco said.

I ignored him, asked the redhead, "Who are you?"

"My name is Peter Grant," he said in a soft, tremulous voice. "You must forgive me . . . when I saw you . . . I . . ."

"Yeah," I said, "I know. You've been having this dream, and somehow I'm part of it."

Grant nodded, his face slack with shock.

"See, De Marco?" I said.

De Marco shrugged. "See what? Dreams are cheap, a dime a dozen." He turned to Grant. "You ever see this guy in York City?"

Grant shook his head, mumbled, "Never."

"Still up a tree, Craig." De Marco grinned. He was sounding more like his twin in Old York by the minute.

"I said, "Maybe." To Grant I said, "In your dream, you're in a place called Old York, Grant, only it bears no resemblance to York City. There are no ramps, no Tela-vistas, no swifties and no one's ever heard of the dole. Maybe the red tape's about the same, but everything else is primitive by comparison. Old York has something of the *feel* of this thirties set, but that's about all. There are no trolleys. No cars. People ride around in horse-drawn carriages they call coaches. There are no radios, but plenty of telephones. They've got a cockeyed way of doing business. The payoff's gone legit. Even the cops get their end of the take and it's strictly kosher. They've set up a whole profession around the payoff: the Double M racket. That's what I was, a registered Double M. In your dream, Grant, you knew me, had some kind of business with me, and were following me around. And when I just now came strolling out of your dream world, big as life, it kind of knocked you for a loop." I looked at Grant knowingly, waited for him to come across with a yes.

If anything, the redhead seemed more fidgety than ever; sweat stood out on his brow. Even in the bar's dim light I could see that his freckled skin had turned a shade whiter, had taken on an almost withered look. Grant shook his head, slowly, quizzically, like a condemned man hearing his pardon had been lost in the mail. He shrugged. "I fear . . . I do not know . . . have never heard of this place . . ."

"Old York," I heard myself say. "Old York."

Grant nodded.

De Marco laughed. "There goes your case, Craig; too bad, guess it's back to the old padded cell, ah, pal?"

I said to Grant, "What about the rest of it?"

"There is nothing there . . . that I recall."

"Take a drink, pal," De Marco advised him. "Looks like you can use one."

Grant tried to smile, gave it up, grabbed his glass and polished off the contents in one gulp; he shuddered.

I said, "You said something about a dream."

"Yes . . . a . . . a *nightmare*."

"I was part of it?"

"Someone who . . . *looks* like you."

"How much like me?"

Grant whispered, "It *is* you. The same build, face, even the voice. *And I knew your name before you told me!*"

"Easy, pal," De Marco said. He nodded to the waiter. "Another one for the gent here." Grant didn't toy with his drink when it arrived, he tossed it down like the first.

"Up to telling us about this nightmare?" I asked.

"I . . . I want to," Grant said. "It is giving me no rest . . . I will be driven insane . . ."

"You've hit the right bunch for *that*." De Marco grinned.

I took a swallow of my drink. Grant mopped his brow with a shaky palm, looked at me with unseeing eyes. "We are running," he said.

"Where?" I said.

"Somewhere . . . somewhere in the woods . . . a forest, perhaps."

"Then it could've been Old York."

"No. Wait. I say to you:

" 'We must turn. There is a lake ahead.'

" 'Which way?' you ask.

" 'Down the hill, farther into the woods; we will come out on the other side by the road.'

" 'Right.' You follow me, ask: 'How far to Newberg, from the road?'

" 'A half mile perhaps. You have a car?'

"We stumble through a maze of roots and branches.

Damp earth and leaves are underfoot. It is autumn, I think. We are being pursued. I do not know by whom, but I am certain there are many of them.

" 'Yeah,' you say, 'parked in Newberg.'

"We continue to run. We reach the road. It is a narrow macadam strip. The woods are on one side, a field of tall grass on the other. We look behind us. Far in the distance small figures are running toward us on the road.

"Suddenly we are in the car. You are driving. Trees, houses, streak by. I lean back in my seat, mop my brow with a hanky.

" 'We're okay now,' you tell me. 'Let's hear what you have to say.'

"Words begin to roll out, over which I seem to have no control:

" 'I have watched them. For four weeks I have lain in wait, spied on them from hidden places. None of their movements has escaped me.'

" 'They never tumbled?'

" 'I was most discreet, Mr. Craig. In any case, my mission will soon be completed.'

" 'Mission?'

" 'I am merely an agent, a representative.'

" 'Yeah?'

" 'Forgive me, Mr. Craig. I must speak with my principal. I must do this first . . . but I am convinced that we are allied in many ways. Tomorrow I am certain I will be given authority to tell all . . . tomorrow . . .'

" 'What's this tomorrow, Grant? I thought we had a deal.'

"I shrug. 'A small number of hours. That is all. What can it matter? Still, you will be disturbed if I leave you with nothing.'

" 'Yeah.'

" 'You know, of course, that Lou Fox is engaged in the manufacture and distribution of illicit liquor?'

" 'That's no news.'

" 'Do you know of a Bugs Moran?'

"You merely look at me; I go on:

" 'He and Fox are in this thing together: I have located two of their warehouses.'

" 'What does this Lou Fox look like?'

" 'Once you have seen him you will never forget. He is hairless—a round, naked skull. His eyes are small, narrow, and they blink. A wide nose and broad, twisted lips. He is an animal, a beast.'

" 'Sounds swell. Your snooping should put you in solid with this bunch.'

" 'It will mark their end, Mr. Craig, not mine. You will see. We will pool our resources, our information. I know we can assist one another in achieving our goals.'

" 'Come on, Grant. Talk sense!'

" 'You are impatient, Mr. Craig. I see that. Very well. If it is facts you wish, I will give them to you. You know there are many ways for goods to enter this country illegally. Doubtless this organization utilizes them all. One of their chief means, however, is through the export-import agency of Lou Fox.'

" 'So?'

" 'Are you aware that Fox is merely an employee? That is right, Mr. Craig. The ownership is under a different name. I will tell you, Mr. Craig, as a demonstration of my good faith, to show I wish to share my knowledge with you . . . to work together . . . to be partners in this endeavor. But the name—you want the name, don't you, Mr. Craig? That business, Mr. Craig, is owned by Al Capone.' "

CHAPTER 24

Alexis Rike

Alexis Rike opened his eyes. He was not in his cell, but on a cot in a small, sour-smelling room. He got up. Not bad, he could stand. He went to the door, tried it. Locked. That stood to reason. That was about all that stood to reason. It didn't matter, he wasn't about to let reason bother him. The voices apparently were real. He had never actually been sure. They had said things the inquisitors might say after one of their sessions. But they had not *sounded* like them. It might merely have been his imagination. But here he was—just as the voices had called it—out of his cell. Chalk one up for reality.

Rike paced back and forth. His last brush with the probe had cleared away some of the cobwebs. Unlike the Greek and Roman Rikes, the East Broadway Rike had known, more or less, what he was doing—a real improvement. The Roman Rike may have known, too, but his mind was nailed shut; no thoughts had leaked out, no clues had been offered. Here there had been thoughts, stray wisps of memory. But what they added up to was—in some ways, at least—worse than no thoughts at all. His luck was lousy, all right.

Time for another go, perhaps, Rike thought.

He lay down again, closed his eyes.

The memories came at once:

Lang was dead.

Rike put down the *World-Telegram;* it lay there partially covering his typewriter.

Morris Hutchins asked, "Something wrong, Alex?"

"Gordon Lang died this morning," Rike said.

"Who?" Hutchins wrinkled his brow. He was a short, squat man in a gray business suit. His partially bald head shone under the neon lights that crisscrossed the office ceiling.

"Gordon Lang, the physicist—the guy who headed the government project."

Hutchins nodded uncertainly.

Rike said, "Found him stretched out on his front lawn."

"Ticker gave out, eh?"

"So they say."

"How old was he?"

"Fifty-six."

Hutchins, who was pushing sixty himself, sighed. "Friend of yours?"

"Nope. Just knew about his work."

"Uh-huh. Don't forget those rewrites," Hutchins said. "Need 'em by four."

Rike nodded.

Hutchins left with a sheaf of papers for his own office. Rike sat staring out the window. He was on the eighth floor of the Morton building. Union Square was gray and overcast down below. Even the neon sign on Klein's department store seemed duller than usual. It looked as though it might rain. Rike frowned. He had an appointment that night. He hoped the rain would hold off until his business was finished . . .

On his cot, Rike had broken out in a cold sweat. He could remember bits and pieces of this Alexis Rike's life, fragments that fit together like clumsy pieces of a jigsaw puzzle. Perhaps the probe had loosened a bolt in his mind, sent the memories tumbling out. Too bad they were such a mess. There was no accounting for any of it. *Rike on East Broadway and this Rike were two different persons.* They looked alike and talked alike, but they weren't the same man. At least he didn't *think* they were. The probe might distort his mind in such a way as to make memory imperfect. That could be an answer of sorts. He didn't like the answer. He didn't much like this new Rike, either. How much time did he have left? The voices had said three hours. He didn't know how much time had gone by. Perhaps an hour or so. There was more to remember. He would try again:

The rain was coming down hard.

For the third time Rike looked at his watch. Late. His contact was late.

The trees kept the rain off him. Even now in early November there were still enough leaves to act as a shield. The night made him part of its darkness. From his vantage point some yards to the left of the park bench, Rike had a clear view of the surrounding terrain, or those parts of it which mattered: the rain-soaked bench and the dimly lit dirt path which wound by it. No one could observe him from the path, but he could see everything. At the moment, everything wasn't very much.

Rike pulled his coat collar tighter, leaned closer to the damp bark and shivered. It was a little shy of one o'clock. Tuesday morning. The buildings behind the low stone wall that separated Central Park from Fifth Avenue were barely visible, their few lights faded into remoteness. The water was beginning to puddle under his shoes. Looking down into the darkness, he could see little; his feet felt wet. Rike's eyes traveled back in the direction of the bench. The road, now a rivulet of mud, stretched empty, back up the shallow hill toward the paved street. Even the sounds of traffic were inaudible here under the steady deluge. Rike shivered again inside his belted raincoat. He had waited this long—almost a full hour—for he hadn't been certain what else to do. Gorbach had always shown up before. A stalled subway? A traffic jam? Illness was only a remote possibility. The little man would have managed somehow. An accident, perhaps . . .? He and Gorbach had met this way tens of times without a hitch. Gorbach was good at his job, kept out of mishaps. Again Rike wondered about the little man. How difficult it was to imagine him ever having been a child, or with a wife and children of his own, or simply holding down an ordinary job in the company of others, complaining, perhaps, about the long hours, waiting impatiently for the coffee break, packing it in after a hard day in the office and heading for home. Home? Did Gorbach have a home? Rike had once asked him his first name. "It is of no importance," the little man had replied. Gorbach at play? Gorbach relaxing? All equally impossible. For Rike, Gorbach would always be a man without a past or future. Small, thin, with a worried frown on his angular face; shabbily dressed with red stubble coating his sunken cheeks and ink and cigarette stains coloring his tapered fingers. Gorbach—peering nearsightedly through his glasses—seemed to exist only for these exchanges, possessing no other life of his own. Gorbach was an enigma.

When Rike looked again at the luminous dial of his wristwatch it was one-ten. He knew then it was done with. Move. It was time to move. There was no longer any reason to wait.

He left the cover of the trees.

He did not see the shadow move behind him.

Alexis Rike lying on his cot did.

CHAPTER 25

The Girl and the Golem

Stuart Hillcraft said, "That was a long time ago."

"Eight years," the girl said.

"Ingram's family would like to know what he was up to," the Golem said.

"They'd also like to positively establish his death," the girl added.

Hillcraft nodded. He was a medium-sized man of thirty-five or so with slicked-back black hair, a thin moustache and round wire-rimmed glasses. He had been head of Ace Investigations for three years. He said, "Our file on Ingram, I'm sure, would contain a detailed description. That would be of use. The problem is, of course, that our files are, of necessity, confidential." Hillcraft smiled.

"We appreciate that," the girl said. "But in view of the elapsed time and Dr. Ingram's death, we hoped you could make an exception."

"I really don't see how," Hillcraft said.

"We are prepared to engage your firm, Mr. Hillcraft, to investigate Ingram's last days," the Golem said. "Money is no object in this matter. Dr. Ingram's family is wealthy. The investigation should be simplicity itself. All it requires on your part, sir, is a perusal of your own files."

The girl opened her handbag. "Would five hundred dollars be sufficient, Mr. Hillcraft?" She laid the money on his desk.

Stuart Hillcraft sat very still, his eyes traveling from the money to his visitors and back again. Outside on West Broadway traffic and pedestrians competed for space. The sounds of horns, motors, voices edged their way through the second-story window.

Stuart Hillcraft said, "Ingram was his real name?"

"No," the girl said.

"Can you give me his name?"

"That, sir," the Golem said, "might needlessly complicate matters."

The girl said, "His family is socially prominent. They could be embarrassed by Ingram's activities."

"And," the Golem said, "they would certainly not wish to be associated with the fire."

The girl smiled. Light from the window caught her

golden hair, making it gleam. "The family is prepared to pay for its privacy."

"Five hundred dollars' worth, sir," the Golem said.

"Yes," Hillcraft said. "You've made that clear. Ordinarily, what you ask would be impossible. However, Ingram's death puts a different light on the situation. I am not acquainted with the case. It may, for all I know, contain data of a sensitive nature. The best thing to do is go and see." Hillcraft got to his feet. "Let me check out Ingram's file. In all probability, we'll be able to do business."

"Business makes the world go round," the Golem said affably.

Stuart Hillcraft left his office.

The Golem rose, went to the window, stood staring out. "Very hectic civilization," he said.

Hillcraft was gone a good quarter of an hour. When he returned, the detective seemed visibly disturbed. "I don't know what to tell you," he said.

"What is the difficulty, sir?" the Golem asked.

Hillcraft seated himself behind his desk, fidgeted with some papers. "Ingram's file is gone."

"Stolen?" the girl said.

Hillcraft removed his glasses. "Your guess is as good as mine. Lost. Stolen. Misfiled. I simply don't know."

"Could it be," the girl asked, "that there never was an Ingram file here, that this is, in fact, the wrong agency?"

Hillcraft began to polish his glasses with a hanky. "I wish it were."

"You are certain then?" the Golem asked.

"Positive."

"How?" she asked.

"Ingram's case is listed on our assignments sheet for March, April and May 1935. The man who headed the investigation is no longer here."

"And those who worked under him?" the Golem asked.

"Stringers. One-shot operators. That was our practice then. The Depression made it possible to employ cut-rate labor."

"Do you have their names?" the girl asked.

"They'd be in the file, of course," Hillcraft said. "And that's gone. As of this moment, anyhow."

"Is there nowhere else to look?" the Golem asked.

"Back pay records," Hillcraft said. "But that's a maybe. They may not even be listed. In those days, not every case was itemized. The case director could withdraw a bulk sum if he wished. Then only his name would appear. It would take some time to go through the records."

"That may not be necessary, sir," the Golem said. "You have the director's name?"

"I do," Hillcraft agreed. "But that appears to be all I can offer you. Are you still willing to retain our agency—for that bit of information?"

"Indeed we are," the Golem beamed.

The girl said, "For one hundred dollars."

"Fair enough," Hillcraft said.

The girl returned four hundred to her purse. Hillcraft put the remainder in his desk drawer. He smiled at his visitors. "The man you want," he said, "is called Mark Craig."

CHAPTER 26

Mark Craig

Grant stopped talking.

Nothing had changed around us. The dim light. The men at bar and tables silently drinking. Only an occasional word or murmur intruding on the stillness.

I looked at Grant.

His eyes were glazed; his mouth hung open like a man suddenly stricken by lockjaw. Peter Grant had run out of steam.

I'd had better moments myself.

If there was a clue somewhere in Grant's tale, I had failed to find it. His story made no sense to me, struck no responsive chords. I was back where I'd started. And that was nowhere. The dice had come up snake-eyes.

Pat De Marco caught my attention, grinned, shrugged, took a swallow of his drink.

I said to Grant, "That's it—the works?"

Grant blinked, stared at me as if one of the bar's fixtures had suddenly nudged him. "No . . . no, there's more . . ."

I asked, "In your dream, you actually called me Craig?"

Grant nodded. He looked sick.

"You're sure?"

"Mr. Craig, I have had this nightmare every night for the past month. Word for word. Always the same. Do you understand? Every night! It is etched into my mind! *I know your name because of my dream!*"

I said, "Who are these other mugs? This Lou Fox, Bugs Moran, Al Capone; you know *them?*"

"I know no one, Mr. Craig."

"What gives with you guys?" De Marco said. "You both take the cake. Everyone's heard of Bugsy and Big Al."

"Everyone?" I said, too tired even to feel much surprise.

"Sure. They're all over the Tela-vista. Big shots. Gangsters from the Prohibition era. You know."

"Uh-uh," I said, "but I'm learning." To Grant I said, "Go on with your dream."

"We are back in the city," Grant said. "I do not know its name. I ask you to drop me at 22nd Street and Tenth Avenue. I have nothing more to say. We ride in silence. It is a quarter past three. The streets are crowded with traffic in midtown, but as we work our way farther downtown, the streets grow quieter, less congested. I tell you:

" 'I will be in your office within twenty-four hours, Mr.

Craig, without fail. Say one o'clock, if that is convenient. How does that strike you?'

" 'That's okay.'

"We pull up to the corner of 22nd Street.

"I nod, reach for the door and am gone.

Now the nightmare begins.

"I am no longer myself. I am a disembodied spirit. I view what follows through your eyes, Mr. Craig. Do not ask me how this is possible—it is, after all, a dream . . . a nightmare . . .

"You drive to Ninth Avenue. Park. Wait.

"I appear on the corner of 22nd Street, cross and continue on to Eighth. You leave your car, follow me. I am unaware of your presence. A part of me—the part that has become an observer—wishes to warn me, tries to yell, but is unable to do so.

"I enter a brown building on Eighth Avenue and 26th Street. You move quietly behind me, see that I have gone into a third-floor apartment. The door is still open when you reach it; you step through.

"I am lying on the floor next to an unmade bed.

"Two holes are in my chest.

"Now there is a screaming everywhere. It is as if the walls, floor and ceiling could no longer contain themselves, must cry out against the agony which they have witnessed.

"You look around startled.

"The room begins to shimmer, to waver.

"You reach into your pocket; a gun appears in your hand. You begin to back up, your eyes searching for the source of the sound.

"They come then, the faceless ones.

"They have heads, you understand, but no eyes or mouths or nostrils; they are hairless. It is as though a large, flesh-colored ball had been attached to their shoulders.

"They come through the walls and floors. Out of nooks and crannies. From under the bed and from behind the bureau.

"You shoot them with your gun, Mr. Craig. You shoot

them and they bleed and fall and others take their place.

"Their hands reach for you; fingers tear at you. Bodies try to crush you.

"You twist around, spy a door behind you. Using arms, shoulders and hips you break a path through the massed bodies, hurl yourself at the door.

"You crash through.

"There is a sudden silence behind you. Turning back, you see only blackness. The house, room and its faceless inhabitants have vanished. Along with my body. Frankly, Mr. Craig, I miss my body most of all. There is a poignancy attached to its loss that is shattering. I wish to tell you of this, but I am still wordless.

"Turning, you survey your surroundings. You are in a corridor of some kind. White walls, floor and ceiling gleam around you. Up ahead, two white glittering doors. You move toward them. They swing open as you approach.

"Behind you the white corridor has winked out. But you do not see this. You are staring at a square nine-foot metal slab; it hovers some five feet off the ground. A gray metal ceiling gleams dully some ten feet above you. Knobs and dials project from the walls. The humming sound which I heard before seems louder here.

"You walk to the slab, look down.

"A man is lying on it. He stares up at you wide-eyed. The man is you."

CHAPTER 27

Alexis Rike

Rain and wind. And the soft glow of street lamps. Even after the isolation of the park, Fifth Avenue was an empty place. There were no people here. Only an occasional passing car. Traffic lights were red and green smudges in the falling rain. Rike pointed his footsteps north, a slim, tired-looking man with eyes half closed against wind and rain; he moved slowly toward 96th Street.

Across the street, a lone figure detached itself from the shadows of the tall buildings, began heading toward him. Rike slowed, came to a halt. No doubt about it, a man was waving at him.

Rike waited.

"Good evening, Mr. Turner," Gorbach said breathlessly as he stepped up onto the curb, a tired, lopsided grin on his narrow face. In his hand he clutched a suitcase.

The neon lights in the all-night diner on 96th Street cast a whitish gleam over the Formica tables, seemed to bleach the small eatery of all color. Rike and Gorbach were its only customers. Rain beat against door and windows. The counterman sat at a corner table, the *Daily Mirror*'s racing section spread before him. Johnnie Ray sobbed a tune over the small white radio behind the

137

counter. Gorbach took a bite of his apple pie. The suitcase lay on his lap.

"You must understand, Mr. Turner, I had no choice, none whatsoever. I am certain I was being followed. Someone knows, Mr. Turner, I am convinced of it. Perhaps you too have been compromised. I could not take the chance. Believe me, you would have acted the same as I."

"Forget it," Rike said.

"Thank you, Mr. Turner. I know I have put you to some inconvenience. I am well aware of that and I apologize profusely. However, when you see what I have brought, I am sure you will be pleased."

"I wouldn't mind being pleased," Rike said. "What have you got?"

"The Lang strongbox we discussed. You will be satisfied, I assure you. I personally can vouch for the box's bona fides. It is my belief, Mr. Turner, that its contents are worth a small fortune."

Rike sighed inwardly, took a sip of coffee. He said, "Look, Gorbach, I only brought this month's pay. There'll have to be some delay on the rest of it. I'll try to make it as fast—"

Gorbach's face grew red; his voice trembled. "Do you think me a fool? Are you not aware of the risks I took? What hardships I underwent to obtain this? Do you think, perhaps, this is a game we are playing? Do you? Money on the barrelhead, Mr. Turner, that's the way it goes with me. I cannot make any exceptions. Not now. I must disappear, Mr. Turner; I must literally vanish. I may have shown my hand in obtaining the box. I do not know who is following me. Is it so hard for me to make you understand? We have always gotten along, Mr. Turner."

Rike sighed, finished his coffee. "What about next week? I could pay you then."

"Impossible."

Rike spread his hands.

Gorbach said, "I cannot give you these documents, Mr. Turner, without, at least, payment in part. Believe me, if there were any other way to do this I would do it gladly.

138

I do not have to tell you that. But I am at my wit's end. It hurts me to say this, but I must. If you do not pay me now, there are others who will. Say to yourself you are dealing with a half-crazed man, a wild man, then you will understand. The money. I must have it at once."

Alexis Rike said, "I'd be sticking my neck out, Gorbach, way out."

"This box is worth it, Mr. Turner."

"So they say. All right, Gorbach, you've got a deal."

"I will get my money?"

"Some of it. More than you'd get here, anyway."

"Thank you, Mr. Turner, thank you."

"Let's get going."

"Where, Mr. Turner?"

"My place, Gorbach. I've got a little extra something put away." Rike smiled thinly. "Saved it for a rainy day. About two thousand worth."

Gorbach let out a long sigh. "Again, thank you," he said. "I've always had the greatest confidence in your judgment, Mr. Turner."

"Yes," Alexis Rike said. And thought: So far, so good. A close one. Gorbach had five thousand coming to him. And if he—Rike—had offered less, the little man would've had a fit. But he'd played him like a fish on the line, promised nothing, then come across with what he had. And Gorbach bought it. Just as well. Otherwise, he would have had to take the strongbox from him. And the redhead might have gotten hurt. *Now, if only the money is still there* . . .

The cold autumn rain, dark and heavy, showed no signs of abating.

The houses—five- and six-story yellow brick walk-ups —on East 96th Street between First and Second avenues were old, shabby. Rike and Gorbach entered the ninth house from the corner. Rike used his key on the front door. The pair climbed four flights. Rike used another key, let himself into his flat. A flick of the light switch revealed a cozy, book-lined living room. It was warm inside. The steam hissed noisily. Rike hung his and Gorbach's coats in the bathroom to dry, went into a yellow-walled kitchen, mixed two drinks, came back, handed one to his guest.

Gorbach said gravely, "Thank you again, Mr. Turner; I want you to know that I am truly sorry for imposing myself on you in this way, contrite even, but under the circumstances, I saw no other way out of my difficulties."

"It's all right."

"Allow me to assure you, Mr. Turner, your secret is safe with me. I know that, in a manner of speaking, I have violated your cover. However," the little redheaded man shrugged, "I am now out of the game entirely. My usefulness is at an end. In procuring Lang's papers, I have rung down the curtain on my career. I shall contact you only once more for the remainder of my payment. And then I shall be gone from your life forever. No one will ever know through me, Mr. Turner, who you are or where you reside."

Rike looked at his guest evenly. "Great. How about a look at the stuff you've brought?"

"Of course, of course." Gorbach unlatched his suitcase, removed a small, metal box. The box had been broken, its lock forced. Gorbach opened it. Two items were inside. He handed both to Rike. "The entire contents. Forgive me, Mr. Turner, but I am afraid you will have to take this offering on faith." Gorbach smiled apologetically. "These documents could mean nothing to you. Even the most advanced physicists would be hard pressed to comprehend them. But trust me, Mr. Turner, these are the genuine articles. By the time I return for the rest of my payment, your superiors will have had ample opportunity to convince themselves of that."

Rike leafed through the papers, paused occasionally before turning a page. "I hope so," he said.

"As for the notebook," Gorbach said, "it is, I fear, worthless. It is not even Lang's. It is the work of a James Ingram."

Alexis Rike put the papers down on an end table, the notebook on top of it, went to one of the bookcases, removed the fourth book from the right on the middle shelf—a thick volume of sea stories—opened it. A square pocket was cut in the center that left no full pages but only a frame. An envelope was there. Rike tossed it to Gorbach. "Two thousand," he said. Reaching into his pants pocket, Rike fished out another, smaller envelope, gave it to the little man. "Month's wages," he said.

"You understand, of course, that two thousand is far from adequate, but I will be patient. I trust you, Mr. Turner, to make the speediest arrangements for full payment. I rely on you for this. I know my faith will not be misplaced . . ."

His head seemed to be splitting. His body was covered by perspiration. Rike stirred restlessly on the cot, stared up at the ceiling. He saw nothing.

There was a place called New York City and he, Alexis Rike, had been part of it in a time known as 1952. He knew with certainty, somehow, that he was no longer in that time period. *What was he doing here?* He couldn't answer.

But he knew what Alexis Rike was up to in 1952.

There was something called a Cold War going on and Rike was a participant: he was a Communist agent for the U.S.S.R. A spy. He lived in threadbare surroundings, held down an assistant editor's post at a small newsweekly. And every so often—doing his best to see that he wasn't followed—he would pick up assorted items from men he met only briefly and pass them on, just as clandestinely, to other interested parties.

Except that Alexis Rike had been killed that autumn night in Central Park:

The rain had been heavy.

Rike had looked at his watch.

One-ten.

Time to go. Gorbach wasn't going to show.

Rike had started to leave the park. He had missed the shadow moving behind him, hadn't heard the quiet footsteps or seen the flashing knife.

Alexis Rike had died, face down, in a puddle of muddy water.

A moment had passed as the assassin hurried away.
Rain. Wind.

And a solitary figure had stepped out of the darkness.
Alexis Rike.

He walked slowly toward the body lying on the muddy
ground, bent, took hold of a limp wrist, held it for a
moment, then let it fall. Rike went through the body's
pockets, took keys, wallet and an envelope. He did not
bother to examine the contents of either, but put them in
his own pocket. Straightening up, he walked slowly toward the park exit, his face expressionless; he thought:
time to meet Gorbach.

Alexis Rike took a deep breath, stood up shakily. The
walls of the small room seemed to be closing in on him.
He used his palm to wipe the sweat from his forehead.
What did it all mean? Probably nothing. He would
awaken soon and find that it had all been a horrible
nightmare. The trouble was he didn't believe that for a
second. He had no idea what he actually *did* believe.
What he felt was fear. It seemed an understandable emo-
tion under the circumstances. Who was Alexis Rike? A
man in Greece? Rome? The Middle Ages? A man in New
York in 1952? He had glimpsed a second Rike in Rome,
one who had died under Caligula's knife. There had been
nothing to make of that. But the two Rikes of 1952 were
another matter. They were connected in some way, but
only the second Rike had known it, had been able to see
into the mind of the other Rike, the spy. *And who am I,
Rike thought, a third Rike? Or the second one?* Everything he had seen had been from the viewpoint of the
second Rike; he had felt something there all along, now
he knew what that something was: *the presence, the all-
pervasive intelligence of the second Rike.* Or was it all a
delusion, nothing more than a series of dreams brought on
by whatever the inquisitors were doing to him? That made
sense of a kind, a lot more than any of the other crackpot
notions he'd been tossing around. Yet sense, he felt, was
the wrong approach to the problem. Too bad he had no
inkling of the right approach . . .

142

The door to his room opened. The inquisitor stood there. "It is time," he said.

CHAPTER 28

The Girl and the Golem

"Mr. Craig?" the girl said.

"Uh-huh."

"My name is Ann Darling, and this is my associate, Reginald Meerlue."

Mark Craig ducked his head, gestured broadly at a pair of chairs. "Make yourselves comfortable."

The girl and the Golem seated themselves. Craig sat back behind his desk, made his face attentive. "What can I do for you folks?"

The girl said, "We were referred to you by Mr. Hillcraft at Ace Investigations."

Craig broke into a broad grin. "No kidding. Old Stu did that, huh? Didn't know he cared. What is it, some case too hot to touch?" Craig laughed. His hair had some gray in it; his forehead was creased and there were dark lines under his eyes. He wore a wide-shouldered blue serge suit which was slightly frayed at the cuffs. His third-floor, West 45th Street office was small, dark and noticeably dusty. "There must be a catch," he said pleasantly.

"On the contrary," the Golem said. "You stand to make a handsome profit, Mr. Craig, with virtually no exertion."

"This I've got to see."

"It's one of your old cases, Mr. Craig," the girl said.

"You mean at Ace?"

"Yes, sir," the Golem said. "According to Mr. Hillcraft, you were the case supervisor. We should like some details about that operation."

"Couldn't Hillcraft give them to you?"

"The case records appear to have been misplaced," the Golem said.

"Ah-ha," Craig said.

"We're willing to pay a hundred dollars," the girl said, "for any information you can give us."

"And that's all?" Craig asked.

"That is all," the Golem said.

"Sounds swell," Craig said. "You've got a deal."

"Thank you, Mr. Craig." The girl smiled. Money changed hands.

"Okay," Craig smiled, "what's the case?"

"The Ingram affair," the Golem said.

"The what?" Craig looked blank.

The girl said, "Dr. James Ingram lived at 465 West 25th in Apartment 4A. He was known to the landlord and his fellow tenants as Tom Logan."

"When was this?" Craig asked.

"April 1935," the girl said.

"That goes back a ways. What did this bird look like?"

"Full head of white hair," the girl said, "gray moustache, around sixty, a tall man."

Craig shook his head. "Doesn't register. What was it all about?"

"We were going to ask *you*," the Golem said.

"On the night of May 15, 1935," the girl said, "there was a fire in Dr. Ingram's flat. Sometime between ten and eleven o'clock. It's believed that Dr. Ingram was working on a project of some sort, one involving experiments. Something went wrong."

Mark Craig broke into a grin. "Relax, folks. I just got it."

"Excellent, Mr. Craig." The Golem smiled. "We were sure you would remember eventually."

"Yeah, huh? Well, it's a good thing you didn't lay odds. It's just a fluke I was in on this thing."

"Indeed?"

"Uh-huh. And even so, there's almost nothing to tell. You're going to be disappointed."

"Have no fears on that score, Mr. Craig," the Golem said. "The most trivial items are apt to satisfy us."

"Fine," Craig said. "It's like this: I was holding down a desk job at Ace. My tag was case supervisor. That meant I lined up the outside help and read their reports. But I didn't go snooping any myself. I was with Ace maybe five years. A thousand cases must've gone through my hands. But if you were to ask me what most of 'em were about now, I wouldn't be able to tell you. Yeah, you'd be out of luck, folks, except this one was an exception. I had three guys on Ingram. He used to work for Norwood Chemicals back in the twenties when the going was good. But halfway through the Depression the racket turned sour and they started cutting back. Ingram got laid off. After a while the brass at Norwood got wind that Ingram was maybe carrying on with some research he'd done at their plant. That wasn't kosher. Ingram had signed a paper when he first went on Norwood's payroll. Everyone there signed that paper. It said that any project they began while in the employ of the firm remained the property of the firm. So Ace was hired by Norwood to take a look-see. I got the case. I put three guys on Ingram. One in the building with him. Another shadowing him and a third to relieve the other two. I wouldn't remember this much, even, if it wasn't for the fire. That kind of made it stick in my mind; you can believe it! On May 15, two of the guys I had on Ingram turned up sick. That wasn't so hot. We'd just about had the goods on him. He'd been stocking up on all sorts of equipment and we'd been keeping tabs on the lot. Ingram had actually rigged a lab in his flat. It looked suspicious as all get-out. But we couldn't be sure. Maybe he was doing some work on his own hook, something that had nothing to do with Norwood. If we blew the whistle on him and Norwood took it to court, we wanted him sewed up, an open-and-shut case. Otherwise Ingram might countersue and we'd all be in the soup. So I'd gotten this guy, an expert, to give Ingram's flat the once-over; he'd know what's what, be able to size up the type of work being done there. If it had any connection at all with Ingram's assignment at Norwood, we'd bring the Johns into it, get a search warrant and go through the flat with a fine-tooth comb. Our expert was set to show up the night of May 15. Ingram usually stayed out late, was sometimes gone till three, four in the morning. It was sort of tricky, this operation, because it wasn't, strictly speaking, legal. We were breaking and entering. Only who would know? Sure, Ace was putting its license on the line, and our expert his neck in the sling—but from where I sat, the whole thing was a pushover. The building's tenants turned in early and Ingram—if he stuck to his routine—would be gone most of the night. The hitch was our two guys were sick. Now we'd worked with these guys before, and for an extra C-note they'd've knocked off their own mothers. Norwood was footing the bill, so there was no sweat on that score either. Only that was out now. It was too late to hunt up other talent, someone we could trust to play along and keep his mouth shut. The guy I'd planted in the building was just a guy, a two-bit pork and beaner I'd put there because he came cheap. But I couldn't trust him on this kind of deal. So it looked like there was only one thing to do. I got my hat off the rack and went away to pop the job myself. The extra C-note didn't hurt, either. I picked up our expert and we beat it over to Ingram's place. There was an empty flat right next to his and that made it perfect. We settled down, waited for Ingram to leave. Only he never did. Instead of him taking off, a whole flock of Joes and Janes showed up. We figured, at first, maybe he was throwing a party. I guess what he was up to was fooling around with some of his lab stuff. I don't know why he'd want that crowd, though. Well, anyway, that queered it for us. We were all set to pack up when it happened: the whole damn place went blooey. The next thing I knew I was picking myself off the floor and there was smoke everywhere. I don't know how long I was out;

maybe a minute or two. I was alone, my expert gone. The dumb palooka had left me there and run off to save his own skin. I never heard from him again, either. He didn't even show up to collect his dough. It didn't matter. That finished the job. Ingram went up with his flat. And that was it. I got out in the hallway. Ingram's door had been blown clean away. I looked in. If ever there was a hellhole, that was it. Just one big mass of flames. I could hear people yelling down below. I felt woozy as hell. I didn't hang around. I hightailed it down those stairs, out the front door and kept on going. We closed the case next day. Norwood settled accounts with us the following week. And that's the last I heard of it. Get your money's worth, folks?"

"Decidedly, sir," the Golem said.

Mark Craig grinned. "You did, huh? I figured maybe I laid an egg."

"No, Mr. Craig," the girl said, "you've given us just what we wanted. There *are* a few more questions we might ask, however."

Craig nodded good-naturedly. "Why not? Shoot."

"What was your profession, Mr. Craig, before you joined Ace?" she asked.

"Ah," Craig smiled, "the plot thickens."

"No, sir," the Golem said, "there are no ulterior motives involved whatsoever. Call it a matter of idle curiosity, if you wish."

The girl said, "It's just that we'd like to know a little more about you, Mr. Craig. To help us place your story in the right perspective."

"Sure. That's okay with me. It's old hat by now, anyway. I was a private eye for a while in the twenties. A firm went broke that owed me and a few other guys some dough. The firm folded. We divvied up what was left. My end was a couple of small, beat-up trucks. That was a break. Some guys I'd done business with were busy shipping hootch all over the place. Sure, it was illegal, but what wasn't in those days? I put my trucks at their disposal and pretty soon I'd made enough dough to buy a couple more. I was sitting pretty for a while. But I was caught by the Depression like a lot of other guys. I'd gone in over my head, borrowed to expand the business, you know; even played the market some. When the crash came, I just about lost my shirt. I hung on for a spell, but it was rough going. I quit the rackets even before Prohibition died. I knew some guys who were palled up with Tammany Hall and that's how I got my license back. I went to work for Ace and stayed there till I opened my own shop. How's that?"

"Fine, Mr. Craig," the Golem said. "It fills in the picture nicely."

"Glad to oblige," Craig said. "That was an easy hundred smackers."

The girl said, "Can you recall the names of your co-workers on the Ingram case, Mr. Craig?"

"Let's see," Craig said, "I can't for the life of me remember the name of the guy we put in the building—"

"He was Harry Henderson," the Golem said.

Craig shrugged. "If you say so. The other two were Max Endicott and Jessie Stover. Mean anything?"

"I think not," the Golem said.

"How did you know, Mr. Craig, that Dr. Ingram actually worked for Norwood Chemicals?" the girl asked.

"How did I *know?*"

"Was there a possibility," the girl said, "that Ingram, in fact, had no connection with Norwood, but was being investigated for entirely different reasons?"

Craig was silent for a while. "It's possible," he finally said. "Only it's kind of farfetched."

"Why?" the girl asked.

"Because I got all my dope from the security man at Norwood. Why would he lie?"

"Did you check his story in any way?" the girl asked.

"No reason to. It sounded on the up-and-up. That was good enough for me. Look, Ace used to get tens of cases like that. And the security chief of whatever outfit it was would call us in. As simple as pie."

The Golem said, "Who was Norwood's security chief, Mr. Craig?"

"A little guy, Pat De Marco."

148

"I see," the Golem said. "And the outside expert you brought in. Who was that?"

"I won't forget that bastard so soon. I hope I bump into him someday—"

"His name," the Golem said.

"Sure. Rike, that was his handle. Alexis Rike."

CHAPTER 29

From the Diary of Dr. James Ingram

May 7, 1935. The channel widens, the "dream" and voice take on new substance. Not only has the Prime been shifted but others as well. As if a house of cards had been scattered. This is the gist of the "message" but what am I to do about it?

May 8, 1935. The voice babbles but does not touch on the main issue, what I must do to ensure the success of my project. Oh no, on this point there is nothing. But the rest seems clear enough: along with these shiftings there has been a widespread dislocation of time and space. (What shape has it assumed? The voice is silent on this, too. One can only speculate.) The Prime moves somewhere within this altered reality. As do those who seek him.

May 9, 1935. I do not think these nocturnal broadcasts are even directed at me. They seem a "natural" phenomenon, a product of the force field, brought into sharper focus by the approach of the black hole. Does this not mean that others may be receiving them as well? And perhaps acting on whatever information is thus revealed? It is my chief hope. For my hands are tied. I see no way to influence the drama which is being performed outside of my reach

May 10, 1935. The dream has undergone yet another change. There are vast explosions as though the universe were being shaken. Now the red glow permeates the dream at all times.

May 11, 1935. The voice has become more explicit. The Prime shifts through time junctures in both normal and dislocated time-space. Or is he perhaps *being* shifted? This is unclear. His shifts affect the others—his pursuers?—who are shifted it seems at random, like a deck of cards being shuffled. Is there no underlying principle?

May 12, 1935. Can it be that the broadcasts are meant solely for me, after all? The voice has answered my question Blind chance is the underlying principle. The Prime is a product of blind chance *But the others are, too!* And all their shiftings—the Prime included—are governed by blind chance! Everything and nothing is thus explained.

May 13, 1935. Now the red glow has been explained too. It is the aftermath of the explosion (*what* explosion the voice does not say). But it is also more than this. The red glow marks an alternate route through the time junctures, one not affected by the shifting of the Prime. Perhaps he can be located through this route. But do those who seek him know of it?

Midnight the same day. I cannot sleep. I have been thinking of the time-space dislocations. Is it possible that the upheavals are so overwhelming that even those who seek the Prime will become befuddled? How will they manage to cope, to function? And what of these dislocations themselves? Are they not as great a threat to time-space stability as the aliens?

CHAPTER 30

Mark Craig

A look of disgust crossed Pat De Marco's face "What a crock of shit," he said.

Grant jerked a shoulder as if trying to shrug off the complaint. "Please . . . What claims have I made? I have no theories. I am at sea in this . . at sea. I merely relate a *dream,* one which has become an obsession . . ."

"Sure," De Marco said. "Well, Craig, now you know, right, pal? You're on this slab lookin' up at yourself "

"Yeah, it's the bunk, De Marco; and your being here every night is just your idea of a swell time."

"Look, pal, I ain't sayin' I ain't nuts. I'm nuts, you're nuts, he's nuts; but the nuttiest thing of all is this dumb dream we're listenin' to like it's gospel."

I sighed. De Marco was right The dream was a mess from the word go. Along with everything that went with it. No way out and there never could be. The three of us were busy beating our heads against a stone wall. We all probably suffered from some unknown disease, some terrible illness that was just starting to make the rounds. Just give it time. We were its first victims, but others were bound to follow. Everyone would end up at Frank's and pretty soon the thirties set would have to expand. They'd take over all of York and keep growing. Maybe in the end, they'd take over the world. How about that? Actually, it didn't seem too likely a prospect. But then what was? I reached for my drink, finished it. "There's more?" I asked Grant.

"Yes, Mr. Craig, there is more."

"Let's hear it," I said.

"Very well, Mr. Craig. You are staring down at yourself. You put out a hand to touch your motionless replica. At that very instant, there is a fierce explosion. The room and its contents are gone. A red haze is everywhere. Through it I see Fox. The bald, shiny head. The small, piggish eyes. The thick, repellent lips. It is him without a doubt! He stands by a table, hands an instrument to a tall, distinguished-looking man with white hair and a moustache. The figures before us spill together and separate in a swirl of red mist. It is impossible to observe their actions now, to know what they are doing. Yet I feel it is of the utmost importance to try. Too late I realize that you-I, still locked in tandem, are sinking. The floor is gone. You shoot your gun into the thickening stream of red darkness. It is as if a wave of congealing blood were sweeping down upon us. Everything is carried away. When the explosion comes this time it rends all in its wake. Believe me, Mr. Craig, nothing could have survived the eruption. This is the thing which I feared most. In the eyeblink before my final demise, I know that I have failed, failed . . ."

Grant was silent. The story he told made as much sense as mine—which was absolutely none—but was probably twice as unnerving. Even if I never found out who I was, after a while the nightmares might grow distant, become as vague as last year's datebook. But Grant was treated to a rerun of his private hell every night. And I was one of its star attractions.

"So you died," De Marco grinned at the redhead, "right, pal?"

"Yes," Grant said, "I died "

"Yet here you are," De Marco pointed out with irritating logic. "See, it's just a dream."

"Not just . . . there is something else."

"Yeah, what?"

Grant shook his head. "I do not know," he whispered.

I said, "How do you account for my being in his dream, De Marco?"

De Marco shrugged. "Look, pal, *I* don't have to account for nothin', now do I?"

"Perhaps," Grant said to me, "we have been subjected to the identical experience, Mr. Craig, something awful. *And then made to forget.*"

"How?"

"Hypnosis!"

"It's a thought," I admitted. "Why?"

"I have no idea, Mr. Craig; however, might not these nightmares be the censored events rising to the surface, so to speak?"

"You really buy that, pal?" De Marco asked Grant.

"No," he whispered.

The lights had grown dimmer. Frank's was closing down for the night. The last customers were filing out the door. I looked at them—a barren and listless bunch hooked on yesteryear. Their day had come and gone generations before they were born. They were as antiquated as a stuffed dodo, but not half as cute.

I covered the tab and we went out onto the fairgrounds. The neon lights were off, the sound tracks of bygone eras at rest. Only a few street lamps lit our way back to the city. We trudged along through the darkness a sour and disheartened trio. Even De Marco kept his lip buttoned. Our talk-fest had turned out to be a dud. We'd each go home alone to face what was left of the night. And all the nights after that. Alone.

I said, "We should keep in touch, at least, see if anything else turns up."

"I am afraid Mr. De Marco is right," Grant said. "What could it all be but some insidious delusion that we three are prone to? A thing purely of the mind, Mr. Craig. And of the senses. I can tell you that I have seen the red haze here in York City itself."

I stopped short. "What are you talking about, Grant?"

"Three months ago, on the day I first came to this

153

city—from a solitary life on the West Coast—I saw the red haze. I was seeking an inexpensive dwelling that would not deplete my savings and had therefore traveled to the north side of York. It was there, Mr. Craig, that I first saw it. The entire section was bathed in a red glow. This was before those horrible dreams. In fact, the red wave that submerges us in my nightmare, Mr. Craig, must have had its origins here. And, as it turned out, the glow was entirely a figment of my mind. At first, you may be sure, I was convinced that I was witness to a conflagration. I was amazed, however, that it caused no stir among my fellow pedestrians. I turned to them, tried to draw their attention to the flames. They rebuffed me, Mr. Craig; they thought me mad. No one saw those flames, no one but myself. It was all I could do to escape attention. I was in dread that someone had summoned the authorities. I have always had a morbid fear of confinement, of being detained. Perhaps that is why I have not gone for treatment before this. It is the prospect of interrogation which frightens me. But I assure you, Mr. Craig, I have had enough. I can no longer endure these nightmares. Treatment of the most stringent sort is called for. Mr. De Marco here is quite correct. And I shall seek it out. I am determined to do so. My advice to you, Mr. Craig, is to put yourself completely in the hands of your physicians. Let them unravel the puzzle. I am sure there is no reality in any of this. None. Only sickness. Some type of devious, hidden malady. God help us all."

I said, "Grant, did you ever go back to this place where you saw the glow?"

Grant stared at me. "Never, **Mr.** Craig. Are you insane? What if I should see it again?"

The moon sent light streaming through my hotel window. The night was almost spent. But I couldn't sleep. I lay in bed staring up at the ceiling. A couple of more days like this and I'd be ready to toss in my hand no matter what happened. Too much had come at me too soon. A simple case of emotional and mental overload. Only nothing about my case was simple. What I needed

154

was a long, quiet rest by the seashore. What I had felt like a noose tightening around my neck.

None of it jibed. Like a bunch of jigsaw puzzles, tossed pell-mell into the same box. The pieces could never be made to fit.

It was one thing to lose my memory. And something else again to have every trace of my past wiped clean as though I'd never existed.

Sure, dreams could seem real. But when the characters out of mine started popping up on the thirties set, it was time to take another look. Especially when my dreams and Grant's overlapped like Siamese twins. We'd both run into faceless men, the red haze and maybe even this Lou Fox. I'd dreamed of a train. And a bald-headed guy was on it. The description fit.

Why? How?

Why not? Was there any rhyme or reason to any of it? Mere caprice was as good an explanation as any. Better than most, probably. Only it left me cold, as out of sorts as a circus seal stuck on a desert highway.

The how part seemed simpler. I was beginning to put more stock in Grant's hypnosis theory by the minute. What else was there? At least it was something that *might* be uncovered. Any other angle seemed hopeless. I remembered my SEC appointment later this afternoon. It didn't take a crystal ball to figure out what they'd turn up. Zilch. And that should have put a damper on the whole hypnosis angle. You can't hypnotize a computer. *But maybe you could rig it.*

Not bad. A bracing thought if ever there was one. Rigging meant people busy in the real world, not in some dark corner of my mind. It meant that I had a flesh and blood foe to contend with, not some poor spook my tired brain had cooked up in an idle moment.

Comforting, but hard to swallow.

I could just see myself trying to sell that idea to the good doctors at State-City Hospital.

Mark Craig, the victim of an all-embracing conspiracy, one that would go to any lengths to keep him from learn- the truth—whatever that was.

My, my. I wasn't exactly sure what they did around here with folks who had such queer notions, but I was willing to bet it wasn't much fun, not on the receiving end, at least.

The thing to do—obviously—was keep my mouth shut. I might be slated for the lockup, all right, but I sure as hell wasn't going to blow the whistle on myself.

Let the powers-that-be hunt my identity, do all the digging they could. *While I did mine.*

They had helpfully given me a city map at the hospital, so I wouldn't lose my way. It had come in handy. Before Grant and I had swapped addresses and good-nights he had pinpointed the location of the red haze.

Tomorrow I'd go take a look-see.

If I saw it too and wound up in a padded cell, at least I'd have Grant for company.

PART 4

Alexis Rike

Time inside a black hole
would assume the aspects
of space—making it quite
impossible to remain immobile.

from *The Notebooks of
Dr. James Ingram*

CHAPTER 31

Alexis Rike stood in the street.
Something seemed to call him.
A voice whispered: go, go, go.
A red glow was in the sky.
Alexis Rike went.

Rike boarded the speed belt, grabbed a seat on the center strip and zoomed off through the tunnel. He wore the face of Clark Gable. Other plasto-change faces—Tom Mix, Plato, Queen Victoria, Albert Einstein—stared back at him. A man on the outside standies strip dressed in the silks of the old 3010s and wearing the face of Commander Neil sneered at Rike. *A period buff, Rike thought: sometimes they ran the loyalty bit right into the ground.* Rike ignored him, fixed his thoughts on what lay ahead. Festival Palace was the largest museum on the East Coast, housed everything from a Ford Model T to the Lone Ranger's mask. The computer engineers who had designed it had left nothing to chance. Fires simply didn't happen in Festival Palace. But this was the height of the gaming season and huge crowds would be reveling for blocks around. Only since when were huge crowds combustible?

Yet Rike felt certain the red glow had come from Festival Palace.

About a mile from his destination, the belt swerved into an auxiliary tunnel: trouble up ahead—whatever it was—was being bypassed. Rising, Rike pushed his way through the standies, hit the slow strip and stepped off.

A red sign spelled out exit. A mobile ramp carried him up to daylight.

The sky was a clear, bright blue—what could be seen of it. Thick smoke filled the air. A red glow flickered through the smoke. Hot gusts of air scooted over the pavements. Bells and sirens seemed to come from all directions.

He was in a catchall residential complex. Streets were tree-lined. Multicolored high-rise and low-rise units of various materials, shapes and bulk were on either side of him, along with a lot of smoke.

People came out of the smoke. Those who couldn't run were limping or crawling. The fire had made a mess of their costumes. Melting plasto-change dripped down their necks and shoulders. Rike heard screams, shouts. He shuddered, coughed. Most of the throng was heading away from Festival Palace. Rike went toward it.

Robot crews hustled around, not seeming to do very much. A couple of blocks, and Rike came to a chain of them blocking the way. Their costumes were torn and singed. Some of their skin coating had been burned away. A pair had begun to totter. "Street closed," the head robot told Rike in a creaky voice. Rike flashed his Guardian's badge. The chief robot looked at it a long time, finally raised an arm to let Rike by.

"What's happened?" Rike asked.

The metal cop rolled his eyes like a cow in the slaughterhouse. He didn't know.

Rike trotted away from there, turned a corner.

What was left of Festival Palace blazed and teetered before him.

Black smoke poured through its roof. Red flame licked at the walls, rose straight into the sky.

One wall was half gone, lay shattered on the broken pavement. Five wide columns had been wrenched from its structure like loose teeth, joined the rubble on the ground. Something had gone wrong with the automatic fire repellent, which now squirted feebly and uselessly

159

into the air. Bodies lined the streets, hundreds of them, some still burning like abandoned camp fires.

Alexis Rike turned and hurried away from there.

A block away, he reached a view booth, stepped in, stuck his rate-card in the pay-slot, punched out the chief's co-ords. The screen remained opaque. Something had gone wrong with the lines, too.

Alexis Rike left the booth, stood indecisively while smoke rose above him, lazily drifted along the street. Up ahead he caught sight of the robot cops. A couple were out cold on the ground. The rest were aimlessly wandering around as if hunting for dropped coins. Their leader, who had spoken to him earlier, was standing stockstill, staring off into the distance as if waiting for some lost ship to turn up on the horizon.

Clark Gable came stumbling into view. He'd rounded a corner and was heading past the robot crew.

This Gable was a small, narrow-shouldered man with a round, sagging belly. A thirties sector was only a few miles away and Gables were in plentiful supply.

The world was about to have one less.

A robot fist shot out as Gable waddled by, caught the little man in the skull. His plasto-change squished. Gable went down under another blow. There was a lot of blood. Gable did not move.

Alexis Rike plucked frantically at the plasto-change that covered his face and felt it come away in one large lump; he chucked it into the gutter, his hands shaking.

Down the block, the robot cop had resumed staring off into the distance.

Alexis Rike knew what he had just seen was impossible. Robots were mild, gentle contraptions, violence as foreign to them as a hangover. There were no recorded cases of a robot being subverted or running wild. *Until now*.

Quietly, Rike edged away from the robot crew. The fact that the little man they had just murdered was his look-alike hadn't quite escaped him.

The belt station Rike had used less than an hour ago

was out of commission. He found another six blocks over that still rolled, slipped his rate-card into the slot and let the ramp carry him down. He made his way across four mobile strips to the center section, sank into a seat. The tunnel rushed by in a dizzying whirl. Up above the sectors would be flashing past: the forties, fifties, nineties, followed by a complex of automat-factory units. Around him a hodgepodge of characters clad in outfits from all the decades came and went.

Rike switched belts at Suncture, got off at Government Square and rode up the ramp.

Trees lined the streets. Squat, round and towering structures competed for attention. Styles from all the ages were on display here. The citizens dashing about on the pavements, high-rise walks and spirals were as dissimilar as their conveyor belt counterparts. Rike went past a playground where kids were shouting, came to a tall bronze building which bore a large gold Guardian's shield. He went in flashing his badge at the robot guard on duty, took the speed lift to the twenty-second floor.

Operations-Center consisted of a computerized filing system and robot clerk. Rike ignored them, headed for the chief's office; the chief wasn't there. The robot sec sent him packing to the director's suite. Rike wondered who the director was these days.

Harry Henderson rose to shake Rike's hand as he came through the double doors. "Glad to see you, Alex. The more the merrier." Henderson was a medium-sized, heavyset man in his mid-fifties, wide-nosed, gray-haired and double-chinned. He had a small scar on his left cheek. He was smoking a cheap cigar. "You know the others?" Henderson asked.

Rike said yes, sat down at the long table. A patch of blue sky showed through the uncurtained window that overlooked the plaza below. He could hear the kids shouting outside.

To his right was little Joseph Berg, about forty-three, with red hair, glasses, a pointy chin. Henderson sat across from Rike. On his left was Joyce Fairchild, a thirty-ish lady with short-clipped brown hair, glasses, a tanned complexion and shrewd brown eyes. Ralph Olenger sat at the head of the table. That made him director. He was pale-skinned, slow-speaking, with heavy eyebrows, bluish black hair over a high forehead and a long, straight nose. He, at least, looked the part of a director. Directors of State Security were chosen by the Master Security Computer. The title was all but honorary, as humdrum a proposition usually as being head of the local ladies' sewing circle.

"Congratulations," Rike told Olenger.

"For what, the hot seat?"

"It's a great honor; at least that's what the manual says. How long have you been director?"

Olenger shrugged. "A couple of weeks. Looking for a promotion?"

Rike waved a hand. "Forget it. I have enough troubles of my own."

Henderson said, "You guys going to sit here gabbing all day while the city burns?"

"It's *still* burning?" Rike heard himself ask in some wonder.

"Damn right," Henderson said. "The thing's out of control."

"Not quite, Harry," Joyce said.

Olenger nodded. "Mobile fire squad's on the job; it's only a matter of time before they get things squared away."

"What took them so long?" Rike asked.

"The lines were knocked out," Olenger said, "no alarm at fire-control."

"All the lines?"

Olenger shrugged. "Whatever caused the blowup packed a wallop."

"Some wallop!" Henderson said.

"What *did* cause it?" Rike asked.

Olenger said he didn't know.

Berg said, "This most certainly does not concern *us*."

"No?" Rike said.

"It is the robot fire squad's business, Mr. Rike," Berg said, "not ours."

"Like hell," Henderson shouted. "When the damn fire repellent goes on the blink, that makes it our business!"

"Don't yell," Joyce told him.

"What evidence is there that anything has been tampered with, Mr. Henderson?" Berg said.

"This is childish," Joyce said.

"Damn right," Henderson shouted.

"You too, Harry," Joyce said. "We've got to stop carrying on this way."

"Miss Fairchild has a point," Rike said.

"Of course," Joyce said, "all the repellent didn't just turn itself off; and, of course, it's our duty to investigate—"

Olenger sighed, shook his head slowly. "Not yet, I'm afraid."

"There's something else we do first?" Rike asked.

"Yeah, nothing, that's what we do first," Henderson complained.

"Look," Olenger said, "it's not my idea."

"If the Guardians are to mean *anything*," Joyce said, "if they're not just a sham, then now, in this crisis—"

"I see no crisis, Miss Fairchild," Berg said.

Henderson turned to Rike. "Everyone's gone nuts."

Olenger wagged a finger. "Look, when my name was tagged for director, the first thing I did was bone up on the constitution."

"And?" Joyce said.

"There's not a thing we can do till the robot squad's gone over the damage. And right now that's impossible because of the fire."

"So later," Joyce said. "Then what?"

"Well, if something turns up, something suspicious, I convoke a Guardians' Council, pronto."

Henderson snorted. "By then, the whole city could be a pile of ashes."

"Do not be asinine, Mr. Henderson," Berg said.

"Look," Olenger said. "I was summoned by computer. You three were out in the field. That leaves one hundred and fifty other Guardians who've got a voice in this too.

We simply can't go charging around without an official say-so."

"Charging around?" Henderson roared. "Man, this is a clear-cut case of sabotage!"

"We do not know that, Mr. Henderson," Berg said, "but let us suppose some lunatic—"

"Lunatic? Jesus, look at the size of this thing; it had to be organized, planned."

"By *whom?*" Berg demanded. "Have you really lost all your reason, Mr. Henderson? Are you truly telling us that a *group* of lunatics has banded together and gone unnoticed by our robot squads?"

"Yeah," Henderson said, "that's what I'm telling you."

"It's never happened before," Olenger said.

"It's happened now," Henderson said.

Olenger smiled sadly. "Even so, Harry, what could *we* do? At best, we're rank amateurs at this, dilettantes."

"The robots," Berg pointed out, "are professionals."

Rike cleared his throat. "I think I'd better make my report now."

He made it.

"You mean," Joyce said when he was done, "you actually saw a robot kill someone?"

"Yes."

"Impossible, Mr. Rike," Berg said.

Rike shrugged.

"If true," Olenger said, "it is unprecedented."

"You have proof, Mr. Rike?" Berg asked.

"No," Rike said.

"See?" Berg said.

The scene began to fade as if billows of fog were obscuring it. Gray turned to blackness. Familiar voices came out of the blackness.

"He is an enigma."

"Has he traversed time?"

"How? He is obviously not the Prime. For the Prime is the great mover. Yet here we see many. And none move."

"His mind depicts the ages."

"His mind? An instrument meant solely to deceive us,

to lead us on a false path. Of this I am now convinced. But we must uncover how he came to be here, through what upheaval. And what is his exact purpose."

"The probe again?"

"Yes. But now set at its deepest level."

"And then?"

"Kill him."

CHAPTER 32

The door to Rike's cell swung open. The short, bald-headed monk stood there in the flickering light of his torch. He was alone. Hastily he pushed the heavy door closed behind him. His voice shook when he spoke. "I can tarry but a moment," he whispered.

"They are going to kill me," Rike said evenly.

"I know." The monk's eyes were round with fear. "They pack now; soon they will leave. I have heard them speaking. There is to be one last interrogation. You are not expected to survive."

Alexis Rike looked levelly at the monk; his voice was calm. "You're my only chance now; without you I haven't got a prayer. You know that, of course?"

"Yes."

"Will you help me?"

"*Yes.*"

From under his robe the monk produced a short seven-inch dagger, gave it to Rike. "Use it only if all else fails. Suspicion must not fall on this monastery. The knife might have been hidden on your person and escaped our search. But it may lead to difficulties if used, nonetheless."

Rike nodded, hid the knife in his garments.

"You are to be escorted to the inquisition chamber by three of our monks. Turn on them. And then flee. It has been arranged. Use the stairs directly to your right. They will lead into the courtyard. The large gates will be left unlocked."

Alexis Rike gravely thanked the monk. Nodding once, the monk turned to go.

"Wait." Rike raised a palm. "You said that I appeared from nowhere."

"It was so."

"Where did this happen?"

"Not far from here."

"Tell me how to get there."

The monk did.

Only two of Rike's escorts were monks. The third was an inquisitor, a tall, cadaverous man in black with a white, pasty face.

"Come," the inquisitor said in a flat, nasal voice.

Rike came.

They went down the familiar corridor, cells on either side of them. The inquisitor walked at Rike's side. One monk led while another followed. The procession to Rike seemed endless. It was as if this foursome had always walked these corridors, always would. There was only the sound of their echoing footsteps on the stone floors, the dark shadows that moved with them along the walls.

Time seemed to have stopped. Yet it was time. Now. Rike's hand shook. He took a deep breath, reached under his shirt, grasped the knife.

The inquisitor half turned.

Rike lashed out, caught the tall man in the midriff, carved a crooked line up to his neck; he fell without a sound.

Rike twisted sideways, ready to defend himself against the monks. Neither moved. Friends, then.

Rike raised a hand in half salute, took off down the corridor.

Alexis Rike ran for his life.

He could hear commotion behind him. He was being followed. He ran faster. The night was around him, small houses on either side of him. He was close to the center of town. Almost no time at all now. He still had his knife. If they caught up with him he would use it, take as many of them with him as possible.

The market square was dark. No light of any kind.

There were only three buildings. Two were nothing more than shacks. Rike kicked in the door of the first, then the second. Both were empty. The third was a barn-like structure. The door was padlocked, but Rike found a window, forced it open. He would be trapped here if he was wrong. He had no choice. There was nowhere else to go.

It was pitch-dark inside. He felt his way along, stumbling often. He could hear sounds coming from outside the building. *They* were here.

He tripped over the cellar door. He yanked at the handle. The door opened with a squeal. Rike closed the door after him. Slowly, silently, he moved down a series of stone steps. The blackness flowed around him like dark waters.

He hit bottom.

Footsteps sounded from the floor above.

Rike stood motionless like the blind man he was.

Now what? Which way should he, could he, turn?

Above him, the trapdoor squeaked open; light splashed down the stone steps.

At that instant, Rike became aware of his surroundings: a totally empty square cellar—an earth floor. Four stone walls. And a tunnel leading off through one of the walls.

The men above were starting down the steps.

Alexis Rike plunged into the tunnel.

Again the heavy, clinging darkness seemed to flood over him. Arms outstretched in front of him, he ran. Sightless. Unheeding. Gasping for breath. Legs pumping furiously. His body wet with perspiration. His mind a vacant, empty place.

The man appeared from nowhere. His body glowed a

dim green. He hung suspended in midair, stretched out on a thin slab of metal.

The man neither spoke nor looked at Rike. His eyes were closed. His face pointed to the ceiling above.

The man was Alexis Rike.

Up the tunnel two glowing headlights appeared. The huge train filled the tunnel completely. No place to hide. No place to avoid its onrushing form. Rike heard the roar of its engines. Felt a rush of air.

The speeding train bore down upon him.

Then there was nothing.

The sound reached him from far away, a harsh buzzing slicing through the brightness of his headset. Pretty far gone. But he still knew what that sound meant.

Alexis Rike pulled off his headset, climbed out of his cushioned chair like a fat man painfully hoisting himself up a long, dangling rope, padded over toward the viewer and after what seemed a very long and arduous trip, got there. It was Joseph Berg.

"—for God's sake," the thin, narrow-boned redhead was saying. His voice, to Alexis Rike, seemed to be coming through a long tunnel. Rike looked closely at Berg's face: it was white, pinched, his eyes wide and staring under the round glasses, his mouth open as though his jaw had become unhinged.

The effects of the headset began to diminish; Rike was sobering up fast. "What is it?" he asked.

"It is Olenger. He is dead, Mr. Rike, dead. Butchered. Killed like some animal in a slaughterhouse. It is horrible."

Dusk crept over the city. Olenger had lived in a north side complex. The area was roped off now, robot squads guarding the entrance. Joseph Berg waited by the corner, a small, huddled figure in a long coat.

Alexis Rike went over to him, nodded, put an arm around his shoulder, steered him toward the building. Rike flashed his Guardian badge at the duty robot and was waved through.

They went into the lobby, a marble floor echoing under their feet.

Using the chutes, the two men rode up.

"Any details?" Rike asked.

"None," Berg said. "Only the notification." The little man was silent as they got off at the thirty-eighth floor. The duty robot stepped aside when he saw Rike's badge. A robot investigator was waiting for them inside Olenger's suite.

"Rike," Alexis Rike said. "This is Joseph Berg. Guardians-on-call."

The investigator pumped their hands, each in turn. "Delighted, gentlemen, delighted," he beamed, "even if under so trying, so tragic a circumstance. What is the world coming to, gentlemen, what indeed? Allow me to introduce myself. I am R-Meerlue. The body is in the bedroom."

R-Meerlue was medium-sized, chubby; his round pleasant face seemed to belie his vocation. His hair was salt and pepper. He had a double chin and chewed an unlit cigar. A brown checkered suit and vest fitted snugly over his slightly protruding paunch.

R-Meerlue opened the bedroom door. The trio stepped into a large, blue-walled room. Olenger was stretched out on the floor, his black dressing gown stained red with blood. One leg was twisted under him. An arm was up over his face as if trying to ward off a blow. Both arm and face were smashed in as if someone—or something—had taken a sledgehammer to them.

The remains were viewed in total silence.

R-Meerlue sighed, cleared his throat. "Obviously it is the work of a demented mind. I ask you, gentlemen, what motive could there be? Is not ours a society all but devoid of blemish? Is not labor—once so demeaning an activity—now a mere trivial nuisance? Why, machines such as I, gentlemen, gladly do the lion's share of the chores. No task too large or too small, as they say." He spread his arms as though trying to show the size of the tasks; he shrugged his round shoulders. "Who but a raving lunatic would do such a thing?"

The three returned to the living room. R-Meerlue smiled. "Standard, of course, gentlemen; what I always say on such dire occasions. Aside from their placating nature, my words have at least one other virtue. Usually they contain a certain amount of truth."

"And now?" Berg asked.

R-Meerlue was apologetic. "By definition, the perpetrator must be insane, but otherwise, who can say?"

"That certainly covers a lot of ground," Rike said.

"Indeed," R-Meerlue said.

"Who found the body?" Rike asked.

"The cleaning woman. She knows nothing. Under sedation at the moment." R-Meerlue removed a lighter from his vest pocket, lit his cigar; he inhaled.

"Quite a trick," Rike said.

"Merely good public relations." R-Meerlue smiled.

Rike said, "How do you suppose the killer got in?"

"A key, perhaps. There were no signs of forced entry."

Berg wanted to know about the weapon.

"The traditional blunt instrument, Mr. Berg."

"It appears almost as if he were struck by a pile driver," Joseph Berg said.

"Nothing so exotic, I'm sure," R-Meerlue said.

"Anything else?" Rike said.

R-Meerlue shook his head.

"It is not very much," Berg said.

"No," R-Meerlue admitted. "But then we have just begun, Mr. Berg, have we not?"

It was dark now. The crowd had grown denser behind the cordon. Street lamps cast slanting shadows over the milling figures. Faces stood out, Humphrey Bogart, Bette Davis, Rin-Tin-Tin. Rike and Berg pushed their way through the crowd. Loudspeakers echoed in the distance. Some sector hawking its wares.

"What if a robot did it?" Berg whispered.

Alexis Rike shrugged.

"I do not like it," Berg said.

"Who does?"

"What shall we do, Mr. Rike?"

"I don't know," Alexis Rike said.

Rike walked the streets.

The city was alive with lights, sound, movement. A blur of people passed him, some in costume, others barefaced. A mini-twenties sector blared at him. President Harding, looking solemn in a huge, glowing portrait, pointed at parts of a newfangled radio set that even a child could assemble. Al Joson sang "Mammy." Neon lights spelled out Houdini, Charlie Chaplin, Krazy Kat. He kept on going. A couple of blocks more brought a measure of quiet. He passed wooden benches, small parks, an old age home. Live in Your Childhood, the sign read.

Alexis Rike sighed.

Through the trees and buildings, he could see the dome of Ingram's Rest glowing a milky white in the distance. He moved toward it. Mist and fog rolled over the pavement, a gift of the weather machines.

Founder's Square was a small island of light, noise, congestion. The milky translucent dome rose sky-high, seemed to gleam down benevolently on the crowd below. A museum, video-library, assorted tech and admin centers surrounded the dome. Even at this hour a line had gathered at its entrance. The guided tours closed shop at five sharp, but the question and answer service went on around the clock. Queries—on all manner of subjects —were fed into a communications link and some five days later, a written reply was posted over the Founder's stamp. Dr. James Ingram's body had been dead these fifty long years, but his mind lived on, a monument to the society he'd helped erect.

Rike pushed through a service door, went up three stone steps, took the chutes up to the fifth floor, went down a brightly lit corridor and found Nona Evers in the archives section.

She was a pert, green-eyed blonde of twenty-six. Her hair was long, eyes wide, gait swinging. She was a Guardian of the Founder's Brain. At certain times, she was

171

known to put in as many as twelve days a month on the job. Which was considerably more than her co-workers. Nona smiled when Rike appeared, joined him at the door.

"Ready?" he asked.

"All set."

She got her bag and the couple went downstairs and out the front door. The line waiting for Ingram's blessings had grown even longer. Rike took Nona's arm and the pair headed off into the night.

"How's the good doctor?" he asked.

"Snoozing away, what else?"

Rike nodded. As a Security Guardian, he knew, of course, that the whole question and answer operation was pure hokum. Computers processed the public's queries. But computers might be of some help to him now.

Rike said, "This may sound a bit strange—"

"Don't give it a thought," the girl said airily. "You never have before."

Rike agreed that was probably true. "What do you think of when I say 'robot'?" he asked.

"Robot? What's so strange about that?"

"Answer the question," Rike said.

"Safety. Labor. Loyalty. Duty . . ."

"What about the word 'murder'?"

Nona made a face. "I'd say obsolete."

"Want to wager a bet?"

"Not especially."

"All right. Now I tell you—incredibly—that the robot cops have gone out and murdered someone. What do you say?"

"You mean my reaction?"

"Yes."

"Deranged."

"The cops?"

"*You.*" Nona smiled. "Wrong answer?"

"Not at all. I admire honesty." Alexis Rike took a deep breath, told her about the street incident, Olenger's killing. He told it swiftly and without feeling; he did not like telling it.

"You mean," the girl said when he was done, "you

172

think you actually saw a *robot* commit murder near the fire and think maybe Olenger was killed by one too? Is *that* what you mean?"

"That," he said, "is what I mean."

"Fantastic!"

"Leaves you kind of breathless, doesn't it?"

"It's fine with me. What do I care? I've known you a long time, Alex, and no one's ever said you're exactly sane."

"That's nice," Alexis Rike said.

"But you better watch out. Go around spreading tales like that and they'll put you away."

Rike nodded.

"You're serious?"

"Unfortunately. The Founder's Brain has an autonomous computer system. Or is that just hearsay?"

"True enough."

"Here's your big chance to help an old friend."

"What am I supposed to do?"

"Relay the story I've just given you to Ingram's computer."

"You don't want much, do you, Alex?"

"What's wrong with that?"

"Nothing. Except that'll get us both in Dutch."

"It shouldn't."

"You've got something else up your sleeve?"

"Yes. Feed him all that as mere conjecture. Your cyborg's heard worse. Tell him you're writing a novel."

"A possibility," the girl admitted.

"Right. Ask if this thing *might* happen. And how? That's all."

"That's enough. But I'll do it. For you, Alex, you great big nut."

"Thanks," Alexis Rike said.

CHAPTER 33

Next morning Rike went to see Harry Henderson. The robot clerk greeted him affably and Rike marched into the chief's office. "Don't you ever go home, Harry?" he asked.

Henderson, in shirt sleeves and open collar, seated behind a small, cluttered desk, shrugged; he looked disgruntled and bleary-eyed.

"You could at least shave," Rike told him, sitting down.

"What for? Charly doesn't give a damn." Charly was the robot clerk.

"*Persons* might drop in someday."

"Swell chance."

"Well, there's always me."

"You're a crank, Rike."

"I suppose so. What's the story on the fire, Harry?"

"What do you think?"

"The worst I'd imagine."

"Uh-huh. That's what it is. The worst."

The two men looked at each other.

Rike said, "Have a Euphor?"

"Nah," Henderson said. Reaching into a bottom desk drawer, he took out a bottle. "Old reliable," he said; he poured out some gin in a drinking glass, drained it in a gulp.

"That stuff is poison," Rike said.

"What isn't?" Henderson wiped his mouth with the back of his hand. "The whole thing had to be carried out like a goddamn military operation, Alex. The dynamite was planted all over the joint. View booth wires were sliced for fifty blocks around the Palace. Hookups to the rescue squad, emergency fire units, robot cops were all shorted. Even the robots on the scene seemed to be weak-kneed, didn't do a damn's worth of good."

"A thing that big," Rike said, "should be easy enough to run down."

"Go tell that to the robot cops. So far, Alex, no one has seen, smelled or heard anything. How about that? And all the evidence went up with the Palace. At least that's the story. You buy it?"

"It depends."

"Hell! When *people* are killed, *people* ought to be looking into it. Not a bunch of damn tin cans."

"The voice of reaction." Alexis Rike smiled.

"Damn right. If there's one thing I can't stomach it's the thought of knuckling under to those rotten contraptions."

"They make abundance possible," Rike pointed out, quoting the manual.

"Why don't you shut up?" Henderson said.

"Think any of this is connected with the Olenger killing?"

Henderson shook his head. "Beats me, Alex. I can't figure that baby at all. Who could've done it? Why?"

"Who set fire to the Palace?"

"Some sweet mess, ha?" Henderson grinned sourly.

Alexis Rike nodded absently.

"If you'd get off that damn Euphor stuff you'd be a lot more worried," Henderson said.

"I'm worried."

"But not enough."

"Well," Rike said, "maybe not enough to remain here all day."

"What else is there, Alex?" Henderson asked with some interest.

"The Yesteryear tube; the headset; why don't you compose a symphony or something; perhaps join a rec-group?"

Henderson snorted. "I'd rather just sit here and read these dumb robot reports; I get more kicks that way."

Rike shook his head. "To each his own. You're starting to sound just like a Purie, Harry."

"And to hell with 'em, too," Henderson said.

Rike went down the hall, taped his duty report. Then he boarded a belt to Founder's Square.

The day was gray, overcast. A group of gamesters, dressed in swirling costumes of the 1780s, swept along. Tourist groups hustled by, each guided by a robot host. A long line of men, women, children waited to ask Ingram's brain for a word of wisdom.

Rike used the side door, took the chutes up to Archives.

He found Nona behind a stack of papers. "Don't work so hard, it sets a bad example."

"For whom, the robots?" the girl asked.

"You've got a point," Rike said. "Let's take a stroll."

The couple went down with the chutes and out onto the square. Soon they were part of the crowd. "Looks safe enough," Rike said.

"Safe for *what?*"

"Darned if I know. That's part of the problem. Well, did you manage it?"

"Of course."

"The suspense is killing me."

"Ingram's cyborg didn't come up with anything world-shaking, Alex."

"What did it say?"

"It said maybe."

"Maybe?"

"Its very word."

"Word?"

"There were others. The cyborg feels that the robots might dispatch someone, *but*."

"Go on."

"But it's not very likely. There are built-in safeguards, checks and balances, and checks on the checks. Including automat shutoffs, should such an unlikely idea persist."

"I know," Rike said. "All that's part of the security training program."

"However," Nona said, "the cyborg suggested deception."

"Who was deceived?"

"You were."

Rike made a face. "The robots weren't really robots but people in disguise?"

"Smart," Nona said. "Right on the button."

"Could be. But all that is supposed to be under control."

"How?"

"Security risks. Folks who've lost a couple of marbles along the way. Soreheads. Cranks. Out-and-out loonies. We keep track of them. That is, the robot aides do."

"What about organized crime?" Nona asked.

"You've been watching too many entertainies."

"No organized crime?"

"None to speak of."

"The robot aides wiped it out?"

"Who needs crime when people can get anything they want?"

"What do *you* want, Alex?"

"Not to worry about all this."

"See," Nona said, "you can't get what *you* want. Maybe there are others."

"Perhaps, but don't hold your breath."

CHAPTER 34

The amphitheater was full. White light shone down on the Security Assembly. Guardians called for the floor, demanding to be heard. Olenger's murder was raked over the coals. The Festival Palace blowup was poked, probed and examined from all angles. A steady stream of speakers strode to the rostrum, said their piece and returned to their seats. Each had a slightly different theory. Robot aides presented what facts there were. Alexis Rike sat back in his seat, tried to keep from dozing. Many of the delegates were in full costume. Some were Sherlock Holmes, others Philip Marlowe or Sam Spade. The entire proceedings were recorded by a branch of the master computer. All theories would be given computer attention. The weather machines had broken down sometime during the night. Rain beat against windows, came down hard on the roof.

Joyce Fairchild said, "Alexis!"

He opened his eyes.

"You're asleep. Wake up."

Rike rearranged himself in his seat. "Why?" he asked.

"They're about to pick a new director."

Rike yawned. "What time is it?"

"Ten to six."

Onstage the computer seemed to cough. Lights began to blink. A spool of paper uncoiled through a slot.

A portly man clad in a Mike Hammer costume stepped up to the machine, removed the paper, handed it to a shorter man.

"Hal Dooley," the short man read in a squeaky, high-pitched voice.

The delegates applauded; Dooley got up and waved from across the hall. No one suggested he make a speech. Dooley sat down. The delegates began to file out of the amphitheater. In twenty minutes it was a dark, deserted shell.

Rike leaned against the doorbell. Rain beat on his shoulders. Lamplights glistened in the damp air. The street was empty. It was nine-thirty at night.

The return buzzer sounded and Alexis Rike pushed open the door. He walked up two green-carpeted flights of stairs, leaving wet footprints behind him. He smelled damp wood, musty linen, coffee, cigar smoke, furniture polish. Dooley lived in a replica brownstone.

Hal Dooley opened the door to Apartment 2A before Rike could knock, ushered him into a small, cluttered living room.

Dooley extended an arm, shook Rike's hand. "Good to see you, Alex."

Dooley was a short, compact man with a square face, thinning hair, mild gray eyes.

Rike handed him his raincoat and Dooley went away with it. A large poster in a black frame showed Uncle Sam pointing a finger into the living room. Buy War Bonds, the caption read. A victrola was playing "One Meat Ball" by the Andrews Sisters. A blowup photo of Raymond Chandler smoking a pipe and holding his cat Taki hung in an ornate silver frame over a flower-print couch. The Cisco Kid and his horse Diablo were in a plain glass frame on an end table. Dooley was a forties buff.

Dooley came back holding two tall glasses. "Got some Pepsi out of the icebox." He grinned. "Hits the spot, you know."

Rike took a glass. "Yes, I know."

"Six full ounces," Dooley said, winking. "That's a lot. Twice as much for a nickel too. Pepsi-Cola is the drink for you."

Alexis Rike wagged his head, took a sip, sat down on the couch.

"Listen," Dooley said, "you want to hear some records of Axis Sally or Tokyo Rose?"

"I don't think so."

Silence engulfed the room. Dooley went to the victrola, removed the record from the turntable, put on another. Nat King Cole began a rendition of "Nature Boy."

"How's that?" Dooley asked.

"Terrible."

Dooley nodded. "Would you settle for 'It Might As Well Be Spring'?"

"Yes. The victrola's the wrong era, Hal."

Dooley switched records. Dick Haymes started to croon. "Don't I know it. It's all I could get. The rug looks dirty," Dooley said, "wouldn't you say?"

Rike glanced down at the rug. It seemed clean enough. "I suppose so."

"I'll vacuum," Dooley said brightly. Getting an old electric vacuum cleaner out of the closet, he began briskly tending the rug. The machine roared.

"Pretty noisy," Rike said.

"You're telling me," Dooley said. He sat down next to Rike, the vacuum growling even louder.

"All this, I suppose," Rike said, "means something."

"Right you are, Alex."

"Mind telling me what?"

"That's what I called you for. We've got troubles. Figure the place might be bugged."

"This racket makes it all right?"

"That's just cover. Got me some electronic gear going that should scramble things pretty good. Anyone giving us the ear, it'll sound like that engine's screwing up the works. Listen, I spoke to Henderson. Right after I got the nod."

Rike smiled. "Harry never gives up, does he?"

"Well," Dooley said, "I don't know, he may have something. He said if you could keep off the Euphors you might be okay."

"Okay for what?"

"I've got a job for you."

Alexis Rike shrugged. "What makes you think I *want* a job?"

"Aw, Alex," Dooley said.

"I'll listen, but that's all; no promises."

"Fair enough. You were born a Purie, weren't you, Alex?"

"My parents lived in the ghetto, if that's what you mean. I didn't actually *choose* to be born there. Anyway, all that is a matter of public record. What about it?"

"Why'd you pull out?"

"Boredom, I guess."

"That was about eighteen years ago."

"Right."

"Folks living?"

"No. They still use fire engines in that place. Had a big blaze. The whole block went up in minutes."

"Figure you can find your way around in there?"

"It's been a long time."

"I'd like you to go back, Alex."

Rike looked at Hal Dooley. "You're crazy," he said.

"Someone's got to."

"Forget it. The answer is no."

"Don't you even want to hear about it?"

"You really *are* crazy, Hal. Sure, the Puries might be behind all this. Think that hasn't crossed my mind?"

"Well . . . ?"

Alexis Rike shrugged. "What do *I* know about undercover work?"

"What does anyone?"

"That's not *my* problem."

"Look," Dooley said, "you were brought up in the ghetto . . ."

"We get enough crossovers each year. Find someone else."

"You're a special case, Alex. Eighteen years on the outside; parents gone, friends moved on; you could get away with it, go unnoticed, have the run of the ghetto. But the important point is you're a trained Security Guardian."

"Trained? Let's not play games. You know what that's worth."

"Headgear," Dooley said. "We could fix you up with headgear. Developed before the robot aides took over security. We've kept them in mothballs. What it boils down to is a crash course. You'd know all there is to know."

"Crash is right. You've been in office about four hours. Mind telling me where you got all this?"

"Henderson."

Alexis Rike made a face.

"He's a dedicated Guardian, the last of the breed, maybe," Dooley insisted.

"Look, Hal. If you've got the headgear, you can train anyone, right? So train anyone except me."

"We need someone we can trust. Henderson and I, we've both known you a long time, Alex. We've got confidence in you."

"That's more than I have. You two really take the cake. All this isn't even legal."

"It's legal. The director can delegate authority, initiate undercover operations."

"When's the last time a director did that, Hal?"

Dooley shrugged. "How should I know?"

"This is juvenile," Rike said. "Headgear, undercover operations. The Puries have their police, too. You have any idea what their prisons are like?"

"No, do you?"

"I've heard stories."

"Alex, as director I have access to the inner vault. The three of us can cook up anything you need. No one else'll know."

"You two are really worried, aren't you?"

"Sure. The robot cops have come up with nothing. The fire, Olenger's murder—it's a washout. *But it shouldn't be.*"

"Give them time."

"That's what *they* say."

"You think the robots and Puries are in this together?"

"I don't know what to think, Alex."

"I do," Rike said. "All this is just guessing. And even if it isn't there's nothing I can do."

CHAPTER 35

Rike sat back in his plush easy chair, closed his eyes. The holograph continued to mutter. His finger pressed remote. There was quiet. Another button activated the Yester-year tube. John Barrymore's voice sounded in his ears. Rike opened his eyes, recognized *Svengali,* a 1931 opus with Barrymore and Marian Marsh. He watched absently for a while, then turned off the set and went to bed.

The warning system roused him some three hours later. Rolling to his feet, Rike groped for the light and buzzer switches, found them. The buzzing under his pillow stopped; light filled the room. Rike looked at his watch: 2:38 A.M.

He reached for a robe, rearranged his bed, extinguished the light, went down the hallway into his office.

He punched on the closed-circuit system, seated himself behind his desk. The center screen brightened.

R-Meerlue was in the hallway, half bent, busily at work on Rike's front door. The robot wasn't having much luck, it seemed. Rike, who had invested a good deal of time and effort on both the front and back doors to his apartment, could understand why.

A short row of ivory buttons lined the desk top. Rike pressed one with a thumb. R-Meerlue straightened as the front-door lock snapped open. Once inside, R-Meerlue moved swiftly through the darkened parlor, making little sound. Rike watched his progress on the left screen. The robot paused by Rike's bedroom, inched open the door.

R-Meerlue appeared on the right screen now. Faint

light shone through a half-opened window, cast angular shadows across the bedroom walls.

The robot cop loomed over the bed, peered down at the blanket-wrapped figure that lay there; he removed a long knife from his pocket, quickly plunged it into the figure. The figure neither moved nor cried out.

Alexis Rike stared at the screen, shook his head, stood up, fumbled in the desk drawer for a small black box, a classified item he had checked out of the arsenal. He carried it and himself back up the corridor, toward his bedroom.

R-Meerlue had just finished pulling the blanket away from the dummy that lay in Rike's bed.

Rike, standing in the doorway, held out the black box.

R-Meerlue gazed from Rike to the box and back again.

Rike said, "Take it easy. This gadget is murder on mechanicals."

"You don't say?" R-Meerlue said in a voice Rike didn't recognize.

The robot cop still had his knife. Grinning, he launched himself at Rike.

Alexis Rike pressed a stud on his black box.

Nothing happened.

Rike dropped the box, managed to grab R-Meerlue's wrist; the two went down together in a tangle.

R-Meerlue put a knee in Rike's stomach. For a robot, it was a feeble effort. This encouraged Rike. He banged R-Meerlue's wrist against the floor. The robot cop dropped his knife. Rike pounded his fist in the robot's face. Blood trickled from R-Meerlue's nose.

R-Meerlue squirmed away, lurched to his feet. Rike, reaching for him, missed. R-Meerlue scampered down the hall, Rike after him.

The front door banged closed. Rike paused long enough to grab a gun. He ran out into the hallway as a chute door slammed shut.

R-Meerlue was gone.

Only it hadn't been R-Meerlue. Had it?

＊　＊　＊

R-Meerlue smiled. "It is an honor, I should suppose. Robots are rarely impersonated. And, naturally, in a society where impersonation plays so large a role, we robots feel the omission keenly."

Rike sighed. "I'd have gotten him, only I didn't have my stunner handy."

The robot grinned broadly. "You thought *I* was the assailant, then?"

"There wasn't much time for thought. But you would have used a fist rather than a knife, I suppose."

"Hardly," the robot cop said with some dignity. "Are you unaware, Mr. Rike, that we are programmed against such actions?"

"I meant hypothetically, of course."

"Ah!"

The two other robot cops left. Rike, who had been sitting on his bed, stood up, stretched. "A mess."

"Doubtless," R-Meerlue said. "But think how much worse it could be if we Guardian-aides did indeed indulge in such bloody deeds. Fortunately, quite impossible. Were it not, we would have to search through our own ranks for Mr. Olenger's killer."

"Yes," Rike said, "I guess you would at that."

Alexis Rike, wearing the face of Cary Grant, checked into the Ritz, after taking numerous evasive steps to make sure he wasn't followed.

"James Knight," he told the robot clerk who was Robert Morley.

"This way, Mr. Knight," the robot bellhop said, taking his suitcase; he looked like Johnny, the Philip Morris callboy.

A group of gamesters staggered by, stoned to the eyeballs. Rike yawned. It was 4:35 A.M.

Once in his room, Rike locked the door, undressed, put both black box and stunner under his pillow and went to sleep.

The following afternoon he called on Hal Dooley.

"All right," Rike said once Dooley had activated the vacuum cleaner. "I'm ready to go."

PART 5

Mark Craig

Ah, but to fall into a black hole. A person who did that would be stretched out like a very thin rubber band.

from *The Notebooks of Dr. James Ingram*

CHAPTER 36

A noise awoke me.

Someone was pounding on the door.

I sat up in bed. My mouth tasted as if I had been chewing on a wad of cotton. My head ached as though it had been substituting for a Ping-Pong ball. My body felt weak and spent as if I'd been running the hundred-yard hurdles and come in last. Aside from that I was probably in good shape. Depending on how you defined good.

"Craig!" a voice yelled.

"A minute," I mumbled back. That encouraged me; I could still talk. Now if I could only get my legs over the side of the bed, I'd really be showing progress. Maybe I'd even make it across the room.

The lights were out and I couldn't find the nightstand lamp. I had no idea what time it was, how long I'd slept. I was sure hitting on all burners. A bit more of this and I'd be ready to hand in my retirement papers.

"Craig." The voice called again.

"Coming."

Whatever this was about had better be important or there'd be the devil to pay. Provided I could reach the door. Who the hell was it?

De Marco?

Grant?

Someone from State-City Hospital?

The SEC?

No one else knew I was here.

I finally got my feet over the side of the bed and

started walking. A chair I couldn't remember almost tripped me up and then I bumped into the wall.

Great.

A grayish rectangle on the other side of the room told me where the door was. I'd been heading in the opposite direction. I changed courses wondering what they'd put in the hootch I'd guzzled at Frank's. Nitroglycerin, probably.

Remnants of my latest dream were still buzzing through my head, adding to the general confusion. These dreams would have to stop.

I got to the door, fumbled with a latch I'd never noticed, yanked it open.

Tim Yancy stood in the doorway.

I looked at him. I managed to get my mouth halfway open. It hung there like a jammed drawbridge. I didn't move. I couldn't have moved if my life had depended on it. I was stuck to the spot as if my feet had sprung roots into the carpet. My intestines were busy trying to squirm up my windpipe. My body was suddenly wet as though I'd been huddling in a bathtub. It was all I could do to keep from toppling over. Any other efforts like thinking or breathing were more than I could handle.

Yancy brushed by me. "Come on, Craig," he hissed, "snap out of it. There's been a foul-up." He reached past me, closed the door.

I turned to face him, slowly, painfully, like a man whose joints had just been soldered together.

"What are you doing here, Yancy?" I heard myself croak in a voice that sounded as smooth and easygoing as two sheets of sandpaper rubbing together.

"Listen," Yancy said. "Gardner's gone loco; he's put the grab on three of my guys. I tried to get holda Littlefield; there's no answer. I can't figure this, Craig. But I ain't hanging around for them to cop me. I'm gonna duck. You're back on the payroll. Find out the score. You need me, call Murray's pub. I'll get the word . . . Hey, Craig, you listenin'?"

I wasn't.

My brains seemed to be going through a fast boil. My

fingers were squirming around like squid caught on dry land. My feet were off doing a slow shuffle toward the window as if they'd decided to go on a private jaunt all their own. Maybe they had their reasons.

I went with my feet.

I had to look out that window. I could have groped around for a light switch and maybe found out that way. But things can happen to rooms and I had to be sure.

This Yancy wasn't merely another Grant or De Marco, a man who might have a mental problem; he was like me: he knew all about Old York.

In fact, he seemed to think he was in Old York right now.

I found no blind on the window—a window which was in the wrong wall. My hand was shaking plenty. I yanked the plain, tattered shade and it rolled up noisily.

Yancy was still yakking, his words flew by me like distant birds—hardly noticed.

Outside, dawn was breaking. The sky was gray, overcast. Few people were up and about. Those who were had on their usual blue denims. A horse-drawn milk wagon was clattering along on the cobblestone street. Dilapidated, peeling tenements greeted my gaze. The local midtown coach—pulled by four horses—rounded the corner right on schedule.

I was back in Old York, as if I'd never been away.

I remembered nodding yes to Yancy. I didn't remember his leaving or my getting dressed and making my way down the stairs. I think I spent the next couple of hours walking the streets aimlessly. I hit the rush hour and denim-clad factory hands filled the pavement. I walked through them. A second wave of office workers came streaming by sometime later. I wasn't sure when. By the time the business execs had boarded their coaches and driven off I had reached downtown and was starting to come to myself . . . whoever or whatever myself might be. My knees were knocking together like castanets and I had trouble keeping my hands from doing the shimmy. Otherwise, I was fine.

It was all really very simple. Either I was bouncing around from one world to another like a volleyball or I had gone stark, raving mad. I didn't even want to think about the first possibility. The second seemed likely enough and would have been quite depressing, if I were still capable of any feeling. I was lucky. I felt as lively as a cadaver and almost as cheerful. A little more of this and I'd be all washed up no matter what happened.

I paused to buy a tabloid and wasn't surprised to see that the three days I'd spent in York had never been. Here it was the morning following my visit to Mrs. Landry. Thinking of kindly old Mrs. Landry gave me an idea. If nothing else, I owed her a return visit. Hospitality demanded it. Only this time I'd take a cannon along. I wondered how she'd explain yesterday's high jinks? Considering everything else that was going on, it hardly mattered; the Landry doings were strictly small-time, run-of-the-mill by comparison.

That struck me as funny and by the time I'd finished laughing I'd attracted a good deal of attention. I got out of there.

Laughing seemed to bring on an appetite—if not loads of good cheer—and I stopped off for a bite at a nearby diner and then a quick shave at Nick's barbershop before hoofing it the rest of the way to my office.

It was nine-thirty. I walked in to the ringing of the phone. None of this was real, I decided, and it didn't matter what I did. Neither breakfast, shave nor hike had raised my spirits in the least. Probably nothing ever would again. I picked up the phone.

"Craig?"

"Yeah."

"Nickerson. You got maybe fifteen minutes to clear out of there. Gardner's on the warpath, is on his way with a flock of Johns."

"Gardner?" I heard myself say, "What's the beef?" My lips were doing all the work; my head was still back in York. I didn't really believe in Gardner. Or anything else. I had become a total skeptic.

"His boys been going over your files here with a fine-tooth comb. They found what me and Watts found."

"I'm still an unperson, huh?" my voice said, smart and snappy just as if I were actually alive.

"Still," Nickerson assured me.

"How'd they get wind of all this?"

"Search me, Craig. This ain't even the DA's territory. Someone musta tipped him. Who's got it in for you, Craig?"

"Just about everyone," I explained. "Thanks."

" 'S'all right. Just earning our dough, right? If you get outta this with a whole skin, Craig, we'll drop by an' pick up a little something."

"Uh-huh," I said.

I hung up. My money was safe, even if I wasn't. The odds of my pulling through were somewhere below zero.

I got an automatic out of my desk's bottom drawer, along with an extra clip, grabbed a fistful of nickels, locked the office door behind me and beat it down the back stairs.

I used a trash can to help me over a fence out back, went through a side alley onto Jennings Avenue and became part of the denim crowd.

I used one of my nickels to dial De Marco's office from a pay phone. It rang nine times before I called it quits. I looked up Mrs. Landry's number in the phone book and just for kicks tried her too. No soap. I dialed Clive Western at the *Daily Sun* but he wasn't in yet. I thought of calling Bridget Mercer and telling her about my dream in which she'd had a star role, but decided to table that one. I used the phone book one last time and looked up Peter Grant. There were four of them. No percentage in phoning. What would I say? I jotted down their addresses for future reference—if there was a future, a doubtful prospect at best in my case—and went hunting for a coach to carry me away.

The day stayed overcast. We rolled past grimy factories, empty lots, dingy storefronts. I took it all in as if I were seeing it for the first time. It didn't feel like home, that was for sure. No place, probably, would ever feel like home again. It was time to face facts. I had blown a fuse upstairs. My mind was taking on the consistency of pablum. The best thing to do was turn myself in at the nearest asylum. Too bad I wasn't back in York, the treatment there would've been neater. Not that Dr. Spiegel had been so hot. Still, who could blame him? Dr. Spiegel and everything that came with him was merely something I'd thrown together in my spare time. Like a large fruitcake. If I really put my mind to it, I could probably dredge up a place where everything came up aces always instead of jokers. The trouble was, Old York wasn't any more substantial than plain York. I knew that now. Nothing, in fact, was real. There was only me. And a lot of silly folks who kept doing unlikely things. Like Assistant DA Gardner, who suddenly sent a team of hired killers to mess up a simple business deal. Or Peter Grant and Pat De Marco back in York, hooked on the thirties strip. Or Mrs. Emma Landry, who could turn herself into a witch in an eyeblink. Or the faceless guy who kept popping up. Or the simple fact that I couldn't, for the life of me, stay pinned down to one world. Little things, but they added up. And that final figure showed that old Mark Craig had flipped his raspberry, was due for a one-way ticket to the local giggle farm. I couldn't put it off any longer. I'd run out of excuses. Only one or two small items to check and I'd be ready to toss in the sponge. Not that I'd really believe in anything I found. I was obviously mad as a hatter. But one last look-see wouldn't hurt anyone. I was curious. What, after all, could happen? For things to happen, things had to be real.

I got off at the last stop, transferred to another coach and continued on my journey. The gun in my pocket felt fine. All I'd probably bag was a lot of phantoms. Even that would give me a rear.

CHAPTER 37

I could hear the barges hooting on the river. The fog was thick, heavy, blending with the gray sky. The tenements— a uniform peeling gray—seemed to lean against each other for support and comfort like aging heart patients. I stepped around the trash cans that blocked the pavements, tried to avoid the blank-eyed, shuffling beggars who shared this terrain with the decaying structures. Then I was on the last block—the waterfront lapping at the concrete—standing in front of the house I sought: five stories of weathered boards and shingles.

I went up three lopsided steps into the darkened hallway. Nothing had changed. But then, why should it? I was here only yesterday.

The door on the third floor was slightly ajar; I pushed it open all the way, and stepped into Mrs. Emma Landry's flat.

The bed, table, two chairs, sink and gas range were all there where they belonged; Mrs. Landry and the thing without a face weren't. But they had left behind some of their handiwork. Little Pat De Marco was stretched out on the floor; his eyes were open, staring at the ceiling. Nothing to see up there, but De Marco wouldn't mind. Someone had done a dandy job on his neck. It was black and blue and nearly twisted off his shoulders. His gun was still in his hand. It hadn't done much good apparently.

I looked at the floor. There were red splotches on it. Blood? The thought of my phantom stalker, Old Faceless, actually bleeding was more than I could stand. Most of this, in fact, was becoming more than I could stand. Too bad there was no way to yell "time out," take a short breather, let someone else run with the ball for a while. I was "it" and "it" always got to play through to the end. At least in this game. Whatever this game was.

I looked down at De Marco.

How was I going to write this off to nightmares?

I'd never much cared for the little guy and yet, for some reason I couldn't understand, he'd gone the distance for me.

Or was this *really* De Marco?

Maybe the guy I was all set to mourn was strolling around York City big as life this very second?

I gave it up. Thinking in circles only hurt my head. And right now my head needed all the coddling it could get.

I crossed over to the window, stood looking out at a brick wall.

End of the line?

Maybe.

If this was all madness, then I ought to call the boys with the straitjacket.

But why rush it?

If York was real in any way, the doctors had already had a crack at me, and what good had it done? Too much was happening to be the work of just *one* disordered mind. Maybe I had a *lot* of disordered minds for company? The notion cheered me a very little bit. A very little bit was the best I could do for the moment. Before I called it a day, I'd take one last stab at finding out the score.

I raised the window, put a foot over the sill and climbed out on the fire escape.

Fog rolled over me from the waterfront. The air was thick with moisture. I was no stranger to these surroundings; I'd been here before.

It had seemed like a dream. Because things like that didn't happen. But maybe they had.

The thing without a face had chased me up these rungs, out onto the roof.

That was the first time. And I'd gotten away.

The second go-round was even better.

Faceless had made another pass at me. This time I'd shifted to York City before reaching the window and Pat De Marco had gotten his.

I'd never finished the trip that second time, never reached the top.

Now I would.

I climbed each rung hand over hand. The structure shook with every step. I passed the fourth and fifth floor. I was all alone out here. For all I knew there wasn't another soul in miles. I could get to hate this place without any prompting at all. In fact, I already did.

I scrambled onto the roof.

I stood there taking deep breaths and looking around. Not much to see. The fog buried most of the view; only a couple of adjacent blocks were visible.

One thing was certain: the dead, empty city I'd glimpsed the first time was nowhere in evidence. Maybe a closer look would change that.

I made my way across the rooftops till I reached the last house. Another block was visible below. Houses. People. A moving coach. I shrugged, not sure what I'd hoped to find here. What I *had* found was nothing. I could have saved myself some time and effort by using the stairs and going out the front door. I began to wonder if everywhere I looked wouldn't be a dead end, a one-way ticket to nowhere and nothing. I should be used to it by now.

I turned to retrace my steps to the fire escape. And stopped.

Far off in the distance, somewhere in the northwest, a faint red glow was rising in the sky. It hung there, neither fire nor rainbow and not even in the right place. The fog should have made it impossible to see. It didn't.

I'd found Grant's haze and the red glow which had haunted my nightmare.

And it was here—right in Old York.

I went back down the fire escape, through the window of Emma Landry's flat. Pat De Marco was still there. Somehow, vaguely, I'd hoped he might have gone away.

I'd been doing a lot of going away lately and I was more than willing to share the honor with De Marco's cadaver. No such luck. I went through his pockets and came up with nothing useful. I frisked the closet and uncovered a lot of junk, including a bunch of old-fashioned black, flowery dresses packed in mothballs—stuff which could have been worn by an old crone like Mrs. Landry. I didn't like it. A flesh-and-blood Emma Landry who actually lived in this dump and palled around with faceless men was more than I cared to think about. I got busy, looking under the bed and in the water closet. When I found nothing there I left the flat, carefully stepping around Pat De Marco, closed the door behind me, went down three flights of stairs and back out onto the street. The street looked like a preview of the netherworld but I was glad to be there. I didn't want the cops to tie me to De Marco's corpse. I went away fast.

I used a pay phone around the corner. This time Clive Western was in.

"Anyone hunting for me?" I asked.

"Not that I noticed, son; why?"

I told him about Assistant DA Gardner.

"Very peculiar," Western said, "but what isn't? Which reminds me, I've done some digging into your alleged past."

"And?"

"You wouldn't believe me if I told you. Drop by the office, perhaps I'll let you take a peek."

"You really found something?"

"Uh-huh," Clive Western said.

"I'm on my way."

By the time an express carriage brought me to the *Sun* building, I'd almost figured out what to do. "Almost" was all I could manage. I didn't feel bright enough for anything fancy. Just getting through the next few hours would be an accomplishment. My best bet, I knew, was keeping my lip buttoned and poking around like crazy. I didn't want to show in the De Marco killing at all. What could I tell *anyone* that wouldn't land me right in the clink? Either the city jail or the booby hatch. Not much of a difference any way you sliced it. One thing seemed clear. The longer I stayed on the loose, the more I might turn up. Sooner or later, someone would probably catch up with me. But at least I'd give 'em a run for their money. Yes, even with Western or anyone else I bumped into, I'd try to be my old, easygoing self. All I had to do was remember not to break into tears. Simple enough—I hoped.

I found Clive Western in his office.

"You're looking jaunty," Western said from behind his desk.

"That's for the sucker trade," I admitted. "Actually, I'm a spent shell."

"You don't know the half of it, son. Frankly, when you first spun that dizzy yarn of yours, I thought it all a lot of eyewash, no more than a bad case of advanced whoop-de-do."

"A perfectly reasonable conclusion," I said, snaring a chair with my foot and seating myself.

"Thank you. So it seemed." He screwed up his eyes. "Nick Chester. Susan Ascher. Sam Noonen. Izzy Greenhouse. Norman Walsh . . ." He went on ticking them off, the Joes and Janes of my elusive past. "They're a fine bunch of upstanding citizens. Only one thing wrong with the lot—they have no present or future. A considerable handicap, you'll agree."

I agreed.

"Yes," Western said, "quite a tidy package. But a bit too neat, perhaps. It certainly strains the limits of credibility."

"Maybe we should both see a doctor?"

"My apologies. It did seem like a decent enough thought at the time."

"I'm sure."

"Tell me about Norman Walsh."

"Walsh? He was a senior op at the Morgan Confidential Agency. I put in about two years there some eight years ago. Morgan was never around much, but since he owned the joint, he could make his own rules. Walsh and two other guys, Izzy Greenhouse and Charles Spero, kind of ran the show. Should I go on or is that enough?"

"More or less. What did Walsh look like?"

"A short, burly character with lots of hair, a brown moustache and horn-rimmed glasses."

Western handed me a yellowish newspaper clipping. "Recognize the gentleman?"

A glance was all I needed. "That's the bird. And an obit, no less. It figures. Maybe I've got some terrible hidden disease that made them all croak."

"Perhaps. But you shouldn't neglect the ones who've merely vanished. Or never were."

"How could I?"

"Exactly. Well, as you can see, you have this Walsh down pretty pat. The description matches. As do the highlights of his life."

"That's something, I suppose."

Western raised a bony finger. "With one exception."

"Oh?"

"Yes. It's really quite a minor point," Western said. "I hesitate to mention it, in fact, but you might take a peek at the upper left-hand corner and see for yourself. Specifically, the date. Your man died three years before you came to the agency, son. There was no way in the world you could have known him."

I moved along the street. People went by. I paid them no heed; they were merely so much motion. I'd pulled it off, managed to hold up my end just long enough to get away from Western. So much for that. My good spirits had gone the way of the two-cent cigar and nickel shoe shine. I wasn't feeling any too well, that was for sure. The yellow and red brick buildings on either side of the avenue had suspiciously taken on the aspect of prison walls. Street lamps were crafty eyes that watched my every move. The creaking of horse-drawn traffic was a snide murmur about *me*. Old Mark Craig had really done it this time, gone completely bananas; next thing you knew, his brains would seep through his ears one night while he slept. His mind was as scrambled as an omelet

199

and just about as easy to put together again. Worse yet, he didn't have a solitary notion in his noodle how to handle this mess. Maybe it really *was* time to hustle over to the nearest hospital.

Maybe.

But a couple of small items kept nagging at me, pieces that didn't quite fit the ding-a-ling web that had sprung up around me:

Pat De Marco *really* was dead; the body I'd stumbled over this morning was no hallucination. *Someone* had done him in.

I still had a scar on my leg that I'd gotten jumping through a window. The faceless man had inspired my jump. Maybe *he* was a hallucination. But the scar, sure as hell, wasn't.

Maybe I had no past. And maybe Norman Walsh and I couldn't have worked in the same office. But he had lived *once,* the obit proved that. And my description of Walsh had fit him to a T.

Small points, but not entirely without merit.

The trouble was that none of these inspiring items added up to a hill of beans. Logic and reason had just laid an egg. And the rest of the mess was even worse. The world-shifting bit had to be pure nightmare, the work of a demented mind. *My* mind, unfortunately. Even if I cleared up the first part of my woes, the second part was sure to get me, put me away in a safe, quiet place for a good long time, if not permanently.

I had a cup of coffee in a greasy spoon and tried to think about absolutely nothing. It wasn't easy, but I managed.

Back on the street, I used a pay phone, dialed police headquarters. It took me a while to reach Nickerson.

"What's happening?" I asked.

"What ain't? You didn't give your name just now?"

"Uh-uh."

"That's good, 'cause there's a warrant out for your arrest."

"Warrant? You're kidding."

"Would I do that, pal?"

"I guess not. What's the charge?"

"Conspiracy."

"Who did I conspire against?"

"Assistant DA Gardner."

I sighed. "That figures."

"He says you and Charley Frost conspired to help Tim Yancy beat the jeweler's rap."

"He'll never make that stick."

"Sure, but think of all the fun he'll have tryin'."

I thought about it. Considering everything else stacked against me, this was child's play. Still, sometimes kids could cause a hell of a mess. "He stake out my office?"

"Uh-huh. Your flat too."

"Great. How long does this go on?"

"Not long. Gardner ain't got the manpower. Lay low for a couple days an' see a good mouthpiece; he'll straighten things out."

"Yeah. Thanks."

"Listen. Call me or Watts before you take up house-keepin' again at either of your hangouts. We'll give you the all-clear. If there is one."

"It's a deal," I told him.

"Right, pal. You're runnin' up quite a bill, but we got confidence in you."

"I appreciate that."

"Sure you do."

We said our good-byes.

I stood there and watched the crowd hurry along. Now what? This creep Gardner was trying to ruin my career. Little did he know that others had already beat him to it. Any other time, this thing would have me climbing the walls. Just now it didn't matter. I wasn't sure what did.

I got my wallet out and counted my dough. I had enough of the folding stuff to last me awhile. If worse came to worse I could always tap my bank account—provided Gardner wasn't there first.

Hopping a local coach, I went off to see my first Peter Grant. The city directory had had four.

Grant wasn't home, but his landlady described a tall,

skinny galoot and I went away satisfied he wasn't my man.

The second Peter Grant was a half hour away. He wasn't home either, but his wife and three toddlers were nice enough to show me his photo: a short, fat man with no hair at all. Two of the toddlers let go of my legs and I went away again.

Two Grants down, two to go.

The third was only fifteen minutes by coach. The horse team brought me to a quiet, tree-lined street. Small one- and two-family houses made this a special section—one populated by the rich.

I found the house without much trouble. No one answered my ring.

Next door, a middle-aged lady told me—after giving my Double M buzzer the once-over—that Peter Grant was a small, slender redheaded fellow with a pointy chin. I thanked her warmly, meaning every word of it, and hurried off to hide behind a tree across the street.

I cooled my heels for close to three hours before getting any results. Results came in the guise of two figures moving rapidly up the block. I watched them with interest, then amazement.

Peter Grant and Bridget Mercer turned into the house across the street.

I went after them.

CHAPTER 38

I resisted the temptation to ring the front-door bell and see what would happen. Probably I wouldn't like it—I'd had too much of that already; now it was someone else's turn; fair was fair.

I went around to the side of the house and peeked through a pair of windows. I was looking at an empty kitchen. I had no use for empty kitchens. I tried the windows to see if they would be more helpful. No dice. Locked tight as a drum. I continued around to the rear of the building, tried the back door. Locked, too. I decided against kicking it open and trotted off to the far side of the house. Here my efforts were instantly rewarded. My quarries were seated in the living room, across from each other, peacefully chatting away.

I ignored my wet, clammy hands; they were shaking so much they were bound to dry in no time. My legs felt like two worn rubber stilts. The old ticker sounded as if it were doing the ten-mile hurdles and losing. The thought of getting this close to what might be an answer had unhinged me. If I waited much longer I'd probably chuck the whole thing.

I brought my gun down against the windowpane, just above the latch, shattered it. I stuck my hand through the hole, turned the latch, raised the window, stepped in over the sill.

Grant and Mercer turned, stared at me. Amazement was on their faces.

Pointing my gun at the pair I said, "Surprise."

Bridget Mercer was the first to regain her composure. "What is the meaning of this, Mr. Craig?"

"That's what I'm trying to find out," I told her. Stepping over to Grant, I said, "You know me, don't you?"

"Mr. Grant is a member of my firm," Mercer said, as if that explained everything.

I said, "He can talk for himself, I hope."

"Certainly. You broke my window," Peter Grant said reproachfully.

"That's not all I'm going to break," I assured him, "if you two don't come up with some snappy answers." Sometimes the simple approach works best.

Grant turned to the woman. "He is insane," he told her.

"This is really intolerable, Mr. Craig," Bridget Mercer said.

"Damn right," I said. "Why were you following me, Grant?"

"Following you?" Grant seemed shocked.

"Two days ago, early afternoon, down by the Hall of Records; you were sticking to my heels like a piece of gum. I want to know why."

Grant tried to get to his feet. I put my palm against his chest, shoved him back into the chair. He sat there looking up at me, the first signs of fear on his face. "This must be some mistake . . . a terrible error . . . I have been engaged in a series of conferences all week . . . a new project, you understand . . . lunch was catered every day . . . I never set foot outside the office building . . . never . . ." His voice trailed off.

I glared at him, made my voice hard, contemptuous; it took hardly any effort at all. "And you never laid eyes on me before this minute, right?"

Confusion showed on his face. "No. Yes. I mean . . ." Peter Grant stopped, stared at me and shuddered. "Yes, Mr. Craig," he whispered, using my name for the first time. "I did follow you. I will not lie to you. Yet up to that day, I had never laid eyes on you, never saw you in the flesh. Only in a dream."

I stood there looking at him. I got this sinking feeling. The one that comes when you go down for the third and positively last time. I had come hunting facts. Now the guy was handing me another dream. If there was one thing I didn't need, it was another dream.

"And what about you?" I asked Bridget Mercer. "Did I pop up in some dream of yours, too? Is that why you came calling on me?"

"Have you actually taken leave of your senses, Mr. Craig? You were recommended to us, as I believe I told you. Now put aside that gun and tell us what this is about."

"I wish I knew," I said, sounding almost plaintive. "Okay, Grant, spill it; let's hear this dream of yours."

"It is awful, Mr. Craig, awful. The dream is totally

beyond comprehension. I have told no one of it, for fear they would think me mad."

"That I can understand," I told him sourly. I sat down in an armchair, let the gun rest in my lap. "Shoot," I said.

Grant said, "You and I are together in a room, Mr. Craig."

"Where is this room?" I asked.

"I do not know. It is, however, nowhere in Old York. In my dream, Mr. Craig, I never leave this room. But there is a window overlooking a street. It is nighttime, street lamps are lit. Our conversation seems to engross me totally. I pay no heed to what is outside that window. But periodically, dark, boxlike things on wheels roll by. They make noise which is similar to that found in factories. Yet I see no engines. Horses do not pull these boxes, Mr. Craig; they seem to move of their own volition."

I said, "You know my name from this dream."

Peter Grant nodded.

I sat and eyed the little man. This was the Peter Grant of York City. Only he didn't know it. In some goofy way, we were trapped in part of the same nightmare.

Grant was talking again. "We are in a room, Mr. Craig, and you are speaking to me; but we are never able to finish our conversation. In fact, I do not even know its contents. There is a pounding at the door. You reach for your gun. 'Who's there?' you shout. Machine-gun fire answers you. The door bursts open. Three men are there. All are armed—"

"Describe them," I said.

Grant described two pugs who might have been anyone or no one. The third character had a bald head, full lips, small piggish eyes. Lou Fox? It seemed a safe bet.

Grant continued his story. "You shoot once, a wild shot. One of the men raises his machine gun. Before he can fire, you turn, crash through the window."

Grant fell silent.

Bridget Mercer laughed. "I didn't know you had such an active imagination, Peter."

"It is a sickness," Peter Grant said.

I said, "What happened to you in the dream?"

"I don't know, Mr. Craig. This is where I always wake up."

"Can't say I don't envy you, Grant. At least you wake up sometimes."

CHAPTER 39

The express coach took me through the city. The whip cracked over the horses' heads, the coach pitched wildly from side to side. I both saw and didn't see the city outside. Whatever trace of attachment I'd once felt for this place was sinking fast, like a bottomless boat in a rough sea. This was strange, alien territory now. Even its inhabitants—including what friends and acquaintances I had—appeared distant, remote. Dr. Spiegel was right: Old York was too peculiar to be real. I grinned to myself. Here was a notion I could fully appreciate and even recommend to others. The more demented Old York appeared, the saner I might be by comparison. I wouldn't mind that at all.

The coach roared through the northeast city gates. I sat back and tried to relax—a commendable goal. But hard to achieve—it was going to be a long ride. Trees, bushes, small houses flashed by. I looked at my denim-clad fellow passengers: two men and a woman; they seemed real enough, but I couldn't even believe in *them* anymore. I'd become a total skeptic.

My chat with Peter Grant had changed everything and nothing. The redhead's cockeyed story rang true. Grant couldn't know it, but what he'd seen through the window

—the boxlike contraptions—were automobiles. *I* knew it, but no one else around here did.

I knew something else, too. Old York, with its coaches and telephones, fit into the history books like a sore thumb.

But York City made sense of a kind. At least there *could be* a York City; anyone who bet on Old York was a goner, bound to lose his shirt. Smart money would go the other way. And I was putting my two bits on the burg with mobile ramps and the Time Festival.

Too bad I was here and not there. Being here definitely put a crimp in my theory.

What I needed was concrete evidence; a little of that would go a long way. But a healed cut on my leg and a lot of dopey memories hardly qualified. Neither did a run-in with Assistant DA Gardner nor a wiped-out past. I wasn't quite sure what *did* qualify. Maybe nothing.

I got off at the last stop, transferred to another coach. This one was more crowded. We bounced and jostled along. Whatever confidence I had was vanishing fast, like a racetrack addict's paycheck. Too much guesswork. And the rest could be no more than an optical illusion, the visual counterpart of my mental troubles. There was no way to know.

Every now and again I glanced out the window. Valleys, small hills, a lot of trees, an occasional farmhouse. We were down too low for the view I wanted. I sat back and concentrated on biting my nails.

Karnap was a small one-block hamlet consisting of a bar, livery stable, general store, courthouse and jail. I stood on the narrow strip of asphalt paving. I looked up at the high hills which rose to the northeast of the town. Beyond those hills was my goal. Or, at least, a goal of sorts.

The man in the livery stable was tall, thin and cadaverous.

"Hello. Rent carriages?" I asked.

"Yep."

"Got any handy?"

"Nope."

"What about that one?" I pointed to the horse and buggy in the rear.

"Reserved."

"Expect another?"

"Uh-huh."

"When?"

"An hour."

"Okay, I'll be back."

"Maybe two."

"Got you."

I went outside and looked again at the hills. Nothing stirring. I ambled around the block for a while, collecting a couple of curious stares from the townsfolk, poked my nose through the door of the general store, avoided the jail house and finally settled for the bar. The whole thing hadn't taken more than five minutes.

"Some of the white," I told the barkeep. He was a short, rotund man in a white apron and smiling face. He brought me a hooker of gin. I put it down, shoved some change at him, asked for another and got it.

"Going visiting?" the barkeep asked.

"Uh-uh."

"Business then?" he said brightly.

"In a manner of speaking."

"Ain't much business around here. Sleepy little place, that's what we got. Dead as a doornail."

"Yeah. What's on the other side of those hills?"

The barkeep shrugged. "Nothin' much. Just a lotta grass and weeds. You got business out thataway?"

"Could be."

"Fixin' to buy yourself some farmland, eh?"

"It's a thought."

"Government owns that stretch. Bet you can get it for a song. Brought your own rig?"

"No. Waiting for a carriage."

The barkeep shook his head. "It'll be dark soon, mister. You won't be able to see a darn's worth."

I told him it didn't matter. The barkeep looked at me, put the bottle of gin on the bar top, told me to help myself but keep track of things, said I seemed an honest sort, and went away somewhere.

I was the only customer.

I took my bottle and shot glass over to a more comfortable table and chair by the back wall, sat down and let the minutes crawl by.

This could have been Frank's Bar at the Time Festival or any of a dozen in Old York. Maybe the one permanent feature everywhere was a bar. Or maybe my disordered mind liked to plant bars whenever it could. There was just a chance—a very slight one—that I'd find out in the next few hours.

After a while the barkeep came back. I left him a half-dollar and strolled out. The street was empty except for an old-timer seated on a stoop and a pair of kids tossing a ball around. I went over to the livery stable. A sign read: Back Soon.

The wide doors were closed. I tried them anyway. Locked. I stood around with my hands folded looking up and down the street. Nothing. I went back to the bar.

"Short trip," the barkeep said.

"Yeah," I said. "The carriage guy often take off?"

"Sometimes."

"For how long?"

"It varies, mister; he ain't exactly got a thriving business here. I mean renting those carriages. Doubles as our blacksmith, too, you know. That's where the money's at."

"I can imagine. What does he do when a real live customer comes along?"

"Shows up sooner or later, I reckon."

I went back to my table. "Some more of the white."

"Right-o."

I sat there nursing my drink, eyeing the window. It was dusty. No one passed by on the street outside. Presently shadows began to lengthen. I hadn't eaten much. The gin sent a warm tingle through me. It was cozy in here. I felt my eyes closing. I began to nod.

I dreamed I was with a guy called Ralph Olenger. He had pale skin and black hair. He was talking to me very earnestly—his lips moved and I heard sounds—but I couldn't understand a word he said. The dream seemed to go on a very long time.

The noise of a door opening woke me.

I opened my eyes, looked around the barroom.

Some small changes had occurred during my nap.

Dusk had turned to night outside. Only two street lamps glowed weakly on the pavement. One small light, up front, lit the barroom. I was seated in back by the wall. Dark shadows were everywhere. The four men who stood in the doorway were peering around them. The barkeep was nowhere in sight. There were still no other customers. My head, cushioned by my arms, was resting on the table. This made me invisible—for about another thirty seconds.

I had never been introduced to Assistant DA Bill Gardner, but I had seen him often enough. He was a round-faced, middle-aged character with sandy hair and a pot belly. Known as a mild, inoffensive assistant DA, he had always played the game, collected his money and kept his mouth shut. Till now, at least. Now, Gardner showed every sign of being a tiger.

He stood in the doorway, dressed in the dark purple denim of the DA's office, the same outfit worn by the other three men. Each of them was armed as though he was out on some kind of safari hunting wild game. There was no game here, of course, just me. I got the message. Gardner had a shotgun; his men carried handguns. I had, maybe, a second left. I used it.

Sliding my hand down under the table, I eased my gun out of its holster. I wouldn't have minded shooting all four of them, provided they didn't shoot back. Probably they would shoot back.,

Very slowly and carefully I took aim at the one bulb glowing over the bar.

Three shots had it in pieces. By then I was running for the kitchen door, doubled over as if I had the stomach plague. Behind me a symphony of gunshots was going full tilt.

I didn't look back to inspect the damage. I dived through the door and kept running. Using the butt of my gun I smashed a couple of bulbs in the empty kitchen; maybe it would slow them down. I left the place through a back door, moving fast.

No alleys were here, no backs of buildings. I was in the great outdoors under a star-filled sky.

I ran away from there.

Just going off in the night had its advantages—but not enough of them to save my neck. I needed some means of transportation to put distance between myself and the gun-happy assistant DA.

I sprinted along till I reached the end of the town's only block, doubled back up the main street.

The assistant DA's carriage was waiting for me in front of the stable. I got the horses loose from the railing, hopped aboard the rig, took hold of the reins and stormed out of town.

Shots rang out behind me. Soon the black night closed over me. I was on my way.

I used the dirt road for about ten minutes, then cut out cross-country.

I glanced behind me, saw only darkness. I figured it wouldn't take Gardner long to dig up the old guy who ran the stable and latch onto his auxiliary rig.

If it took any time at all.

Someone had tipped Gardner that I was here: the barkeep or the bird in the livery stable. One or the other. Maybe both. For all I knew, the whole town was in cahoots, keeping its eye peeled. The logistics of such an operation escaped me for the moment—like a lot of things lately—but I'd probably find out sooner or later. And hate it when I did.

Not that Gardner didn't fit a kind of weird pattern.

Whatever was fooling with me had left a watchman behind:

Gardner.

I was to be let alone. Unless I started nosing around, stirring things up. Then I'd be squashed like a bug. Gardner wasn't acting as assistant DA just now—uh-uh. He was chief executioner.

I looked over my shoulder again. Still no sign of company. Tracking me through the fields was no cinch. Maybe I'd managed to shake them.

One thing was clear: I was through in Old York, as used up as a charwoman's bargain washrag. The thought of striking out across the globe, penniless and maybe a fugitive to boot, didn't give me that needed lift I'd been counting on.

I glanced up toward the hills. Much nearer now, but nothing to see—yet.

Maybe never, a voice seemed to whisper in my ear. The voice of doubt. A voice based on reason and logic. Reason and logic would have to go by the boards.

This had to be the place.

A setup. Karnap was primed for my appearance—a booby trap if ever there was one.

But I'd made it through Karnap. And I was going even farther.

The sound of horses' hoofs, rolling wheels and creaky wagon springs blended with the night: crickets, animals, the wind rustling through trees and foliage. It didn't quite put me to sleep. Maybe I had things on my mind.

We began to climb.

The coach rocked from side to side; roots, branches, stones and ditches got in the way of our wheels. I vaguely thought of unhitching one of the nags, riding on bareback. Nuts. It was too much effort. I didn't mind the jolts—they gave me something real to hold onto.

The moon peeked out from behind a cloud, giving me a chance to see where I was going. The hill inched up at a lazy incline. It was a natural hill and not meant for wagons. Over to the right, clumps of bushes, trees. And something else. I stood up just to make certain. Sure enough: a dirt road.

I guided the buggy in that direction. Soon I was heading topward in relative comfort. I still could see nothing of interest above me.

A rifle shot cracked once.

Splinters went flying a foot from my head.

I ducked, yelled giddy-up for all I was worth and gave the horses their head. We took off lickety-split careening up the hill.

Five men stepped out of the darkness.

I didn't get to inspect them at close range as the carriage charged past, but none of them seemed conspicuously familiar. For people I had done nothing to, they were certainly itching for a scrap. I didn't stop to ask why. I fell back in the coach and huddled behind a seat. Bullets pelted the carriage walls. My horse team put on a burst of speed. We were going like nobody's business. Except for a few shouts and shots, the welcoming committee faded back into the darkness—where, for my money, it belonged.

The gunplay had all but ruined the carriage, but had done worlds for my spirits.

Someone had gone to a lot of trouble to see that I—or anyone—didn't reach the top of that hill. So I must be headed in the right direction.

The road twisted, turned a corner and I was on top.

I caught my breath.

Below me was a valley.

And the red haze spread like a glowing, twinkling blanket across its floor.

I started to point the coach down toward it—whatever I'd come to find was down there.

I never got that far.

CHAPTER 40

The red glow rose to meet me, enveloped me. The coach was gone. I was in a train hurtling through darkness. I tried to move. Some force held me. Other figures, blurred and indistinct, were in the car, too. Time seemed to be frozen. I couldn't breathe, couldn't think; I tried to scream.

The grind of wheels on rails seemed to wake me. Had I dozed? I looked out through the window. The train was pulling in at a station. Thick steam rolled past the window, partially covered the platform.

Brakes caught at wheels. The train shuddered. The engines seemed to cough. The train had come to a halt.

Doors cranked open.

The passengers began pouring out onto the platform. I got up on feet which seemed to belong to some chump too dumb to have rolled with the punches, and moved with the crowd. My brain felt as if it had been put through a meat grinder and then slapped, pell-mell, back into my skull. I stood on the platform swaying, listening to steam hiss from the engines, watching the backs of the crowd as they headed for the exit stairs.

Bold letters on thick columns spelled out: Grand Central Station.

I moved with the crowd as a sleepwalker might. I neither thought nor felt. I moved. I was lucky to do that much.

Outside I headed west, drifting along with the pedestrians. Two blocks behind me an el train roared by overhead. The York Time Festival had had one in a large gilt frame. If the sight dredged up any other stray thoughts in my faltering cranium, I failed to notice.

Square-topped cars rolled by in the streets. Wide running boards seemed to snatch at people as they raced against the traffic lights. Horns honked. Cars backfired. Bells clanged on the trolley cars. Double-decker buses lumbered by. Tumult was having a field day.

I lost all track of time. Time and I had fallen out of step. I walked in a daze-like stupor past small shops, gray office buildings, a conglomeration of blinking neon lights, flashing advertisements, jutting marquees. I paid no attention to where my feet carried me. I didn't know what

I was doing here. I had no notion where here was. I moved through the din like a man lost in his own private night.

Slowly, as if mist were rising over the pavements, laying them bare to me for the first time, I began to take stock of my surroundings. It was anything but night. A bright sun beat down coldly from a blue sky streaked with small white clouds. I had left the neon lights behind. I was in a residential section. The gutters were full of drying brown, red and yellow leaves. The trees were starting to look gaunt and desolate.

It was autumn then.

Shouting kids in knickers, peaked caps, kicked up the leaves, sent them swirling, played tag, catch, stickball. Clotheslines dangled between red brick tenements, held shirts, pants, white sheets, long johns. A horse-drawn ice wagon creaked by. The sound of radios came through half-open windows. A fruit and vegetable wagon had stopped on the corner of Ninth and 33rd.

I kept walking.

By now, the mental haze had all but blown away. I was beginning to remember. But the more I remembered, the worse it became.

York.

Old York.

The headlong swing into the valley of red mist.

And then nothing.

I'd figured the mist for some kind of bridge, one that connected York and Old York. Or maybe the other place—with its faceless thing and dead city. I'd spotted the red glown there. And the small redhead, Peter Grant, had described the same setup in York. Pat De Marco, Grant and myself were all displaced persons, lost in a two-cornered maze: York. Old York.

But this place was neither.

In a way what I saw resembled Old York. Only it wasn't. No trains in Old York. And the buildings had been dwarfs compared to what I saw here. I'd known the streets and back alleys of Old York pretty well. These streets were different, more like the ones depicted on the thirites strip in York.

But this was nothing like the thirties strip. I was in a real city here.

Where the hell was here?

I searched my pants pockets.

Empty as yesterday's dreams.

Dreams?

I could believe that. Already York, Old York were beginning to fade. Along with the train that had brought me to this place.

I didn't mind.

How could I ever have believed in any of it? It was all sheer delusion. As nutty as a gorilla doing the tango. I was—obviously—suffering from some terrible mental aberration. This time I'd do it: turn in at the first hospital I came to, find help while there was still time. *If there was still time.*

My decision cheered me.

Standing there in bright daylight, giving an ear to traffic, watching kids and grown-ups hurry by, seeing the garbage men at work with their long-handled brooms, made me feel almost chipper. Here was a friendly spot. Without faceless killers. Lunatic assistant DAs. Men who remembered things which never were. *At least I hoped so.*

I took a deep breath. The air smelled clean, fresh. I was probably part of this city. And as soon as my mind quit horsing around, I'd know who I was and where I belonged.

Up ahead I saw a newsstand. That would be my first stop. Maybe I couldn't afford a sheet. But I'd learn plenty just scanning its front page.

Ambling over, I nodded at the old duffer seated behind the stacked papers, glanced down. My eyes settled on *The New York Times*.

I grinned. Could you beat that? *New* York! I'd touched all the bases, it seemed. Old, new and in between. Too bad it meant nothing.

I started reading: Jimmy Walker was mayor. Lindbergh was making a ten-thousand-mile flight. Hoover was President and talking about peace hopes.

It was Thursday, September 19, 1929.

I looked closer, hunting for more tidbits of knowledge.

I didn't find them on the printed page. I couldn't even *see* the printed page. Something was happening to the newsstand. Or me.

"You okay, mister?" the old vendor asked.

I heard myself say yes. There was no truth in it.

The world was spinning around like a carousel with a juiced-up engine. Vendor, papers and newsstand were breaking some kind of record for locomotion.

I managed to stagger away.

I looked back and the newsstand was two blocks behind me. I'd covered ground, all right. But I was back where I'd started: as loony as a tanked-up jaybird. I thought I'd shaken the worst of it, cut loose from my world of nightmares.

No such luck.

Even now, on the sunlit early morning streets of New York, the derangement seemed to be going full tilt.

A second set of memories had begun to sprout up like weeds in an abandoned lot. I could recall walking these streets before, a shabby rooming house with a cracked window, an office in midtown. Great, huh? There was only one small hitch. The Mark Craig who belonged to these memories was a totally different person.

I sat down on a stoop, waited for my mind to simmer down. Any second now I was liable to go on a weeping jag. No one would blame me.

This new flood of memories was a bust.

I had learned just enough to know I was still crazy. But not enough to know what to do about it. Or how to get around this New York place.

I wondered if I'd bump into Pat De Marco, Peter Grant or any of my other pals from the "good old days." I wondered if there was a Mrs. Landry camping around here too somewhere, waiting to pounce. But most of all, I wondered what to make of these new memories, how to put sense into them. Nothing was clear. There were faces in my mind's eye, but the view was blurry. Things were happening, but I couldn't make out what. Names, dates and places were a jumble.

Thinking about it didn't seem to help any. The world outside had stopped jiggling like a jelly cake. That was nice. Inside, things had quieted down, too. No new data came to jog my memory. I had conjured up a mystery Mark Craig. And a mystery, it looked like, he would remain.

That wouldn't do.

I got to my feet. A cigar store was up ahead. That was as good a place as any to see how much Old and New York were alike. Inside, near the phone, I found the Manhattan directory I was hunting for. Only one Mark Craig was listed. He lived on 28th Street between Ninth and Tenth avenues.

I went back to the street, continued hiking. My feet had been carrying me in the right direction all along. Now I would finish the trip.

PART 6

The image of a person who had plunged into a black hole would remain—phantom-like—long after the person himself had thoroughly disintegrated.

from *The Notebooks of Dr. James Ingram*

CHAPTER 41

Mark Craig

The street sign said Ninth Avenue and 28th Street. I turned toward Tenth.

My legs felt heavy, as if someone had planted weights on them. I was breathing like a lunger in the terminal ward, hard and gasping. I wasn't looking forward to what I would find next. No use kidding myself. This Mark Craig and I could have nothing in common. He would probably be a little squirt of a guy, bald-headed and paunchy with a hammer-faced wife and a brood of squealing kids. Or a whopping fat man. Or a razor-thin bird with a long white beard. He could be a dozen different types. But none of them would be anything like me. Not a chance. So what was I doing here?

I stopped thinking about it. I stopped thinking about everything. I was too busy staring at the two-story, yellow brick building in the middle of the block. I didn't have any witnesses in my noggin. There was no way I could prove it. But this had to be the rooming house I'd pictured in my mind's eye, right down to the cracked window on the first floor. Not fifteen minutes ago. *Before I'd ever seen it.*

The mere sight would've shaken me up like a malted milk, if I wasn't in that condition already. As it was, I just stood there gawking at it like a teenager seeing his first nudie show at the local burlesque house. I wondered if that numb feeling would ever wear off. It did a second later, and I marched up to the building and rang the bell. It took guts.

I had no idea what I was going to say; I'd wing it and hope for the best. I had a notion the best might be none too good.

The door opened.

The woman who stood there was short, squat and somewhere in her sixties. She was white-haired and wore an apron. I didn't have to ask her name because I already knew it. Mrs. McCarthy was the landlady here. It just popped into my mind.

"Mr. Craig," she said.

I wagged my head at her, parted my lips to say something. Nothing came out. I was too stunned to talk. I felt as if someone had conked me over the noodle with a baseball bat.

"Land sakes, what are you doing home at this time of the day?" she asked.

A good question. I started to stammer out an answer. The trouble was I didn't have one.

"And ringing the bell, yet!" Mrs. McCarthy chided. "Now you haven't gone and lost your keys, Mr. Craig, have you?"

"Right," I managed to say in a choked voice. And tried to grin. Whatever came out on my face must have satisfied the landlady because the next thing I knew I was walking up the maroon-carpeted stairs hanging onto the banister for all I was worth. Mrs. McCarthy had gone back to the kitchen after hunting up a pair of duplicate keys for me. She hadn't offered to guide me, but then why would she? I was an old tenant, right? I didn't complain. I knew my room was on the second floor, first door to the right. It had just come to me out of the blue. I wasn't sure whether to slap myself on the back or start screaming. I decided to put off doing anything until I got some privacy. Feet that felt like last year's models brought me to the door.

I turned the key in the lock, pushed the door open and there I was. Only where?

One room. A bed covered by a rust-brown blanket. An old black dresser with a mirror over it. A flowered easy chair by the windows. That was all. It was enough. I remembered this room now as though I had lived in it all my life. But from where? I'd been in Old York yesterday. And a couple of days before in York City. *Or had I?* Maybe both had been so much baloney, the result of too much hootch or a knock on the bean—and *this* was the real McCoy? Could be. By now I was all set to acknowledge that *anything* could be. Why not?

I stood still and tried to remember more, hoping that some miraculous cure was in the works. No more came, as if some malign force had stuck a plug in my memory tank. The room was very quiet and I could see dust specks twirling in the sunlight which came through the lower half of the windows. I raised a window shade all the way, gazed out at more houses, trim backyards, some trees, a bit of foliage. That too fell into place. As if a picture had been suddenly reassembled in my mind. By now, though, I'd lost all confidence in my mind. All this meant nothing so far.

Abandoning the window, I began to frisk the dresser. A lot of starched, neatly folded shirts, underwear, socks. Under the socks, my fingers touched something. A bankbook, one in the name of Mark Craig. That was me, all right, I hoped. I flipped the pages to see how much I was worth. I stopped at the final figure and stared in open admiration. A cool twenty-five grand! How about that? I'd finally hit pay dirt—a world where I was flush. About time, too. If I could only stay put here, I'd be on easy street—a place I'd meant to visit long ago but never had the chance. Unless, of course, money had taken a nose dive here. I didn't even want to think about it. I had started to chuckle. Greed was making me simpleminded. Greed or hysteria.

I went back to shaking down the dresser. Under some sports shirts I came up with another bonanza: a key ring, a five-dollar bill, some loose change. I put these finds in a little pile on the dresser top and went to inspect the closet. Coats, suits, sport jackets, pants, two hats and a cap on the lower shelf, five sets of shoes. A gray cardboard box on the top shelf turned out to hold business envelopes and stationery. The address, in bold letters, was 160 East 53rd Street. The name over the address was Mark Craig. I went through some coat and pants pockets, but only turned up a few hankies.

I leaned up against the closet and took in the whole setup, slowly this time. I used my hand to wipe the sweat from my forehead. I didn't get it. The room was respectable enough, but hardly the place you'd expect a guy with my kind of dough to hang his hat. I closed my eyes and tried very hard to think back, to dispel the phantom worlds I'd been imagining and remember what I'd really been up to. Fat chance. Everything I'd seen so far seemed familiar now. But beyond that I'd hit a blank wall. I shrugged. Big deal. I was better off than I could recall ever being before. Maybe the pieces were really starting to come together. And before I knew it, I'd be back to normal—whatever that was.

I got a blue terry-cloth robe out of the closet, found some slippers under the bed and padded down the hall to the bathroom, where I hunted up my shaving mug and long-handled straight razor, shaved and showered. I spent some time eyeing a toothbrush that probably had my fingerprints all over it—Lord knows, it looked familiar enough—but ended up using tooth powder and my finger. Some things can go too far.

Back in my room, I got into fresh underwear, a clean pair of socks, a white shirt. I wrapped a stiff collar around my neck, climbed into a spiffy blue pin-striped suit, chose a blue and black tie, black shoes and a tan belted raincoat. I tried on a brown peaked cap and I was ready. As done up as royalty.

I gave myself the once-over in the mirror. Everything fit to a T. But then, why shouldn't it? I knew if I thought about it long enough, I'd probably come up with a reason. I didn't exactly feel like a million yet; more like twenty-five grand. But I had no kicks coming: it was all easy money. Too easy, maybe.

I pocketed my bankbook, locked up behind me, left

223

the house and strolled over five blocks to the address on the bankbook. The bank was there. I went in, put my John Hancock on a withdrawal slip, waited in line, handed it to the teller and waited for bells to start ringing. Instead, I was handed two C-notes. All but tipping my cap in gratitude, I left.

I had breakfast in a greasy spoon, shelled out two bits to a hobo on a street corner, caught a trolley to 50th Street, transferred to another, got off at Lexington Avenue and hiked the last three blocks. I stood across the street from 160 gazing up at the four-story brick building that housed my office. Sure, I seemed to remember it now, but somehow—like everything else I'd seen this morning—it seemed vaguely out of focus. I wondered why I recalled so little of what went on up there in my office. I could see myself sitting at a desk, going through some papers. But there was no knowledge in that. Maybe I was making the whole thing up?

Only one way to find out.

I started to cross the street. My gaze casually drifted to the building's front door.

And stayed there.

The man who had stepped through the front door was tall, broad-shouldered with thick black hair over a square, tanned face. He wore a gray suit, red and blue polka dot tie. Turning on his heel, he headed west.

The man was me.

CHAPTER 42

Alexis Rike

Alexis Rike crawled out of the sewer. It was a few hours before dawn. His guide, a pasty-faced individual, replaced the sewer top, glanced around hurriedly, whispered, "I go now," and went.

Rike moved off in the opposite direction.

The streets were dark, empty. Small, shuttered houses offered no lights at this hour. Sparsely placed gas lamps made dim yellow holes in the night.

Puriville stretched for miles, a living monument to man's yearning for simpler days. Rike knew each inch of this territory; headgear had imprinted it on his mind. But the knowledge did nothing to ease his loneliness. Already, he regretted his mission here. It could only end in ruin: at best, he would wander around these streets and learn nothing; at worst, the Puriville cops would land him, putting a swift end to his career as undercover man. Rike wished he had taken a Euphor with him; just one would have done worlds of good. But a Euphor in Puriville would have been a dead giveaway.

Rike wore gray pants, a gray jacket; his wallet held some Purivllle gray-backs, identification papers. That was all. Hardly enough to see one through, Rike thought. The whole thing seemed like madness now. A waste of time and effort.

He had intended to check in at a small hotel some five

blocks away, catch up on a few hours' lost sleep. Now he abandoned that plan. He would walk the streets, watch the sun come up over Puriville, try, once again, to become acclimated to this place. Eighteen years was a long time; too long, perhaps. Even with the headgear imprints, he still had a lot to learn . . .

Rike walked east. His footsteps echoed on the deserted sidewalks.

Puriville.

The city was a graveyard of lost hopes, of dreams curdled and gone sour . . .

Funny he should feel that way; his job hardly begun and already he felt spent and empty. He had hated it here in his youth; the narrow streets, dreary tenements, the gray *sameness* of everything. Why then this mood of loss, of misty-eyed nostalgia?

More and more he recognized the neighborhood. Even Puriville was capable of some change of scene. Here the streets had turned from drab, shuttered two- and three-story houses to dour, crumbling tenements. Rike almost smiled; the city fathers were bent on preserving the old ways, yet all they had really managed to capture was their poverty.

Rike turned a corner. Dilapidated five-story tenements. A barren, weedy lot. A burnt-out factory across the street. Nothing had really altered. It all looked incredibly old and worn down. But there was no mistaking the place. This was where he had lived after his parents had died. This was home. He went toward the building. It was still and black in the dark night. The gas street lamp lit his path; in the yellow light he felt the years wash away and the memories flood back.

He went through the front door of the third house from the left, climbed stairs. No light on the second floor. He groped his way up to the next landing. He stopped before a green-painted door. A single gas jet picked out the decal over the peephole: 3C. Below it a small card read L. C. Banning. Rike's knocking resounded in the stillness.

The man who came to the door had much more white

hair than Rike remembered. But his shoulders were still straight with no stoop to them. He was dressed in a brown robe over blue pajamas, a tall, thin man with a white moustache somewhere in his mid-seventies. He rubbed the sleep from his light blue eyes with an open palm.

He looked at Rike. No recognition showed in his face. Rike hoped it was just the bad light.

"Yes?" Banning said.

His full name was Lester Carmichael Banning, but his friends, Rike knew, had given him another one.

"Doc," Alexis Rike said softly.

Banning looked surprised. Leaning forward, he stared at the man who stood in the doorway. Recognition—mingled with disbelief—came slowly. "By God," Banning whispered. A grin split his face. Seizing Rike by the hand, he dragged him into the flat. "I can't believe it," L. C. "Doc" Banning said. "After all these years! It's you, Mark Craig, isn't it? It's you!"

CHAPTER 43

The Girl and the Golem

The Golem said, "Thank you for seeing me, Mr. Kessler."

"Quite all right, Mr. Meerlue; what can I do for you?"

"I am trying to trace the whereabouts of one of your former employees."

"Yes?"

"I represent the law firm of Golden and Schwartz."

"Of course."

"It is a matter of a will," the Golem explained. "A small sum is involved. But as they say, every penny counts." The Golem chuckled. He had on a three-piece, checkered brown suit and yellow tie. He chewed an unlit cigar.

Kessler nodded. "And who is this person?"

"Pat De Marco."

"What did he do here?"

"Security director."

"When was that?"

"1935."

"That shouldn't be too hard." Mr. Kessler pressed one of a row of ivory buttons on his desk. A secretary came through a wide door, was given instructions, went away and shortly returned with a manila folder which she laid on Mr. Kessler's desk. Kessler leafed through it. "H-m-m-m. Your Mr. De Marco resigned his post here at Norwood Chemicals May 16. I see he gave no notice. The only address we have, Mr. Meerlue, is from 1935. Perhaps he is still living there."

The Golem nodded. "Did a Dr. James Ingram ever work here?"

"I can check," Kessler said, "if you wish."

The Golem wished.

Again Kessler pressed a button, issued orders to his secretary. She returned presently, her hands empty this time.

Kessler turned to the Golem. "Never," he said.

"You've come to the right place, Miss Darling. Alexis Rike used to teach at City. Knew him well, in fact. You are a relative?"

"Yes," the girl said. Her blond hair was tied back by a red ribbon in a neat bun. Her smile showed very white teeth.

"He was with our chemistry department for six years," Dean Dropkin said.

The girl nodded. "I tried a number of private firms first. That seemed hopeless. No one had ever heard of

228

my cousin. But I knew he was an expert in his field and that he sometimes served as a consultant."

"I was unaware of that," Dean Dropkin said.

"Well, that's what my aunt told me."

"His mother is living?"

"Oh yes; a very spry seventy-eight."

"And she had no idea he was teaching here?"

"None. He stopped writing her years ago."

"How very strange."

"I decided to canvass the colleges in the area," the girl said. "Columbia. New York University. Yours was the third on my list."

"Blind luck," the dean said. "Paid off too—up to a point."

"I don't believe I understand." The girl crossed one leg over the other, revealing an ample, rayon-clad calf. She had on a wide-shouldered, dark navy-blue suit. Her blouse was red. She had put on lipstick for the occasion.

"Let me get Rike's file," the dean said. When he returned, he carried a blue folder with him.

"Alexis Rike," he said, "vanished off the face of the earth sometime in the latter part of May 1935."

"There was an investigation?"

"When he did not show up for classes, when we could not reach him by mail or phone, we called the police."

"My aunt never knew what had become of him."

"Neither did the police."

"What sort of a man was he, Dean Dropkin?"

"Retiring. Shy. Even timid. The last man in the world, Miss Darling, something like this might happen to."

"Old Pat? Sure I remember old Pat." The man winked at the Golem. He was short, stooped; two days' growth of beard coated his narrow face. He wore a peaked cap and an old army field jacket. "What's it worth to you, sport?"

The Golem slipped him a five. The man huddling in the doorway of the boarded-up grocery store pushed the five into a pants pocket with one hand, pointed with the other to a two-story wood building across the street. The Atlantic lapped at the Coney Island shoreline two blocks away. "He used to live right there, old Patty did, right on the ground floor."

"And what became of him, sir?" the Golem asked.

"Old Pat, he moved on, he did. He rose in the world."

"Then he is still alive?"

"Alive, sport? What kinda question is that? Of course he's still alive."

"Ah!" The Golem beamed. "I am gratified to hear that. What, specifically, does he do?"

The man laughed. "Old Pat, he's got his finger in a lotta pies. But if you asked for just one thing, I'd say the food business, that's what I'd say."

"And what aspect of the food business would that be, my friend?"

"The black market, sport."

"Indeed," the Golem said. "How may I communicate with Mr. De Marco?"

"Now that ain't easy, I'll tell you. Not for the likesa you and me, it ain't."

"Mr. De Marco secludes himself?"

"Now that's a hot one, sport. Listen. Old Pat, he's a busy guy. He got a lot on his mind, old Patty does."

"Yet, I trust, he *can* be reached."

"You can try."

"And how would I go about doing that little thing?" The Golem sounded exasperated.

"I'll tell ya, just hold your horses. Listen. You go to the Surf-side Saloon. You get me, sport? That's on Surf Avenue, three blocks over. You go between ten and eleven at night. You ask for Mike, see?"

"Mike."

"Yeah, sport. Mike. For the right price, he can get you a steak, maybe. Or anything else you want. You ask him nice, maybe he'll pass the word on to old Pat."

"He works for Mr. De Marco?"

"Yeah. But it ain't like they're thick or somethin'. Old Patty, he's a big man now."

Night and fog hid the Coney Island boardwalk. The smell of salt water rolled in over Surf Avenue. Streetlights were dimmed. Shades pulled. Neon lights extinguished. The city was in semidarkness. Fear of enemy bombing had doused its glow. *Thank Your Lucky Stars* with Eddie Cantor was playing in the darkened Surf-View Theatre on the corner. A bell sounded somewhere out to sea. The girl stepped through the door of the Surf-side Saloon.

The bar was crowded with women, middle-aged and elderly men, a couple of young 4Fs. The girl asked the bartender, "Is Mike here?"

"The fat guy at the corner table, lady."

The girl made her way to Mike's table, seated herself.

Mike was a large, pasty-faced fat man in a wrinkled white shirt. Sparse black hair was slicked back over a glistening scalp. "Whatsit gonna be, miss? You name it, I got it."

The girl put a white-gloved hand into her purse, withdrew a fifty-dollar bill, pressed it into the palm of the fat man. She said, "I want to send a message to Pat De Marco."

The fat man shrugged. "Go ahead, miss, you tell me, I tell it to the right party. Maybe Mr. De Marco gets it. Maybe he don't. When it comes to the boss, miss, I can't guarantee nothin'."

"Tell him it's about Dr. James Ingram. Tell him there's a large sum of money involved. For him."

"How large? He'll want to know."

"Ten thousand."

"Okay. What name should I give him?"

"My name doesn't matter."

"He know you?"

"I don't think so."

"How do I get back to you, miss?"

"I'll be here tomorrow, same time."

"That's good," the fat man said.

Twenty minutes after the girl had left, the fat man crushed a cigarette against a black ashtray, rose ponderously to his feet, waddled over to the coat rack, wrapped himself in jacket and long wool coat and stepped out into the chill night air. He headed south. The Golem slid out of a doorway, began trailing after him.

CHAPTER 44

From the Diary of Dr. James Ingram

May 14, 1935. The voice has become a shout and the dream has turned bright red. Have I become unhinged? I must disregard everything but the work at hand. There is no way to encompass the Prime in my equations. I have begun to doubt the dream's veracity. I move ahead with my original plan.

CHAPTER 45

Mark Craig

I stood there, out in the middle of the street—about as mobile as an ice cube—staring at the receding back of my double. Cars swerved around me, pedestrians were busy giving me the eye and lip. They could have saved themselves the trouble. I was too far gone to lift a leg. I had managed to take world hopping in my stride; except for an occasional bout of depression and the screaming mimis, I was almost human. But there was something about seeing myself stroll down the block that I could've done without.

The traffic stopped for a red light, I got my legs moving again and managed to navigate across the street.

By then the other me was gone.

I thought of chasing after him, but I didn't have the stomach for it. Besides, the way I was feeling now I couldn't've caught my own shadow.

Get hold of yourself, Craig, I said to myself earnestly; maybe you were imagining things. Maybe this was someone else. You've got a pretty active imagination, you know.

Active? Demented is more like it. Nice try, Craig old buddy, I told myself, but it won't wash. If there's one thing after all these years I can recognize, it's me. And that, brother, was me.

No doubt about it, I'd gone around the bend for sure. But so what? I'd been doing it so often lately I might have been riding a merry-go-round.

I chuckled to myself, a low plaintive laugh with just that touch of nuttiness that comes before total madness. People were starting to look at me. That's all I needed, a lot of attention.

I pulled myself together. I'd come here to inspect my office. Just because I shared it with another me was no reason to change my mind now. In fact, it might prove even more interesting this way.

I went into the building. The wall directory had me on the second floor. I used the stairs. One of the keys I'd found in the other Craig's flat let me into a stuffy, one-room office.

I looked around, and again it was as if I'd spent my whole life here. *I knew this place.* And, maybe, with a little luck, I'd even find out what went on here.

Another key opened a green metal filing cabinet. The

desk drawers weren't even locked. Sheets of paper, singly and clipped together, of various sizes and colors were waiting for my inspection. As an old Double M—even if it was in another world—I knew what to do. I got busy doing it.

Three quarters of an hour later, I'd learned a couple of things and could guess at a few more.

My look-alike owned a piece of a trucking line. The trucks carted things across state lines, like bottled soft drinks, breakfast cereal, furniture. The cargo seemed innocuous enough. Like the toys in a kiddy's playpen. It wasn't. Al Capone and Bugs Moran were just some of the names I turned up. My jaunt through York City's Time Festival had filled me in on these two birds. At least, a little. I seemed to remember more now, none of it very pretty. A newspaper clipping and photo showed police raiding a speakeasy—the Half Smile. One Lou Fox, the story said, was being held for questioning. Lou Fox was the man Peter Grant had told me about. I looked at the photo: a fat, bald-headed guy with small piggish eyes. A real beaut.

I put everything back in its place, relocked the filing cabinet and office door and went back down the stairs into the street.

The Mark Craig who could have been my twin brother but wasn't was some kind of a crook. There was no explaining this Mark Craig, or anything else that had happened to me. But maybe I could find out something about Lou Fox. And through Fox, something about me. I'd like that.

I went down three stone steps and rapped my knuckles against a thick wooden door with a peephole in it. After a while an eye looked out at me from the peephole, a lock clicked, the door swung open.

"Hiya, Mr. Craig." He was a slender man with a long nose, deep-set eyes and short black hair. He wore a blue vest and striped shirt; his pants were neatly creased and his black shoes had a gleam to them. I looked at him. And knew his name was Charley Hooker. I was positive.

Knowledge of this sort should've had me doing a jig. Instead, it took everything I had to keep from turning tail and beating it down the block. The damn thing was giving me the shakes.

Nodding, I stepped past Hooker, went into the Half Smile.

It wasn't open for business yet. All but three lights were off. Chairs were stacked on tables. A bartender was straightening up behind the bar. The windows were covered by heavy curtains. The entire joint seemed to be decked out in an artificial night.

"I want a word with you, Charley," I said. I tried to keep my voice level, matter-of-fact; it was no one's business that inside I was turning to instant jelly. I hoped Hooker and I were, at least, buddies.

"Sure, Mr. Craig." Hooker grinned, showing long white teeth. "What can I do for you?"

"I've got a few questions," I said. "Think you can come up with some answers?"

Hooker shrugged. "Try me."

We sat down at a table near the soft glow of a pale lamp.

"Tell me what you know about Lou Fox."

Hooker screwed up his eyes. "Fox?"

"Uh-huh."

"Aw, come on," Hooker grinned, "what's the gag? *You* know Lou better'n me, Mr. Craig."

"Let's say I don't."

Hooker chuckled. "That's goofy."

"So kid me along."

Hooker stopped grinning, took a close look at me, then shrugged. "It's your show."

Hooker waved away the barkeep, who had started over, and for the next half hour regaled me with the sleazy tale of Fox's crookedness: the bald-headed fat man was a kingpin in the numbers racket, a veteran of the gang wars, a rumrunner. The other Craig was somehow cronied up with Fox. At the moment, our subject was stowed in the state pen on an assault rap which he might or might not be able to beat on appeal.

Hooker was done. "Want anything more?"

"Uh-uh," I said. "Thanks." I was tempted to ask about *me,* but common sense and prudence dictated against it. Enough was enough.

"Why this third degree?" Hooker asked.

"Just checking what's public," I told him, "and what isn't."

"Like that, huh?" Hooker said, looking skeptical.

"Yeah."

"That's jake by me." Hooker lit a Fatima, motioned to the barkeep.

"What's your poison, gents?"

"Some barley broth," Hooker said.

"Make that two," I said.

The barkeep brought whisky.

Hooker drank, said, "You hear about Bugsy and Scarface bein' on the outs?"

I ducked my head noncommittally.

Hooker grinned. "You buyin' that, Mr. Craig?"

"Maybe."

Hooker waved an arm. "That's the bunk. All this row talk is for the rubes."

"Yeah?"

"Take it from me, Mr. Craig, they'd be chumps to wrangle now. Together they're sitting pretty. The other way, it's a cinch one of 'em takes the fall; maybe both."

I shrugged.

"Listen, Mr. Craig, it's in the cards; you watch. Bugsy and Scarface on top of the world—like duck soup."

Some world that would be, I thought gloomily. I rose to go. "Thanks. I'll be seeing you, Charley."

"Sure thing," Hooker said.

I left.

The Time Festival at York City had told a different story about Bugsy and Al. They'd been at each other's throats for months now; their feud would end up in the St. Valentine's Day massacre. But Hooker had them working hand in glove. Maybe the Time Festival was just so much hot air. I didn't know. I was no better off than before. Nothing I had learned could explain the why or how of my twin selves. Or anything else for that matter. The other Craig would get home sometime tonight and find out a guy who looked like him had run off with his bankbook. There'd be hell to pay. I could go up against him then. Or do a fast fade. Or maybe just keep prowling around. I could do a lot of things, but what good would it do?

I'd been giving my legs a workout, while I tried to think up something smart. Smart had managed to elude me completely. My legs felt brittle, like dead branches. My clothing was sticking to me like flypaper. The buzzing in my ears sounded like a permanent short circuit. I called a halt to my wandering, looked around to see where I was.

Times Square.

Crowds. Noise. Blinking lights. Sputtering traffic. Grimy tall buildings. One hell of a place to have ended up. Casually, I raised an eyeball skyward.

Far off to the north, the sky was a bright red.

I gazed at it too tired even to react. Around me people were going about their business as usual. Only I could see the flames rising a mile high. Nothing strange in that. The red mist had come to a boil.

Two blocks over I caught an el. The train rattled along over the city. The flames rose and fell in huge sweeping waves. Sides of buildings and rooftops reflected bright red. Inside the car, passengers stared dully out of sooty windows or into space. Some leafed through newspapers, the *Daily News,* the *Graphic,* the *Herald Tribune.*

The train took a curve away from the flames. I got off, went hunting for another el headed in the right direction. The fire was always there to guide me. I changed trains twice more before reaching it.

A towering ball of flame spread over what looked to be half a mile. Adjoining trees, cars, houses should have been nothing more than blazing heaps of rubble. Any living thing caught inside those flames should have been reduced to charred meat. No such thing happened. Everything stood as before. This was a frozen flame, one that only I could see.

What did I have to lose?
Slowly I walked into the fire.

CHAPTER 46

Alexis Rike

Doc Banning was talking, pumping Alexis Rike's hand, squeezing his shoulder and taking his jacket all at once. Then they were in the living room and Rike was seated on the couch. Doc put a big glass of liquor in Rike's hand, drew his easy chair up closer, lit his pipe.

Rike could not taste the whisky, but he could feel it burning down his throat and chest. He could feel the steel springs in the old couch under him. He could see Doc's lips moving and hear his voice, but he could make no sense of his words.

Aleixs Rike shifted.

Nothing had changed in the room. Doc Banning still puffed on his pipe, leaned forward eagerly.

Rike reached under his shirt, removed the package. The brown paper was soggy in spots from his perspiration. He leaned far over and dropped it on the lamp stand next to Banning.

Lamp stand? Something seemed to tug at Rike's mind, a mere wisp of thought. *There had been no lamp stand here an instant ago.* The thought vanished.

Alexis Rike was only twelve years old.

Smoke rose from Banning's pipe. When he spoke, his voice was an echo. "I don't want it, Mark."

"It's a gift," Rike said brightly in his high-pitched child's voice.

Banning's voice was a scream: *"Take it away!"*

His face and body were thinning out, growing longer; he was beginning to waver as though a strong wind were shaking him.

"You don't understand," Rike said. He reached over. His hand clutched the package. He began to remove the wrapping. "I'll show you."

"No! No!" Banning's voice screamed. His body may have become elongated, but smoke still curled peacefully from his pipe.

Elaine, Doc Banning's niece, ran into the room, her long golden hair trailing behind her. She was only nine years old. Tears streaked her cheeks. She made a grab for the package. Rike held it out of reach. Laughter came from his mouth. He pulled the last of the wrapping away. Rike's laughter and Banning's screams filled the room like steam escaping through a broken pipe. Elaine's eyes were round coins. She clawed at Rike's arm. He shoved her away, sent her spinning off through the open doorway.

The screams and laughter had died. The body and face of Doc Banning, impossibly thin, fluttered like wind-blown wash on a clothesline. In the silence, the paper wrapping fell to the floor with a sound like crackling flame.

In his hand, Rike held a book, a small hardbound volume. The binding was dull red leather and the title was stamped in gold on the spine. Rike couldn't read the title. Smoke was suddenly filling the room. Red flames shot up from the carpet, covered the floor. A man stood in the doorway. His hat was pulled down low over his forehead, his coat collar turned up. Both hands were jammed into his coat pockets. Stepping through the flames he began moving toward Alexis Rike.

Rike shifted.

He was still in the room. Banning was back to his normal size. No sign of the fire. Elaine had not returned. The man in hat and coat was gone.

The book lay on the end table.

Doc reached for it. "There's got to be something here," he said.

"What?" Rike heard himself ask in his child's voice.

"I don't know, Mark." He was thumbing through the book. "Blueprints of some kind. And writing. A scientific treatise, it says. Gobbledegook. What good is all this? As dry and dusty as old bones. There's nothing here to even interest a junk peddler."

"There's got to be," Rike said.

"We'll see." Banning held the straight razor in his hand. He swung the gleaming blade free from its ivory handle, spread the book face down. The leather on the spine opened up like the belly of a fish under the sharp steel. Banning peeled it away from the stiff cardboard covers inside and out. There was nothing there.

Nothing.

"Who gave you this, Mark?" Banning asked.

"Norman Walsh," Rike said.

"Who?"

"He's a senior op at the Morgan Confidential Agency. He said it was important."

Banning nodded. He sat back in his chair, absently flipping the pages. Lifting the book, he held it near the lamp so the light shone through.

Nothing.

He went back to the text, his brow wrinkled, his mouth moving silently as he read. After a while he gave it up.

Nothing.

Then the flames were all around them, licking at the walls. The book was on the end table again. Banning was stretched out like a long piece of spaghetti. The man in the hat and coat was coming toward Rike.

Alexis Rike could see his face.

A long, crooked nose. A brown moustache. A furrowed brow. Black lines under gray eyes.

It was Fuller, the man who worked for "the Agency," who wanted him to kill a senator and blame it on the Reds. *What was Fuller doing here?*

The face changed.

It was Gaius Sabinus, the colonel of Caligula's guards who was in the dungeon for plotting to kill the mad emperor.

The face changed again.

The nameless monk of the monastery, bald-headed, thick-lipped, was staring at Rike with small, piggish eyes. His face began to melt.

He was Gorbach. Red hair, glasses, a pointy chin. Gorbach was Joseph Berg. But Berg was someone else. Rike remembered the square in plague-ridden Athens, the small redhead in a group of people he had wanted to avoid.

Gorbach's face was gone. Through the smoke and roaring flames Alexis Rike saw his own face coming toward him.

And remembered.

He knew what the blueprints in the red leather volume were. He knew that the title stamped in gold on the book's spine read: *The Notebooks of Dr. James Ingram.*

The man with Rike's face was very close now. He stretched out his hand toward Rike. Only an inch separated the two.

Rike shifted.

Alexis Rike, full-grown, was walking down a street. He was dressed in denims. It was nighttime. A single neon light glowed red far off in the darkness, spelled out Eat. A bearded hobo slept in a doorway. A block away, a thin, angular woman in a tattered raincoat stopped under a street lamp, a bulky sack hanging over her back. Rike could hear the clatter of a wagon sounding from some side street.

Rike turned a corner and found himself on Linebrook Avenue, an ill-lit, dour block of hulking brick buildings. This was the warehouse district, a no-man's-land whose interiors belonged to musty cartons, unswept floors, barred windows and padlocked doors.

Rike went down a narrow alleyway, stopped at the rear of 192 Linebrook. The beam of his flashlight found the wires he sought. A pair of rubber-handled shears cut them. The alarm was dead. Next, he set to work on the two locks.

A picklock opened them. Pushing in the door, Rike found himself in a musty corridor. Stairs took him down to the basement. The building personnel should be long gone. Rike located the light switch; an overhead bulb began to glow.

A door opened down the hall. Brighter light spilled over the floor. A voice called out, "Who's there?"

Soundlessly, Rike stepped behind a column.

A tall man in uniform—the night watchman—stepped out of the lit room, a gun in his hand. Alexis Rike stood very still. The watchman moved slowly through the basement, past Rike's column, his eyes darting in all directions.

Rike tiptoed out from behind the column. Three steps and he laid a sap against the back of the watchman's ear. The watchman folded. Rike dragged him back to his room, helped himself to his key ring and locked him in.

Alexis Rike began a methodical search of the basement. Some thirty minutes later, he had found nothing.

The elevator took him to the top floor. Using the watchman's keys, he let himself into one room, then another. Blinds covered the windows. Nothing would show in the streets below. He flipped on the lights as he worked his way through the building.

He found the door on the third floor. It appeared to be a closet. He opened it.

A long, dark tunnel stretched before him. Alexis Rike stepped through and began to run down the tunnel.

Behind him the door swung shut.

Old York was gone.

CHAPTER 47

The Girl and the Golem

The Golem sat patiently in an all-night diner. From time to time he took a sip of coffee from his cup. It had grown quite cold. The Golem didn't mind. He sat by the plate glass window staring idly into the dimly lit street. Faint light shone behind a drawn blind on the second floor of a squat, four-story brick building across the street. The jukebox played "Comin' In on a Wing and a Prayer." The Golem did nothing when the second-story window went dark at a quarter to one. Presently, three men emerged through the building's front door. Each went his way. The largest of the three had been Mike, Pat De Marco's henchman. The Golem put a nickel down on the table, left the diner, crossed over to the building. The front door was locked. The Golem pushed. The door snapped open. The Golem closed it quietly behind him, turned right at the stairs, climbed two flights. The third door in the left corridor said: Lumbard Social Club. The Golem placed a hand on the knob, leaned a shoulder against the door. Wood splintered. He stepped into a darkened office, snapped on a desk lamp, seated himself. The desk drawer was locked. The Golem pulled. The drawer ripped open. The Golem found Pat De Marco's name, address and phone number in a black address book under the initial D. He neglected to jot it down; he would remember. The Golem rose to leave. A tall, husky man stood in the doorway. "You ain't goin' nowhere, mister!" the man said. The Golem moved toward him. "You asked for it, buddy." The man made a fist, swung at the Golem's head. Fist and head connected. The man let out a yelp. The Golem casually lifted him off his feet, tossed him across the room. The man landed in a heap, didn't bother getting up. The Golem went away.

The girl said, "Mr. De Marco."

Pat De Marco sat bolt upright in bed.

Moonlight made long rectangles on the bedroom walls. Outside, ten stories below, the half-darkened street lamps of Fifth Avenue were indistinct smears in the night.

Pat De Marco said, "What?"

The Golem snapped on his flashlight. De Marco's face was framed in a white circle of light. De Marco squinted, thrust a hand up to shield his eyes. The light died as suddenly as it had appeared. "You may relax, Mr. De Marco; we mean you no harm."

"We want to know about Ingram," the girl said.

"Ingram?" De Marco snapped. "What kinda crap is this? Listen, you punks, you askin' for trouble, you'll—"

"Mr. De Marco," the Golem said, "you are hardly in a position to threaten us."

"We're only interested in Ingram," the girl said. "We want to know what happened. That's all."

"You have our word, sir," the Golem added.

"Who are you, jokers?" De Marco said.

"Friends of Ingram," the girl told him.

Pat De Marco peered into the darkness. "You're the dame who was askin' to meet me?"

"Yes."

"Hell. This is for the birds. What's wrong with you creeps? I was gonna see you tomorrow, lady."

"This way is simpler," the girl said.

"Yeah, for who?"

The Golem said, "What was your role in the Ingram affair, sir; how did you become part of it?"

De Marco sneered, "You clowns really take the cake. You bust in here in the middle of the night and start yappin' about this Ingram nut. You know when that was? I ain't thought of the jerk in years."

"You may make up for that omission now," the Golem said.

"Wise guy," De Marco said. He settled back against his pillow. "How'd you tag me? You tell me *that* and maybe I'll spill the rest of it."

"Mark Craig," the girl said.

De Marco grinned. "Sure. Who else. Okay, I'll give you what I got. And a fat lot it is. I was with Norwood. You know that much?"

"Indeed we do," the Golem said.

"Well, I was security chief. This was in '35."

"Ingram was never at Norwood," the girl said, "was he, Mr. De Marco?"

"Nah," De Marco said. "Up till I was braced by this Olenger, I ain't never heard of Ingram."

"Ralph Olenger?" the Golem said.

"Jeeze," De Marco said. "How'd you tumble to that?"

"We are acquainted with the general situation," the Golem said.

"Yeah, so what're you pumpin' me for?"

"Why, to get the complete picture, of course, Mr. De Marco," the Golem said.

"Uh-huh, if you say so, pal. Anyway, this Olenger guy pops up in my office one day."

The girl said, "He wanted you to hire a private detective agency to spy on Dr. Ingram."

"Right as rain, lady."

"You were to make up a story," the girl said.

"Yeah, a cock-and-bull yarn that this Ingram was maybe cheatin' on Norwood. What's your racket, buddy? I ask him. He won't say. What's in it for me? I ask. This guy takes a roll outta his kick that could choke a horse. We talk scratch. This Olenger comes through with a bundle. You can bet I make the deal."

"You went to Ace," the girl said.

"I done business with 'em before. Craig got the case. I strung him along like Olenger said, fed him a line. And that was that. The Ace boys poked around; Craig sent me the reports and I passed 'em on to Olenger. Then the fire and this Ingram got fried. Olenger never showed no more. But his dough came in handy. Tha's what set me up in the rackets. Okay?"

"There is perhaps one more item," the Golem said. "You were in Ingram's house the night of the fire, were you not, sir?"

"Big deal. What about it?"

"Why?"

"Why not? I wanted to know the score. Wouldn't you, pal? This Olenger was shelling out plenty."

The girl said, "You began watching Ingram yourself."

"Sure. I figured maybe I could get a slice of the pie—if there was one. I rented a room in that dump. Ace was okay, but me, I'm better, right? Forget it. I didn't learn beans. Maybe I shoulda put in more time on it, ah? So who's got that much spare time? How'd you make me at that fire?"

"You were seen coming out of the building by one of the Ace operatives," the Golem said. "Harry Henderson. He recognized you."

"Henderson, ah? Can you beat that? Listen—"

De Marco closed his mouth, squinted into the darkness. The man and woman had been vaguely discernable in the moonlight an instant ago. Now he could see nothing.

Pat De Marco groped for the lamp on his nightstand, clicked it on.

The room was empty.

CHAPTER 48

Mark Craig

I was riding a roller coaster. There was nothing above me, nothing below me. Just the soaring flames. I was the only passenger on board.

A booming voice coming out of nowhere kept repeating: "I am Dr. James Ingram. I am Dr. James Ingram." I didn't know any James Ingram.

That voice was really too much. Everything was too much!

I'd done it this time, put the skids under me with a capital S, gone from hideous to unendurable in one easy step.

I closed my eyes tight, put hands over my ears, tried to block everything out. I wanted just one thing—for the flame and tumult to go away.

Something seemed to shift.

I opened my eyes slowly, cautiously, as a patient might after a delicate eye operation.

The flames were gone.

I was back in the train. The one of my nightmare.

Again the darkness pressed in against the windows like a sea of black ink. The wicker seat rocked under me. Engines roared. I could smell old cigarette butts, stale air. The overhead light cast a pale sickly glow through the car, over the other passengers who still had their backs to me.

I had been to weak to move the last time I'd been here. But not now. My loop-de-loop jaunt through Hell should have squeezed me dry like a used lemon. Left me as played out as a cadaver. Only it hadn't—another one for the books. Waves of raw energy were pulsing through me. Something had turned on the juice. I was a live wire. I was ready to take on worlds. Too bad there was only the train and the scattering of passengers up front. I'd make do somehow. I got to my feet, glanced around. Sure enough, the cars behind me and up ahead were both empty. My options were shrinking fast like a block of ice left out in the desert sun; in an instant there'd be nothing left.

I settled for a chat with my fellow riders before they took off, too.

The first one I reached was Peter Grant.

I called his name. No answer.

I stood looking down at the little redhead. I looked closely. Glasses. Pointy chin. Small hands folded neatly in his lap. It was all there. Only one thing wrong, in fact. Peter Grant wasn't breathing. He might have been a plaster cast for all the life that was in him.

Reaching out, I put a hand on his shoulder. My hand went right through him. As it would through smoke. I yanked it back as though I'd touched a burning stove.

I stumbled up the aisle.

I was all alone. None of this was real. I was trapped here forever!

I stopped, leaned up against an empty seat; *it* seemed real enough. I took a deep breath; hot air stung my nostrils. I waited awhile and slowly began to simmer down.

Things could be worse; they had been only a minute ago.

I could go to pieces later. The thing to do now was look over the rest of this crew. The effort would cost me nothing. Nothing was a price I could afford to pay.

I'd known Grant was here because back in my nightmare—or whatever it was—I'd spotted his reflection in the train window.

But who were the others?

A couple of steps brought me an answer.

Bridget Mercer, for one.

Some surprise. She'd been farther away, less distinct than Grant. But her black hair and glasses had been a dead giveaway.

The green-eyed blonde next in line was a stranger. So was the chubby guy with the checked suit and cigar seated next to her.

I walked on.

Pat De Marco.

Another sure bet. He'd popped up in both York and Old York, hadn't he? That made him somebody. The little guy sat staring out the window. Just as if he were really alive and there was something to see.

The next three were all strangers.

One was a tall, skinny galoot with white hair and a white moustache.

A heavy-set guy with a wide nose, gray hair and a small scar on his left cheek was a few seats away.

The last of the trio was a slender lad in his late thirties. He had sharp delicate features, green eyes under heavy lids, thick black hair parted on the right.

I had no idea what to make of them, didn't know where they fit in. But then, I didn't know where *I* fit in, either, did I?

The last group was something else again.

I'd never met the short, fat man with the bald head and small piggish eyes. But I knew who he was, all right. I'd seen his picture in a newspaper in the other Craig's office:

Lou Fox. Capone's stooge.

The bird next to him had come out of my dream. I'd been in Karnap, a jerkwater burg some miles from Old York. I was waiting for a rig to carry me to the red haze. I'd fallen asleep and this pale-skinned guy had spoken to me in a dream. I'd even known his name—Ralph Olenger. That's all I'd known.

The pair at the end were even more familiar.

One was Emma Landry, the old crone from my nightmares.

The other was me.

After a while I got tired of just standing there and went over and tried the car door. It wouldn't budge. As if it'd been spitefully soldered to the wall. I peered through the grimy window: cigarette butts, bits of refuse littered the floor. Nothing to write home about.

I ambled back to the Mark Craig spook. That got me nowhere.

I walked down the row of seats with their worthless cargo and wondered if I was better off now than in the flames.

I stopped in front of Peter Grant. The little guy with the dreams. He'd sure had plenty. In York and in Old York. And judging by the setting, some of them were about New York. He'd managed to touch all the bases, it seemed. I'd been right along with him in his dreams. Yet I hadn't known him from a hole in the wall.

Was there any clue in what Grant had told me?

I tried to remember the dreams. The first one had been somewhere in the country, hadn't it? Grant and I were running . . .

I was standing in the woods. The train was gone. I was alone. I could see a clearing through the trees. Dry leaves were on the ground. It was autumn. Two figures were running toward me.

I stood very still, stared at them.

Mark Craig and Peter Grant were coming closer. I was partially hidden by the trees. They didn't see me.

Grant gasped, "We must turn, there's a lake ahead. We cannot go that way."

"Which way?" Craig asked.

Grant said something. I didn't hear what it was. I was too busy trying to keep from going under. Any second now I'd give up the ghost for keeps.

Thoughts from Craig's mind were beating at me like enraged wings. It was all I could do to stay on my feet. They came at me from all angles.

Something burst around me, like a huge tidal wave. Craig's mind engulfed me.

I knew this:

Craig was counting on turning a fast buck with a couple of trucks he owned. Prohibition made booze running a going concern. Some guys who worked for Lou Fox said they'd show him the ropes, give him a fair shake. Craig said swell. Only he didn't trust 'em, did some snooping on his own, turned up the gang's still. And Peter Grant as a bonus. The little redhead had been poking around, too. The pair attracted attention. Craig and Grant took to their heels . . .

Someone was yelling. I looked around, not sure I knew where I was. Craig and Grant were small figures on the far side of the clearing. Five men were racing toward me. They all had guns. I knew where I was, all right. I'd just been mistaken for my look-alike.

I ducked behind a tree. Bullets bit pieces out of it. I turned to run. I had to get out of here.

The woods vanished.

CHAPTER 49

Alexis Rike

The black tunnel closed in on him, seemed to squeeze against his body.

A booming voice muttered: "I am Dr. James Ingram." The voice said it over and over again in an idiot's monotone.

Alexis Rike kept running.

The train coalesced around him. He was in a car with the other passengers. The ghostlike seated figures stared at him vacantly. One of the figures was himself.

He was back in the tunnel.

Back on the train.

The twin scenes flickered on and off like a dull neon sign.

Alexis Rike was in Athens.

The small redhead at the far side of the square pointed at him, screamed, "Poisoner!"

A mob spilled out of the side streets.

Rike turned and ran.

He was in the tunnel. The train. The tunnel. As he ran something peeled back in his mind:

The fountains had been poisoned.

That had brought on the plague.

And he—Alexis Rike—had turned up with the antidote, poured it into each of the fountains. *He* was no poisoner. But someone else was.

Who?

Not the redhead; he was a mere henchman, an unwitting tool.

Someone else!

Alexis Rike shifted.

Cassius Chaerea stood in a darkened corner, his face covered by his crimson cloak. The slave who hid in the doorway could not identify him. But he could see Gaius Sabinus clearly. And he could hear them plot the mad emperor's death.

The slave moved furtively down the hallway; he would denounce Sabinus to Caligula.

Alexis Rike stepped up behind him, swung a club.

When the slave came to he was bound hand and foot, lying face down in a damp cellar. By the time he was found, Caligula would be dead.

The slave had also been a tool.

Alexis Rike was in the tunnel. If he could only stop and think for an instant. The pale light of the train glowed down on the passengers. Rike saw they were growing taller, thinner.

He was in an empty cell. In the monastery. Hastily, he tapped a message on the wall:

You are not alone.

And shifted.

It was Monday, November 10, 1952, 1:30 P.M.

Alexis Rike left the cafeteria, began walking in the direction of Union Square. Fuller was still seated at the table, would remain there for another fifteen minutes.

Rike did not glance over his shoulder. He knew he was being followed.

Presently, he stepped into a phone booth, deposited a coin, dialed a meaningless number which rang and rang. The door of the phone booth was left partially ajar. A crowded midday street. The short, pudgy woman who had been tailing Rike hovered near the phone booth, pretended to search her handbag for some lost item. She could hear his words clearly:

"Yes," Rike was saying, "Fuller swallowed it hook, line and sinker. He thinks I'm going to play along with him." A truck came by, drowning him out for an instant. "No," Rike was saying, "some senator. They want him killed. Probably a liberal." Rike laughed. "Don't worry. I'll get his name. For all I know they want me to pull the trigger." A group of children passed, talking loudly. The woman moved closer. Rike was saying, "They're trying to frame Comrade Bruno." Rike listened for a while, yes-yessed the phone a couple of times and hung up. The woman faded back into the crowd as Rike left the booth. He exchanged a nickel for a *New York Times* at a newsstand, glanced over the headlines. The Korean War was in full swing. Philip Murray, the CIO chief, was dead. Weizmann was mourned in Israel. Rike folded the paper under his arm, crossed the street against the light. The woman followed when the light turned green. But Rike was already gone. She didn't mind. He could always be picked up at his Union Square office. What she had to do now was report back to Fuller. He would know how to handle this. Rike knew too much. The woman hurried away.

Another Rike had watched the entire proceedings. He, too, was now gone.

A third Rike sat in his shabby Union Square office reading the obituary of one Gordon Lang, physicist. This Rike, who was, in fact, a member of the Communist party, knew nothing of the other Rikes. But they knew about him.

The train became the tunnel became nighttime in Central Park. It was raining.

Alexis Rike waited for Gorbach to appear. The trees kept the rain off him. But his feet were getting wet. He shivered. When Rike looked again at the luminous dial of his wristwatch it was one-ten. Time to go. Gorbach had failed to appear. Rike turned to leave the park.

He did not notice the man behind him who stepped out of the bushes in a half crouch, did not hear his quiet footsteps or see the flashing knife.

Alexis Rike lay dead, face down, in a puddle of muddy water.

Fuller wiped the knife clean on some leaves, put it in his pocket and strode up the path toward Fifth Avenue.

Alexis Rike stepped out of the darkness, walked slowly toward the body of Alexis Rike. He would take his keys, wallet and an envelope containing money, and then go off to meet Gorbach . . .

A third Alexis Rike had watched this all. When the second Rike left the park and turned north, Alexis Rike waited a moment, then stepped out on Fifth Avenue.

He could see Fuller—a lone figure—walking toward the eighties.

He hurried after him.

Fuller crossed at 86th Street, headed for Lexington Avenue and the subway. There was more traffic here; this section of town was still alive. Fuller stopped at a trash can near Madison Avenue, removed its cover. Something went from Fuller's pocket into the can. He continued on his way.

By the time Fuller stepped off the curb at Park Avenue, Rike had reached the trash can, fished out the knife.

Rike began to run after Fuller.

Fuller heard his name being called, turned to look.

The awful apparition which greeted him made Fuller scream.

Alexis Rike, not ten feet away, was lunging toward him. His eyes were wide, bulging, his mouth twisted in a terrible grimace. His hand clutched Fuller's knife.

Fuller screamed again, twisted sideways, darted blindly into the traffic.

Brakes squealed, wheels skidded on wet pavement.

Alexis Rike was the first to reach Fuller; he slipped the knife back into his pocket. A handwritten note—which bore Rike's name and address—instructing Fuller to meet him at midnight in Central Park went next to the knife.

A sparse crowd was gathering. Rike shouted over the rain and wind, "He's still breathing. Someone call an ambulance."

Others were leaning over Fuller now. Rike moved to the back of the crowd. He turned the corner at Lexington Avenue, headed toward the seventies.

Fuller was a tool, too, he thought.

And shifted.

The booming voice had grown louder, more irritated: "I am Dr. James Ingram," it bawled.

The train and tunnel blinked on and off like a shorted light bulb.

Rike was talking to Elaine and Doc Banning. In his hand he held a red leather volume. Something about the book was important. If he could only think . . .

The man with the melting face was moving toward him.

Rike shifted.

He was breaking into a warehouse on Linebrook Avenue. Nighttime. He worked with a flashlight, shears and picklock. He was dressed in denims. He carried a blackjack in his hip pocket, one which would help dispose of the guard.

Why was he here?

The Notebooks of Dr. James Ingram had indicated this city—Old York—this place—192 Linebrook—and the tunnel that reached outward. He had to get somewhere through that tunnel.

Rike shifted.

He was in Athens. He wore a toga, spoke Greek. In his hand he held a bottle of antitoxin.

"Poisoner!" the redhead yelled.

Rike shifted.

Caligula plunged the dagger into the man's chest. He came tripping, stumbling toward Rike.

Rike saw himself.

The scene faded, was replaced by another.

Gaius Sabinus and Cassius Chaerea hacked away at a screaming Caligula with their swords.

The crowd scattered in all directions.

Rike stood at a distance, watching. He was dressed in long robes. He spoke Latin. He saw Alexis Rike running with the crowd. He knew this Rike would live out his days as a Roman citizen, knowing nothing of other Rikes. *But he might dream . . .*

Rike shifted.

England. He was in the marketplace. It was 1250. He wore coarse brown robes. He itched. He watched.

Thunder clapped. The earth shook.

Alexis Rike, wearing trousers, white shirt and factory-made shoes seemed to erupt from the ground. He was flung skyward, fell back again; he lay unconscious.

The folk of the marketplace began to scatter in terror.

Something's wrong, the watching Rike thought.

And shifted.

An Alexis Rike followed Gorbach down the street. The little man was nervous. Glancing back, he saw the figure behind him. He increased his pace. *Someone had found out about him.* He must evade this surveillance, lose himself in a crowd somewhere. But what if Turner were being watched too? He would not go directly to the meeting place tonight in the park. He would wait, make certain Turner was not being followed . . .

Gorbach was carrying a suitcase. Inside, Rike knew, were the Lang papers. And Ingram's notebooks—one colleague's gift to another. Rike wondered if he should snatch the suitcase now.

But he already knew what was in Ingram's notebooks, didn't he?

Rike shifted.

What was happening? Rike didn't know. He could not even remember his destination now—if he had ever known it.

He was running faster than before. The train, tunnel and shiftings had become a dizzying blur.

Puriville.

Old York.

Athens.

Rome.

England.

New York.

They went around and around.

Alexis Rike was trapped in an endless whirling circle.

CHAPTER 50

The Girl and the Golem

The train fled through the darkness.

The Golem said, "What happened?"

The girl shook her head. "I don't know. The process has speeded up."

"You did not plan our leaving Mr. De Marco in such an abrupt manner, I take it?"

"No. We were pulled."

"You have lost control?"

"Partially."

"Then a crisis may be at hand?"

The girl bit her lip. "Yes."

The Golem took her arm; together they moved to the head of the car. Twelve unblinking figures stared back at them. "We must choose one," he said.

The girl nodded. "During the circuit shift, when you were stranded in Prague, I was able to find most of their multiples."

"They did not impress you?"

"I'm convinced none are the Prime."

"But you cannot be certain?"

Green eyes under blond lashes searched the Golem's face. "No. But you've seen some of them yourself now. What do you think?"

The Golem sighed. "If the Prime was among them, I failed to notice."

"Only one of these eluded me."

"Indeed?"

"He seems to have vanished in the initial explosion. Certainly there was no trace of him in 1943."

"You mean Alexis Rike?"

"Yes."

"He or his multiples may very well be in territory closed to us."

"True."

"Or he may be dead. Some in that building appear to have perished."

"I know."

The Golem smiled. "You are right, of course. His very absence creates suspicion. Is 1943 still the closest we can come to May 1935?"

"I'm afraid so."

"It is not close enough."

"We're moving faster," the girl said. "It may mean—

sooner or later—we can reach new territory. Or that the whole system itself will become unstable."

The seated figures had begun to thin out. The Golem eyed them gloomily. "What do you suggest?"

"The possibilities. The flickering images. What might have been. And what was."

"At which juncture?"

"The house on West 25th Street. Where the explosion occurred. We didn't approach it in 1943."

"It seemed futile," the Golem pointed out. "Whatever possibilities are there will be weak, confused, perhaps indecipherable."

"Of course. But that was before we had a subject. Now, at least, we know whom we're looking for—Alexis Rike."

4:30 A.M.

Only the hall lights were lit at 465 West 25th Street. The rest of the building was in darkness.

The girl and the Golem stepped out of the shadows. They were on the top floor. There was utter silence. The pair stood very still as if listening. The girl closed her eyes.

And the train materialized around them.

It was a train without substance, flickering transparently on walls, floor and ceiling of the narrow hallway.

The girl and the Golem remained immobile. Things happened.

Dr. James Ingram pulled a switch.

The room exploded.

Five Ingrams spun off in different directions, vanished.

Bugsy Moran and Al Capone shook hands. Lou Fox grinned.

"Yeah, a great day," Capone said, puffing on his cigar.

"This is better," Bugsy said, "than tryin' to stand you off, Al."

"Sure," Capone grinned, "it was some scrap. But now we got the kicks squared, we're like brothers."

"Brothers," Bugsy said, putting his arm around Capone's shoulder.

The other ten men seated around the long table in the

high domed room stared at Bugsy, Capone and Lou Fox. All ten were dressed in black, form-fitting garments. Their faces were white, pasty-looking. Bright light seemed to shine directly from walls and ceiling. The tall, narrow-chested man in black at the head of the table spoke in a flat, dead voice.

"Now we shall divide the world between us."

Mark Craig ran down the corridor. White walls, floors and ceiling glowed around him.

Up ahead, two white gleaming doors seemed to beckon. Craig ran toward them. They swung open as he approached.

He was in a shabby room. Two windows looked out on a rusted fire escape. A tall, thin man had his back to Craig. Dr. James Ingram turned and smiled.

Craig ignored him, his eyes fixed on a glittering spiral strip which unwound through the walls of the building and out into darkness. At its farthest tip a room quivered and pitched. This room was far away, yet near. Knobs and dials projected from its walls. A gray metal ceiling shone dully overhead. Machines crowded the floor. The girl and the Golem bent over one of these machines. They seemed totally engrossed in their efforts.

In the shabby room Dr. James Ingram pulled the switch.

The room burst into flames.

The spiral strip seemed to jump.

The room winked out.

The girl and the Golem spun off together into the darkness.

In the darkened hallway the Golem turned to the girl. "The possibilities are clearer than I expected; too clear."

"The system is undergoing rapid change," the girl said. "We're in some sort of upheaval. I don't know what it is. Or what it will do to us."

Ralph Olenger stepped out of the last door in the darkened hallway. His hair was white, his face wrinkled. Each trembling hand held a gun.

"I've been waiting for you." Olenger grinned with tooth-less gums.

Two guns jumped as he opened fire. The narrow hallway shook with sound.

The Golem stood before the girl. Bullets struck his metal frame, bounced off.

The train became solid around them, shot through the blackness. Ralph Olenger and the dark hallway were gone.

"A rather enfeebled booby trap," the Golem said.

"We are still tied to the building on 25th Street," the girl said.

"Can you maintain control?"

"It's slipping from me."

Images rose and fell like giant waves beating aginst the train walls:

The Golem was in Prague. He put a foot against the door; it cracked in two. The Golem charged into the large hall. The white-faced, black-clad men were there; they rose to meet him. The girl appeared behind the Golem, an energy weapon in her hand. She aimed at the men in black, pressed the stud. Blinding light flashed. Stray wisps of black garments drifted toward the floor.

The Golem told the girl, "We have tracked them—but their plan here is already in motion."

"Can you counter them alone?"

"Assuredly. I have only their puppets to contend with; if I am correct, they plan attacks against the Jews. Then the nobility and church. They hope to alter this juncture completely. They will fail."

"I'll return for you," the girl said. "There is still unexplored territory. The Prime could be within reach."

"Be careful."

The scene shattered.

Dr. James Ingram pulled the switch.

Harry Henderson whirled into darkness. Pat De Marco followed him.

The girl's hand moved to the brass knocker. The man who presently opened the door wore a black robe and yarmulke. The girl went past him into the house, moved up a darkened staircase toward the attic.

The Golem stood in a far corner.

She touched him. "Come."

The scene splintered.

Dr. James Ingram pulled the switch. Mrs. Emma Landry twirled into black night. Peter Grant spun at her heels. Lou Fox drifted after them.

The Golem said, "Your history and mine seem to be emerging quite intact. But the rest is mere fragment."

"The system has changed. Our presence here is affecting it."

Dr. James Ingram pulled the switch. Bridget Mercer sped into the darkness. Alexis Rike went with her.

"There!" the Golem said.

The girl closed her eyes. The train veered.

Mark Craig came crashing through the train wall like a flaming comet.

He had a head, but no face.

The train plunged downward after him and Alexis Rike.

CHAPTER 51

From the Diary of Dr. James Ingram

May 15, 1935. The day has come! In a matter of hours I shall pull the switch. Let come what may!

CHAPTER 52

Mark Craig

I didn't make it back to the train.

I was out in the great black beyond. Or something that could pass for it with no trouble at all.

I was hanging in midair as if suspended by a long, invisible rope. Little starlike lights winked on and off in a vast expanse of darkness. That didn't bother me one bit. I could see everything plain as day. My vision extended for miles. I let my eyes scout around; there was plenty to see, all right.

I had found my faceless man. And thousands of his kin. They floated lazily in the giant pool of night. They were above and below me and on all sides. They drifted by me like so much flotsam, their heads smooth ovals, their bodies wrapped in black form-fitting garments. If there was an alive one in this bunch, I couldn't spot him. Far, far away in the distance, high above me, something metallic seemed to glitter. In the other direction, down below, a tiny light flickered and flared.

I wondered what the metal thing was.

And shifted.

It glowed a dull gray. It hummed softly to itself as though expressing quiet satisfaction in its work. It seemed a mile high. It was some kind of machine.

I hung in midair and gawked at it.

Faceless men floated out through wide holes on its

surface. They weren't any improvement over the ones I'd seen below. They might have been wind-up toys. Or just so much dead meat.

While I hung there, something began to change. The space around me seemed to shudder. The faceless men began popping out faster. As if someone had speeded up an assembly line. I hoped it wasn't for my benefit; I didn't need any faceless men. I wondered what I did need. As I watched this whole crew started to twitch. As if springs had snapped inside the lot, knocking them out of whack. Their black garments melted before my eyes, became business suits, togas, long robes, leotards, an assortment of duds that would have done the largest clothing store proud. Something had annoyingly begun to murmur in my mind in a flat, dead voice: . . . *to complete your urgent mission. You will assume identity 705. You will seize the bridges. At the right moment, you will detonate the explosives. You will also bribe or seduce . . .* The murmur was a jumble; it went on and on. It had a lot more nifty advice to offer. I ignored it. Time to get a closer look at these cigar-store dummies. I waited till one floated by in a tweed sport jacket and gray slacks and grabbed his ankle. I pulled him to me. He had a wallet in his hip pocket. A driver's license identified him as Jack Sanderson. He carried a Social Security card, a Diners Club card and fifty bucks. I was busy reading the small print on the back of a dollar bill when the giant machine did something that sounded like a burp. The wallet, cards and dough vanished from between my fingertips like so much sawdust. The murmur stopped. The jacket and slacks were gone, too, replaced by the old black outfit. I let him float away. All of his pals had also changed back. The machine burped again as though it were just warming up to its job; the floaters began to change again. The murmur started from scratch. A voice whispered in my mind, "Unstable." I could believe that, all right. The voice had sounded like mine. I wondered how I knew. I wondered if I could be trusted. I wondered what the flickering light had been down below.

I shifted.

Flames were around me. I wasn't going to let that bother me; the flames were painless. It gave me time to rummage through my brain. I needed that.

I'd been on the train and thought of a dream. It hadn't even been mine, but Peter Grant's. It didn't matter. I'd found myself in the woods of Grant's dream. I'd wanted out and ended up in the big black. The machine caught my eye and there I was. I saw the fire and landed in it. I was a guy on the go. All I had to do was think about it. Why not?

I thought of Old York.

And shifted.

Four guns erupted at me.

I hit the ground, rolled over in the dust and crawled back in the alley. Pieces of flying brick chipped off the hotel wall in a hail of bullets.

I raced down the alley, turned a corner. I barely glimpsed the four figures dashing after me.

But a glimpse was all I needed.

Two males. Two females. Their faces white. Their clothing black.

I'd tried for Old York and hit Hornsville instead. Frost would be lying dead up in the hotel room. Tim Yancy's records would be in my pocket. Two pair of identical twins—right out of some nightmare old-age home—would be gunning for me.

Except Frost had killed one of the twins, blasted him through the hotel window.

Only now he was alive again!

I knew why, too.

He wasn't human.

None of them were human.

I recognized them now. They were the faceless things the giant machine had been spewing out. Somewhere along the line they'd come up with features, become animated. I'd missed that part of the show. But to see them once was to know them always. And hate them.

The machine had burped and the floaters had started to wiggle like worms; had the burp resurrected the fourth killer, too?

265

I was out on the main street now, running for the livery stable.

The four rounded the hotel.

A bullet winged by my left ear, brought me up short.

What was I doing here?

Time to move! But could I still do it, now when I needed it most?

I thought of York City.

And shifted.

I was back in my hospital room in State-City. Lying in bed wearing pajamas. I tossed off the blankets in a hurry, got up. I had no intention of hanging around. My clothes would be in the closet. I opened it. A gagged Dr. Spiegel rolled out, bound hand and foot.

The hall door jerked open.

Dr. Spiegel stood there. He was short, chubby, with a round face and white hair.

Only it wasn't Dr. Spiegel.

He had a leer on his lips and a long, shiny knife in his hand.

"Welcome back, Mr. Craig," he said and lunged at me.

I shifted.

Lou Fox had his tommy gun leveled at Peter Grant and me. Two other goons were backing him up. Outside, on the street, I heard the sounds of traffic. I'd made it back to New York. The right town. But the wrong setup.

Grant was babbling, "You must believe me. It was not I who initiated these actions, Mr. Fox. I am a mere representative. I mean you no harm. I will gladly tell you who my principal is. Your argument is with him and Mr. Craig here, not with me. It was he who had you watched. His name is Alexis Rike. I swear—"

"Go shove it," the bald-headed fat man grinned. His finger tightened on the trigger.

I shifted.

Blindly.

I'd run out of places I wanted to visit.

York.

Old York.

266

New York.

Each was a death trap!

The machine had been dozing, the floating goon squad dead or dormant. Then I'd popped up on the scene. And all hell was breaking loose—most of it aimed at me. Some change. It almost made me yearn for the simple days when all I did was bounce from one world to the next like a stray tennis ball.

I came drifting out of the darkness. I was rising like a beach ball under water. A red haze glittered all around me. Nothing was substantial. A voice rang out: "I am Dr. James Ingram."

Old York flashed by:

Carriages, horses and Double Ms.

New York next:

Cars, trolleys, gangsters, bootlegged booze.

York:

Glittering buildings, mobile ramps, the Time Festival.

I didn't know if I could stop at one if I wanted to. I knew I didn't want to. I was more than glad to give 'em the cold shoulder. I wished the voice would shut up.

I rose out of the Time Festival.

Another world came into view; it seemed to sprout out of the Time Festival itself. Not bad. Another world might be just what I needed.

Haze obscured it from me. What the hell. Kicking around nowhere was a bust. If I bobbed up in the world and things got hot, I could always take off again. I hoped.

I let the thought whirl through my skull. I concentrated on the new world.

And shifted.

Broad daylight. A street sign said: Founder's Square. A huge dome-shaped structure bore the inscription: Ingram's Rest. There were other buildings, too. That was all the sight-seeing I had time for.

I was suddenly very busy.

Guns, cannons and machine guns were wide open all around me. Rays, missiles and roaring flame were joining in the fun. I'd landed in the middle of a full-scale war!

I ducked for cover, scampered through an entrance of

a small building off to one side. A sign read: Video Library. I hit the floor as glass shattered behind me. Twisting around, I saw that the double doors I'd come through were gone; someone had scored a bull's-eye. I peered out through the wreckage.

The ruckus outside was centered around the domed building. Its defenders were either done up in armor or part of their heads and bodies were made of metal. Something that should have been skin but wasn't had peeled off their hides along with a lot of clothes. What was left looked like fried rubber.

Another troop was going at them tooth and nail. This one had a lot of citizens dolled up like refugees from the Time Festival—in fancy getups, business suits, long capes, along with the usual phony faces. Mixed in with this crew I spied the black-clad floaters. They had faces now and weren't floating. But they didn't fool me; I could spot 'em a mile away. I'd had practice.

A ray or something swooped my way, put the torch to the video library. A screaming shell took the roof off it.

That did it.

I thought of the red haze again.

And shifted.

I'd aimed for the excursion-special, the one which had shifted me through the various Yorks and left me front and center at this latest bloodbath.

I never reached it. Something pulled sideways. The voice of Dr. James Ingram chuckled. "You've been linked to *them* now for some time, you know."

I came down hard on the bare wooden floor. There was the bed, the gas range, the sink and kitchen table.

The odor of rotting wood came from the walls.

The old crone was in her chair rocking wildly. Burning eyes laughed at me. Toothless gums grinned out from a seamy face. "What kept you, Mr. Craig?"

I knew what was coming next.

The door burst open.

It stood swaying in the doorway.

Its head was turned toward me, but it had no face.

It wasn't dressed in black like the others. There was

something familiar abouts its clothes. No time to take stock.

It started toward me.

It'd looked like a giant the first time I'd seen it. But I'd been sick, dead tired, drained of strength.

Now I was wound tight like a coiled spring. Blood was pounding through me. Time had cut this creature down to size. I was done running. I would stand my ground.

I could hear the howling laughter of the old witch behind me.

The thing was at arm's length now.

I grinned, balled my fist and smashed it in the face.

The room exploded.

I was drifting very slowly through the blackness. No snail ever moved slower. That was aces with me. I liked it out here. I had lots of time. I had come through the machine myself now. I had no face. But I would get one soon enough. *Along with them*. We'd all get faces. Wallets full of cards where cards were important. And memories to go with them.

My name was Mark Craig. I was a registered Double M, a middle-man, one of the many who discreetly handled the numerous payoffs . . .

I'd get a suitcase full of papers to prove it. All produced out here in the blackness. The papers would say I'd come from another city, another state, another country. A lot of my references would turn up under tombstones if anyone checked. But one or two would come through. Because one or two would be *them*. Or their stooges.

It was slick, all right, and that made me laugh. The floaters and I had plenty in common. We were all composed of molecules. We'd all gone through the big machine. There was only one slight difference, in fact:

I was alive and they weren't. I was born and they were manufactured.

The machine had *made* them, had given them memories and a mission. The machine was part computer, too. And part seeing-eye. It had spied out all the data it needed for clothing and memories and phony papers and sent it along with *them*. I understood. I had come through the machine.

Some machine.

I laughed and laughed. Because the machine should have been perfect and wasn't. It had tripped up.

I was Mark Craig, a Double M in Old York. My records were foolproof. The machine had burped. My records were gone.

That was nice to know. It was funny and made me laugh. I laughed to show I could appreciate a funny thing.

I stopped laughing and wondered what else I knew.

That Pat De Marco in Old York was a tool of *them*.

I'd paid him to tail Peter Grant. But the day I'd gone to Emma Landry's, Grant was nowhere in sight. Yet De Marco had shown up.

He'd hired a rig and tailed me.

He'd come in shooting at Old Faceless, because Old Faceless was me, fresh out of the machine.

De Marco didn't want us to touch.

Why?

I knew the answer to that one, too, and it made me scream with laughter.

If we touched, there'd be an explosion. I'd be reprocessed by the machine, turn up somewhere else.

And maybe remember.

They didn't want that. Pat De Marco was working for *them*.

But the other De Marcos hadn't cared one bit. They were lost. Just like the other Craigs.

I wondered what I wasn't supposed to remember.

"Not about me," the voice of Dr. James Ingram said. "That would make no difference at all." Only now it sounded like my voice.

I was back in the red haze again.

Dr. James Ingram had started to laugh. I didn't like his laugh. It sounded nutty. It seemed to fill all of space.

I was rising again like a balloon.

Old York.

New York.

York.

Founder's City.

The name had popped into my mind. Along with another name:

Alexis Rike.

I kept rising.

What did I know about Alexis Rike?

Not much. Nothing that seemed important. But things were still a bit woozy.

I thought hard.

He was a Security Guardian in Founder's City. He took Euphors. Watched the Yesteryear tube. Liked the ladies—especially Nona Evers. Preferred loafing to work.

Hell, the guy sounded like me.

That made me laugh.

The voice of Dr. James Ingram said, "See, you *are* remembering. But you're wrong about poor Pat De Marco. He *had* worked for them in Old York. Oh yes, indeed; but they were long gone, you know. The machine had lost contact with them. They couldn't survive; the stations kept opening and closing so *very* fast. The machine which reached you in Old York was a pale shadow of its former self: it even forgot its mission; you yourself controlled it in part, and never knew. Ah yes, it gave you an identity, it created documents. But it was too frail to bring *them* back. Except the four twins, of course. It burped them out. They lived. It burped again. They died. But now they're back. Many, many are back.

"Yes, Pat De Marco *forgot* their mission. But when you appeared in his office, part of his mind remembered. The mission, you know, had been *implanted;* oh my, yes. They'd have done better just *buying* him, like they did Assistant DA Gardner and the others, wouldn't you say?

"Poor Pat De Marco; he remembered to follow you, but his mind was *confused.* He was only to *watch*, an old directive.

"He fired because he was afraid, so *very* afraid."

Big deal, I thought. I looked out through the red haze. I was passing New York. *Again.*

This red stuff and all this yakking were getting on my nerves. I didn't want it as a steady diet. Maybe time for another try at the Yorks.

"But you *can't* go out there," Ingram's voice said.

"Why?"

"I've already told you you're *linked* to *them* now."

"Linked?"

"Anywhere you emerge, they'll be waiting. To kill you."

"Anywhere?"

"Anywhere."

"What should I do?"

Ingram cackled. "What *can* you do? Nothing. They win. Soon they'll find you even here. Just as they'll find your friend, Alexis Rike."

"Can't you help me?"

"Me? What could I do? And anyway, I *like* them."

Peals of laughter rang through the haze.

This James Ingram was worthless. I needed help, someone I could trust. *They* were hunting Alexis Rike, too. That put Rike and me on the same side. Alone they'd pick us off like sitting ducks. Together maybe we'd have a chance.

I thought of Alexis Rike.

I made it a good, long, hard think.

I shifted.

It was different this time.

I could see the train below me.

I was drifting after it in something which felt like a sea of jelly. I moved very slowly. But not as slowly as that train. I was being drawn toward one car. I approached it from the side. I put a hand against the wall. It crumbled like a cracker. I swam in like a fat man under water. All the stock characters were there, in their usual places. Along with two extras: the young blonde and the chubby guy in the checkered suit; they were up and around. I'd hit two live ones. I didn't have time to chat. A force was carrying me forward. I went the way I'd come, through the train wall. I plunged down. I was in a tunnel. A train.

A tunnel. A man ahead of me. Running. This would be Rike. I stretched out a hand, touched his shoulder.

That was a mistake.

The explosion sent me careening into darkness.

I knew what to expect: the big machine. I'd be reprocessed again. And then I'd be drifting in the red haze, back on the York circuit. Except *they* would be there too this time. And I'd have no place to hide.

Oh, I knew a lot now. The explosion had jogged my memory, lent me wisdom. Only it was all a bit late.

There was more than one Craig. The Craigs were unstable. They couldn't touch each other without the explosion, without being repelled.

I'd guessed that already.

What I hadn't guessed was that Alexis Rike of Founder's City was me.

CHAPTER 53

Alexis Rike

Alexis Rike tumbled lazily, head over heels, through the darkness.

He had no face.

A white light seemed to have exploded in his mind. Things were fuzzy—but he remembered. And knew he was doomed.

He was Alexis Rike.

He was Mark Craig.

He was also someone else.

"Me," said the voice of Dr. James Ingram.

That's right, Rike thought. I'm Ingram; and Ingram's gone mad.

"Tut, tut," Ingram said, "is that a *nice* thing to say? Besides, I'm not really you. Only part of me became you and that was a long time ago, wasn't it? We've all changed since then, haven't we?"

It didn't matter, Alexis Rike thought. The aliens would be waiting in the red haze. Waiting to get him.

"Oh no," the voice of Dr. James Ingram said. "Not the aliens. There are no aliens. None at all."

None?

Alexis Rike remembered the City of Silver and Gold.

Dr. James Ingram stood in the white-walled, shimmering laboratory, a tall thin man with black hair and a black moustache. He looked tired and worried. The sounds of combat were very close now. "We haven't much time," he told Nona Evers.

The blond girl nodded. She had been Ingram's associate for more than three years; they had trained for this moment. "The black hole," she said, "will re-emerge in five point six minutes. We'll make it."

Ingram strode to the long metal table, climbed on, stretched out on his back.

Evers moved to the west wall control panel.

R-Meerlue—Ingram's security robot—peered through the window. He could see the driveway below. Bursts from the energy weapons shook the city. "It will be close," he said. "Fortunately, they are poor fighters."

"They *aren't* fighters," Ingram said from the table. "They are programmed puppets. The enemy's *creations*."

R-Meerlue slid his handgun loose from its holster. A troop of black-clad "men" were racing up the driveway. R-Meerlue raised the window, fired. The "men" scattered for cover.

"Three point two minutes," Nona Evers said.

"Listen," Ingram said. "When the switch is thrown, this laboratory will go out of phase with the city. We will become part of the force field; we will be linked together— my body serving as the field's conductor. I won't be able to communicate with you. But we should be safe here no matter what happens."

R-Meerlue took aim, fired again.

Nona Evers said, "And if you fail to deflect their tunnel?"

"Then you two will carry on. Trust no one. Work alone. Remember, their tools are everywhere."

Footsteps sounded on the stairs. R-Meerlue rushed to bar the door.

Nona Evers pulled the switch.

Dr. James Ingram vanished.

Alexis Rike drifted in darkness.

He had not been part of Dr. James Ingram then. And he was not totally part of Ingram now. But there had been a time when he and Ingram were one.

The aliens had planned carefully, had tracked the course of the black hole, had determined the instant it would collide with earth.

And triggered their energy system at that very instant.

There was a tunnel through time.

No aliens ever appeared.

Only their puppets, the simulated men.

They were not even good simulations. They fought when they had to. They did not like to fight and were not good at it.

They had other plans.

They hoped to move through time and change earth history. In this way they would triumph.

"Oh yes," the voice of Dr. James Ingram said, "they were sneaky little devils." He laughed gleefully. "But I foxed them. I hooked onto their energy system. I would have closed it, too, you know. But something went wrong. Something *always* seems to go wrong."

"What was it?" Alexis Rike asked.

"I don't know." The voice of Dr. James Ingram was peevish. "Their system was unstable. Perhaps I miscalculated. I was whisked to 1900. The tunnel sealed closed behind me. I was trapped in the past. But if I could not get in, they could not get out. I decided to start all over."

The blackness began to lift, to turn gray.

"The black hole was tied to their energy system, you know," the voice of Dr. James Ingram was saying. "That hole kept popping up. Pop. Pop. Pop. I calculated it would re-emerge through space-time in 1935. I began work. I would build my laboratory again, even under such primitive conditions. I would take time. But I had lots of time, didn't I? They didn't know where I was, weren't sure what I had done to their system. Their agents were clustered around 1935. The tunnel opened only there in this time juncture. Even if they found me, they would move carefully at first. Because I had become a link in their system, and to kill me might have disrupted everything. Besides, they thought me an incompetent; they bided their time. Oh yes, I had it all planned; I almost succeeded . . ."

Alexis Rike was in the red haze. Back again. Where they could reach him. How many minutes did he have left?

Dr. James Ingram had pulled the switch . . .

May 15, 1935.

He—Alexis Rike—had accompanied Craig to Ingram's building. It had seemed simple enough.

A chemist.

A private eye.

A scientist stealing company secrets.

The first two would catch the third in the act, earn their night's pay.

Dr. James Ingram had pulled the switch.

There were twelve of them:

Rike.

Craig.

The three Ingram had hired to assist him: Olenger, Mercer, Grant.

The Ace op—Henderson—planted in the building.

The pair of tenants: Fox and Mrs. Emma Landry.

De Marco.

Ingram himself.

276

Nona Evers and R-Meerlue—from elsewhere . . .

Alexis Rike could see Old York rising through the red haze.

"Shift!" Mark Craig's voice called out. "Shift, and keep shifting—they're in the haze!"

Blackness was all around them.

Mark Craig and Alexis Rike were adrift in endless night.

"We'll be okay here for a while," Craig said. "Maybe."

"You can't get away," the voice of Dr. James Ingram wailed. "You can't, you can't . . ."

"Some song and dance, huh?" Craig said. "The old gink's lost his marbles; he won't stop yakking." Craig laughed. "Remember when the blonde braced you, Rike? In Athens, right? Well, that was *him*. He did it with his mind. The Ingram who had dreams in 1935 was being talked to by the Ingram on the slab. Can you beat that? He was nuts then, too. But part of him was on the up-and-up. He tried to keep you in Athens, out of harm's way. He even tried to warn himself. The old guy was down and out, but *something* was still in there pitching—his unconscious. So, in a way, he never stopped yakking."

Alexis Rike said, "I don't think I feel too well."

"Take it easy," Craig said. "Just listen. I know a couple of things you don't. You've got this operation pegged as a flop. Well, it's too soon to knuckle under. We still got an even chance to go the distance. Listen.

"When Ingram threw the switch, he caught us all, himself included. Everything got messed up. The blast divided us into multiples, into different selves, right? The ones who stayed in the thirties never caught on. The rest were sent packing through the time tunnel, their memories fragmented, distorted. The big machine processed them, gave 'em identities, an overlay of new memories. Some hung on to their old names; others didn't. Some knew more. Others less. And a few became tools of the machine. But only a few. The blast and what followed played havoc with the force field, put the machine on the blink.

"When two or three of us landed in the same time

juncture, we'd be drawn together, would meet. We were linked. We had dreams, memories we couldn't place. But we were different people in different places. Lou Fox was a goon in '29, a scared monk in the thirteenth century; and somewhere along the line, a tool for them. Bridget Mercer knew nothing. And even less as Joyce Fairchild. De Marco was *their* stooge in one spot, just a guy in another. Grant, whether he was Berg or Gorbach, was only a bit player. Henderson, too. Olenger seems to've gotten the biggest dose of the machine before it went on the fritz and was their pawn right from the start. Nona Evers was completely changed in Founder's City. She was a kid called Elaine, somewhere else. What you don't know is that Ingram was the Prime. *Along with you and me.* That's why we could 'read' our other selves, link up with their memories."

Alexis Rike said, "I know most of this as soon as you tell it. I can read you, too. But things are still a bit cloudy."

"You'd get it all after a while," Craig said, "just like I did. But we haven't got time. We've got to move and move quick if the floaters show up. And you've got to know the score. We're tied together, Rike; you, me and Ingram. Out here, we soak up each other's thoughts like a sponge. Only I've got the edge on you because I've been here longer.

"The old guy threw the switch and everything got scrambled. But you, me and Ingram were caught in the same energy flow. It could've been any of the others, but it was us—just blind chance. Along with Ingram, we became conductors of the aliens' force field; we could switch their time tunnel to different junctures.

"Ingram's aim was to finish the floaters. But the explosion had put him on ice. He was stuck, back on his metal slab. Part of him had already been there, a link in the alien force field—now he merged with himself. This other Ingram had spent too much time being fed the aliens' line. The machine had given him the works. He was flipping his wig.

"The new Ingram got the message; he was out for the count. But he hadn't gone bananas yet. He transferred his

278

data to you, Rike; you took over his job. You used the tunnel; the machine was automatic; you could control it, make it hand you the lingo, the clothes, the IDs. You hunted down the floaters and their stooges, queered their play.

"Ingram was all set to give me the treatment, too, but he never made it. His mind snapped."

"Shame! Shame!" the voice of Dr. James Ingram called.

"Shut up," Craig said. To Rike, he said, "We may be coming out of the black soon. I'm ahead of you. Get set to shift if I give the word.

"Yeah, Ingram went loony. And maybe that saved the day. Because odds had it you wouldn't've been able to stand off the floaters alone. Not for long, anyway. Ingram had done more than just hook onto the force field that second time; he'd changed it, diverted it. The energy flow sidetracked a slice of history, Ingram's mind *fashioned* it. He had the power; he'd tapped their system, tapped the black hole, merged both with his own setup—the dingus he'd switched on. Try to read me, Rike."

Alexis Rike, in his mind's eye, saw York. Old York. Founder's City.

"Uh-huh," Craig said. "The old boy had gone native; those thirty-five years he'd spent in New York had left their mark. He built Yorks. The kickback got a big play during Prohibition, so he built Old York around it, threw in coaches and phones because he liked it that way. He built the Time Festival in York and it grew into Founder's City—*his* city. Ingram *liked* the past, the twenties, especially the thirties. He was nuts. His vision was changing everything; he'd own the future by and by. A future where everyone babbled the old lingo, watched the Yesteryear tube and did nothing. A dead end. But it wrecked the floaters."

Craig began to laugh. "You know what that damn train was, Rike? It was *their* force field, their tunnel through time. That's how Ingram saw it. And that's what it became—a train with stations. The 'stations' kept closing on the floaters, stranding them in history. They'd be cut off from their energy flow and dry up. Their goons would be left holding the bag. Without the floaters to direct 'em, they were nothing.

"The floaters never figured what was gumming the works. They didn't know where Ingram was. Maybe he'd gotten to like 'em, but he was still keeping his trap shut. He couldn't've helped 'em anyway. Know what was closing those stations, Rike? *We* were. We were Primes, conductors of the energy flow. Ingram was nailed down on his metal slab. But we were mobile and linked. Each time you shifted to one spot, I shifted to another. Involuntarily. The floaters never had a prayer in York or Old York. Those stations were the first to go. The two Yorks became self-enclosed. They were Ingram's worlds. Only the stooges were left."

"Oh no," the voice of Dr. James Ingram said. "You're wrong. You've forgotten Founder's City—that was my world too; my *grandest* creation. But none of my creations were *quite* self-enclosed. Remember the red haze, the flames?" Ingram chuckled. "The black hole, the alien energy system—they collided and left their imprint: the red glow was their reflection. *They mark the alternate stations on the time train, the other exits into history.* Only the floaters couldn't find them; the machine was so feeble, so unstable.

"But it isn't now.

"*They* come in the back way, you know. Through Mrs. Landry's room. Oh yes, I'm there too, in the very same room; in another juncture, I'm L. C. Banning and, as such, I know nothing. But I don't need to, do I?

"For that room is outside of time. It shifts open and closed. It is *very* unstable. When it's open it's a gateway to the Yorks, to Founder's City. When the floaters are there, it's a perfect trap. *And I can shift you if I want to. And I do!*"

Craig and Rike blinked in the dull light.
They were back in the room.

A single lit lamp on a nightstand. A kitchen table, chairs, a bed, a sink, a gas range. The old crone sat in her rocking chair. She was laughing. She would laugh forever. The door burst open. The floaters poured in.

"Shift!" Craig yelled.

Alexis Rike was running down a long dark tunnel. Mark Craig was at his side.

The floaters were behind them.

The voice of Dr. James Ingram howled through the tunnel. He was laughing.

"Shift!" Craig yelled.

L.C. Banning held out the red book in a trembling hand. The room was spinning wildly. The floaters came through the door. They were dressed in black. Their faces were chalk-white, their eyes dead.

"Shift!" Craig yelled.

They were running through the tunnel. The "men" in black were behind them and gaining fast.

Rike spoke as he ran: "This tunnel leads to Founder's City. Ingram is there. Under Ingram's Rest. The red book is his; it gives directions. He produced it through the machine; he scattered it through time."

"Before he went nuts," Craig said, fighting for breath.

"Before. It held his calculations. I got my hands on it. In the 1950s. And again in Old York. *The first time.* When I worked for the Morgan Agency. But I was mostly you then, wasn't I, Craig?"

"Shift!" Craig yelled.

It stood in the room. It had no face. It turned on the things in black. Behind it Craig was yelling, "Shift! Shift!"

Again they were in the tunnel. Running. They seemed to be running always. "That's us," Craig gasped, "without a face. That's both of us. Together. We'll keep turning up there forever, faceless, fresh out of the cockeyed machine. The 'moss-covered cave' I thought I landed in between York and Old York—that was *inside* the machine: I was faceless and never guessed! The room keeps pulling a multiple of our faceless self through it; when one of us is there the attraction is doubly strong. It wants to touch us, Rike, that first faceless us. It wants to *be.*

"Yeah—together, Rike. In Founder's City you were

almost me. Your body. My temperament. Your name. And in Old York, once. *Your* body, Rike, *my* name. *Someone* shifted. And we divided again. You crashed through the Middle Ages. I landed in a later York with some of your memories in tow. I remembered Norman Walsh who'd died three years before I even joined the Morgan outfit."

"Who shifted us? Ingram?"

"No. Another Prime. Our ace in the hole. Shift!"

The floaters poured through door and windows. Craig had used the machine, conjured up a gun. The old crone laughed and laughed. The thing without a face charged through the door, went down in a tangle of floaters. Craig opened fire. From far away he heard the sound of an engine. He began to laugh. There were too many floaters. "Shift!" he yelled. "Shift!"

They ran in the tunnel, the floaters behind them. The roar of a train filled their ears.

"She's coming!" Craig screamed.

The train—the nightmare express—thundered down on them.

CHAPTER 54

The Girl and the Golem

The girl and the Golem saw them—two running figures in the tunnel.

"There!" the girl said. Blond hair streamed behind her, green eyes blazed. The train swooped down on the pair, enclosed them.

Three Primes rode the nightmare express.

Craig turned to the girl. Sweat glistened on his forehead. "Listen. You control this force field. That makes you a Prime. You didn't know it. You do now."

Rike said, "Ingram's at Ingram's Rest."

"There's a war on," Craig said. "The floaters are taking over. We've got to shift."

Rike told the girl, "Don't touch either of us. We're all Primes. We'd end up back at the machine. You can read me. I'm going to picture Ingram's Rest. Shift when we do."

Nona Evers nodded once. "I'm ready!"

He floated in midair. He lay on a metal slab. His face kept changing. He was Dr. James Ingram. He was Mark Craig. He was Alexis Rike. He was Nona Evers. *He was the Prime-plus.*

The voice of Dr. James Ingram echoed through the huge underground cavern. "You're all fools," he told the four figures who stood below him. "You'll die here. Run, save yourselves!" Dr. James Ingram laughed—his eyes fixed on the ceiling, his lips never moving. His voice boomed, "Dear me, but you were so wrong, Nona; you thought me lost. But *here* I am. I've been here all along. And I couldn't close the tunnel even if I wished to. *They* have broken through to Founder's City, you know. Now, finally. Oh yes, they're in complete control. Their energy flows through me. Their mission is mine. And now they storm Ingram's Rest. They'll be here in a moment. And they will guard me forever. I'm their lifeline, you know. But you they'll kill." Mad laughter scaled the chamber walls.

Three Primes gazed at the hovering metal slab. They were Alexis Rike, Mark Craig, Nona Evers. But they had also been—for a short time—Dr. James Ingram. And they *knew.*

"The metal slab and Ingram's body," Rike said slowly, "are part of a self-enclosed energy system. Ingram's the prime conductor. *Break the circuit, move the slab and the tunnel will dissolve.*"

The voice of Dr. James Ingram roared with laughter. "Listen, you can hear them on the stairs now. *They* come. How will you break the circuit? How? You can't even touch me! *We're all Primes!* And Primes repel one another!"

"Not I," said R-Meerlue. "I'm no Prime. In fact, I am not even human!" He reached up for the slab; he twisted sideways with all his strength. The slab moved.

Bright flame seemed to split walls, floor and ceiling.

The metal slab fell to the ground.

The noise echoed through an empty chamber.

They walked down the tree-lined street.

Nona Evers said, "What do you think happened to him, Mark?"

"Ingram?" Craig shrugged. "Beats me. Maybe he landed back in the future."

"Which one?"

"Who knows."

Rike said, "We never did find out who killed Ralph Olenger."

R-Meerlue smiled. "From what you've told me, I would surmise it was my other self. Olenger was, after all, a tool of the floaters. The most dangerous one."

"Poor man," Nona said.

"We can never be sure," Rike said.

"So what?" Craig said.

"True," Alexis Rike agreed. He took Nona by the hand. There was no explosion. She smiled at him. The day was mild, sunny. An ice wagon clattered by on West 25th Street. A car backfired. In the distance the rumble of an el could be heard.

It was May 15, 1935.

Isaac Asimov

John D. Mac Donald

"The king of the adventure novel" John D. MacDonald is one of the world's most popular authors of mystery and suspense. Here he is at his bestselling best.

☐ CONDOMINIUM	23525-4	$2.25
☐ ALL THESE CONDEMNED	13950-6	$1.50
☐ APRIL EVIL	14128-4	$1.75
☐ AREA OF SUSPICION	14008-3	$1.75
☐ BALLROOM OF THE SKIES	13852-6	$1.50
☐ THE BEACH GIRLS	14081-4	$1.75
☐ BORDER TOWN GIRL	13714-7	$1.50
☐ THE BRASS CUPCAKE	14141-1	$1.75
☐ A BULLET FOR CINDERELLA	14106-3	$1.75
☐ CANCEL ALL OUR VOWS	13764-3	$1.75
☐ CLEMMIE	14015-6	$1.75
☐ CONTRARY PLEASURE	14104-7	$1.75
☐ THE CROSSROADS	14033-4	$1.75
☐ CRY HARD, CRY FAST	13969-7	$1.50
☐ DEAD LOW TIDE	14166-7	$1.75
☐ DEADLY WELCOME	13682-5	$1.50
☐ DEATH TRAP	13557-8	$1.50
☐ THE DECEIVERS	14016-4	$1.75
☐ THE DROWNERS	13582-9	$1.50
☐ THE EMPTY TRAP	14185-3	$1.75
☐ THE END OF THE NIGHT	13731-7	$1.50
☐ A FLASH OF GREEN	14186-1	$1.95
☐ THE GIRL, THE GOLD WATCH & EVERYTHING	13745-7	$1.50
☐ THE LAST ONE LEFT	13958-1	$1.95
☐ A MAN OF AFFAIRS	14051-2	$1.75

Buy them at your local bookstore or use this handy coupon for ordering:

FREE
Fawcett Books Listing

There is Romance, Mystery, Suspense, and Adventure waiting for you inside the Fawcett Books Order Form. And it's yours to browse through and use to get all the books you've been wanting . . . but possibly couldn't find in your bookstore.

This easy-to-use order form is divided into categories and contains over 1500 titles by your favorite authors.

So don't delay—take advantage of this special opportunity to increase your reading pleasure.

Just send us your name and address and 35¢ (to help defray postage and handling costs).

FAWCETT BOOKS GROUP
P.O. Box C730, 524 Myrtle Ave., Pratt Station, Brooklyn, N.Y. 11205

Name _____
(please print)

Address _____
City _____ State _____ Zip _____

Do you know someone who enjoys books? Just give us their names and addresses and we'll send them an order form too!

Name _____
Address _____
City _____ State _____ Zip _____

Name _____
Address _____
City _____ State _____ Zip _____